RANSOM

BENSON SECURITY 4

JANET ELIZABETH HENDERSON

It was wise to call John Garcia by his street name—Beast. Calling him John reminded him of the asshole who'd fathered him, which tended to bring out his violent streak. He supposed he should have legally changed the John to something else, but he liked having an excuse for being the Beast. The nickname fit with the life he lived in the underbelly of Atlantic City. And it worked well with his profession —cage fighter and sometime bodyguard. Although, according to the four guys who knew him best, it was time he stopped using his face as a punching bag and got a new profession.

One of those four guys was the reason for Beast's current visit to the Amazon rainforest—Joe Barone had married into a UK acting dynasty, and his new family had arranged a week-long wedding party to celebrate. Week-long. Beast shook his head at the thought. Where he came from, wedding receptions took place in an evening at the local bar.

"Is there anybody here who isn't famous?" Noah Merchant, one of Beast's four closest friends, leaned back against the bar, his eyes on the crowded dance floor. Noah was an Atlantic City cop who'd flown down with Beast. Neither of them had been able to take the full week off work to attend the entire event.

"Us." Beast raised an eyebrow at the sight of two ageing Hollywood directors as they tried to line-dance. They were laughing hard while holding each other up. At least somebody was having fun.

"This is too weird," Noah said. "I never thought Joe would marry into a bunch of celebrities. I thought he'd end up in jail."

Beast chuckled his agreement. It was hard to get past the fame in Joe's new family. His father-in-law was an Oscar-winning director, his mother-in-law a multiple-Oscar-winning actress, his brother-in-law was an action movie star, and his sister-in-law...

His eyes found Belinda Collins, yet again. She was magnetic and he was cheap-as-dirt tin. She pulled him to her, the same way she pulled the eyes of most every man in the room. And each and every one of them looked at her with a need to possess, something she seemed oblivious to as she danced with sensual abandon. The woman moved like smoke. Elusive. Sensual. Provocative. She was messing with his brain and making him sound like a weird fragrance commercial.

Noah caught the direction of Beast's gaze and shook his head. "She's not for the likes of us, Beasty-boy."

There was no need to reply. An MMA fighter who lived in the underbelly of society and a Hollywood princess? Yeah. Wasn't going to happen. Unless...she fancied slumming it. But then, even if she did, Beast wasn't about to lower *his* standards to appease her curiosity about the rougher side of life. His life wasn't a tourist destination. He'd spent enough time as a kid dealing with well-meaning outsiders who treated him like a curiosity, or worse, a charity case. As far as he was concerned, if the Hollywood princess wanted to see how the other half lived, she could look elsewhere. He wasn't giving any tours.

"Doesn't cost anything to look," Beast said.

It was the mantra of his life. Plus, if a Hollywood actress wanted to put on a show, he sure as hell wasn't going to pass up the chance to watch.

"Looking is all any of us can afford with this crowd. What the hell are we doing here?" Noah drew Beast's attention away from Belinda's long legs.

"Damned if I know." If Joe had given a crap about their friendship, he'd have eloped and sent an email telling them *after* the fact. Hell, the ceremony hadn't even taken place in Peru. That had been a tiny event in Scotland. Now, if Joe had stopped with that, Beast would have been more than happy.

"We're here to support Joe," Harvard said as he sipped his girly champagne. Out of the five childhood friends, Michael Carter, a.k.a. Harvard, was the only one who'd gone to college. Ironically, his big brain had earned him a full scholarship at MIT, but it had been too late by then to change his nickname. "And, hopefully, get laid." He grinned. "I call dibs on Morticia."

Their heads turned to watch the woman Harvard couldn't take his eyes off, Rachel Ford-Talbot. She was mega-rich, related to British royalty, and an ice-cold bitch. She was also one of the owners of Benson Security, the firm Joe worked for and wanted his friends to join.

"She'll freeze your balls off," Beast warned.

"Yeah, but what a way to go." Harvard grinned. He put his glass on the bar beside him and tugged at the cuffs of the white shirt where they poked out from the sleeves of his charcoal suit. He ran a hand over his shaven head and turned to them. "How do I look?"

"Black," Noah said. "And I don't think the princess does homeboys."

"You know what they say about going black…" Harvard waggled his eyebrows at them. He was six feet six inches of pure muscle and genius brain, but he was also a horny black man with his eye on the prize. "Wish me luck. I'm going in." And with that, he sauntered through the crowd and straight towards Rachel.

"Ten bucks says she eviscerates him within five minutes." Noah reached for his wallet.

"When are you gonna learn that you never bet against Harvard?"

"Next time."

"Fool."

"You taking the bet or not?"

"Hell yeah, I'm taking your money."

Beast shook his head. It was a miracle Noah had become a cop instead of the world's worst gambler. And growing up in Atlantic City, the pressure was on to become the latter. Not for the first time, Beast thanked God that they'd all been roped into a church boxing group when they were teens. That group had saved all of them.

"Nice to see how the other half live," Noah said as he surveyed the crowded ballroom. With its floor-to-ceiling windows and view across the Amazon, it was a far cry from Noah's own wedding reception, which had been held at the local Irish bar. "Guess this is what happens when you have more money than sense. Do you know what Julia's mother told me?"

Beast shook his head. A better question might have been whether he cared what she'd told him.

"That they chose Peru for the party because it had

romantic significance for the couple—they fell in love here." Noah shuddered at the thought.

Beast was in complete agreement. That was the kind of pink, girly crap that made a man want to find the nearest underground fight and let off some steam.

"Joe know she's telling people that?" he said.

"Joe doesn't give a crap. Look at him."

The newlyweds, Joe and Julia, were slow dancing to a techno tune over in the corner by the bar. The place could have blown up and they wouldn't have noticed.

"How the mighty fall," Beast said, with a shake of his head. "What'd you get the happy couple for a wedding gift?" He put his empty glass on the bar behind him. He was done for the night.

"Dinner plates with the flag printed on them."

"The American flag?"

Noah's eyebrows shot up. "Is there another one? What'd you get them?"

"Matching pistols." Noah laughed hard, and Beast shrugged. "It was before I met Julia. I figured if she worked at a security company she had to like guns. Now I've met her, I realise I should have bought her a whiteboard."

"She does like her lists."

Joe had sent them photographic evidence that they were on several of Julia's lists, which meant they had to turn up for the wedding. There had almost been a whiteboard meltdown when Beast made it clear he could only attend the last couple of days of the reception. Julia had been forced to write new lists, and Joe had not been pleased.

"What do you think Joe's in-laws got them?" Noah pointed to the dance floor, where Julia's famous family were holding centre stage. Each of her siblings were competing with each other, and their mother, for the spotlight. It was hard to believe they were related to the painfully shy bride.

"Gold-plated bathtub?"

Noah choked on his beer, and Beast thumped his back.

"That doesn't help," Noah said when he could breathe again.

They watched the dancing for a few minutes, and Beast found his eyes constantly straying to Belinda Collins. The actress was wearing a shimmering silver lace mini-dress that hugged her curves. She'd kicked off her shoes hours ago, and the silver toe ring on her left foot kept snagging his attention. Her hair was down, skimming her shoulders in a cut that probably cost the average person a year's wages. But, he had to admit, just looking at those silky tresses made him think it was worth the money. And the way she moved brought on all sorts of visions involving satin skin on silk sheets.

"You gonna take the job?" Noah's question snapped Beast's attention back to his friend.

"Dunno. You?"

Noah looked down for a second. "Yeah. There's nothing keeping me and the kids in Atlantic City now Therese is gone."

Beast slapped a hand on his friend's shoulder and squeezed. Cancer had taken Noah's wife two years earlier, leaving him with a broken heart, and two young boys to raise.

"London will take some getting used to," Beast said, because he didn't know how else to comfort his friend. "Don't think there's any baseball."

"I'll survive. Well, what do you know?" Noah pointed to the other side of the room. "Looks like I might win a bet for a change."

Beast groaned at the sight of Harvard receiving a lecture from his crush and pulled a ten out of his wallet. "Guess this means Harvard will follow his dick and take the job too."

"She's an incentive, but he's ready for a change. He's done with the government. He wants a new life."

They watched as Rachel slapped the big guy's face and then strode away with her nose in the air. Harvard stared after her like a puppy watching his owner leave the house.

"Here's hoping he lives long enough to enjoy it," Beast said.

"It'd be good if we were all together again." Noah used a suspiciously light tone that told Beast he was trying not to pressure him.

"I don't know if I can follow orders, and Callum McKay sure likes to bark them at his team." They looked over at one of the four owners of Benson Security. He was standing at the edge of the dance floor, feet apart, arms folded, glaring as his wife danced with a British actor. Every time Isobel caught his eye, she burst out laughing. But the actor was beginning to sweat under Callum's threatening stare.

"I don't think he realises he isn't in the army anymore." Noah took a sip of beer before casting Beast a sideways glance. "You're going to think about it, though, right?"

"Told Joe I would. Although if that"—he pointed at Belinda's bodyguards—"is the standard at Benson Security, I think I'll take a pass." The two men were too busy flirting with the wedding guests to pay any attention to their charge.

"They're a different crew," Noah said. "Julia's trying to get her family to fire their teams and take on people from Benson Security."

"They need firing." Beast scanned the crowd and spotted Belinda staggering towards the exit, shoes in hand. "They haven't even noticed their charge is leaving."

Noah's eyes swung to the movie star. "You head her off and I'll go kick their asses. She can't head out of here alone."

Their five-star cabanas were dotted all over the large acreage of the resort. And although it was an isolated location, there was always a chance someone would want to get a little too close to a film star.

"No, she can't." Beast scowled at the thought. "Meet you in the lobby. Kick them hard."

He took off at a jog, pushing his way through the partying crowd. One of the newer Benson Security team members was covering the door to the ballroom—overseeing the hotel's security staff, and the private protection brought in by the celebrity guests.

"Belinda?" Beast called to the woman. She barely topped five feet and yet still managed to look deadly.

She glared at him, as though his one-word question was a criticism of her ability. "She's meeting the third member of her team, the driver, at the main entrance. I have a hotel security officer escorting her there." She was of Chinese heritage, with a thick Scottish accent that did nothing to soften her angry demeanour. "Because the arseholes who should be watching her are nowhere to be found."

"They're busy hitting on women on the other side of the ballroom."

She muttered some curse words that Beast didn't catch.

"I'll cover her until they get here," Beast said. "Noah's rounding them up."

"Roger that. I'll inform the team." She pressed the bud in her ear and mumbled into her throat mike.

Beast didn't wait; he jogged through the resort corridors, hoping he picked the fastest route to head Belinda off before she left the building. She was a celebrity, recognised the world over, and she should have known better than to go anywhere without her complete team—even if she was surrounded by family and friends. Just because you were familiar with people, didn't mean you should trust them. Beast knew exactly how evil the people closest to you could be.

He ran down the stairs, skipping several at a time, and rushed into the lobby, just as Belinda went through the main doors and out into the night. The third member of her team, the driver, greeted her with a smile that was as fake as a two-dollar bill. Alarm bells blasted in Beast's head. Every instinct he had told him something was wrong. He just didn't know what it was—yet. His eyes scanned as he ran, looking for the threat. Adrenalin honed his skill and instinct until he noticed every detail surrounding the actress. But still he couldn't spot the threat.

Belinda said something to her driver as she laughed and patted his chest. Clearly, she knew him and trusted him.

Beast didn't.

The hotel security guard who'd escorted Belinda nodded to the driver—transferring his charge over to her team. The driver smiled as he opened the rear passenger door. With his other hand, he produced a handkerchief and wiped his brow. He was far too nervous for a man inside a secure compound. A man with a team at his back.

And then the threat became clear.

If Beast hadn't been studying the scene so intently, he would have missed it. As Belinda climbed into the car, she slumped forward. The driver positioned himself behind her, blocking the passenger door from the main entrance. But he didn't block all of it. Beast saw hands reach for Belinda. Hands that shouldn't have been inside the car. In a matter of seconds, someone dragged the actress into the darkness of the vehicle.

They were kidnapping her.

A wave of adrenalin surged through Beast. With a roar, he barrelled through the doors and lunged at the driver. The man spun, his hand coming up to fend off the attack. Someone called from inside the car. Beast grabbed the driver's jacket and tossed him out of the way. Something sharp slammed into his chest. He reeled back. There was a metal dart sticking out of him. A strong hand grasped his upper arm as his knees gave way.

His last thought, before the world went dark, was *Son of a bitch drugged me.*

CHAPTER 2

Belinda Collins woke to a terrifying realisation—she wasn't in her hotel room. She knew this because her hotel would never have allowed the heat to gather in her room to the point where she felt like she was in a sauna with a sumo wrestler sitting on her chest. No, the exclusive resort on the edge of the Amazon rainforest was all about air conditioning, thousand-count sheets and beds that made you feel like you were sleeping on a cloud. And she definitely wasn't lying on a cloud. It felt very much like she was lying on a carpet of Lego.

But worse than the heat and the lumps beneath her was the presence of a large body lying beside her. The body was breathing, hopefully sleeping, and Belinda didn't dare move or open her eyes until she remembered who that body belonged to. Which, considering the fog in her head and the throbbing pain in her temples, could take a very long time.

She vaguely remembered staggering out of her sister's wedding reception, on the last night of a week filled with rainforest tours and poolside parties—all to celebrate Julia marrying Joe. Then she remembered heading for one of the cute little golf carts the hotel used to transport people around the resort. She remembered being disappointed that a SUV was waiting for her instead. She remembered her driver opening the door for her, ready to transport her to her cabana. And then…she remembered nothing at all. Nothing. Absolutely blank nothingness. She didn't have a clue where she was, how she'd gotten here and even worse, who she was with.

This was bad. Really bad. As in international-news bad. This was worse than the time she'd gone skinny-dipping with the cast of her first movie and the paparazzi had plastered the photos of her very naked, and un-Photoshopped, backside over every tabloid in the world. It had been cellulite-ageddon. And now, here she was in trouble again. How could this have happened? She was so careful now. She was past the getting drunk and blacking out stage of her life. She was mature—okay, mature-*er*. She was a serious actress. An Oscar nominee, for goodness' sake. She was also very much stuffed.

"You might as well open your eyes. I know you're awake."

Belinda's eyes popped open at the sound of the deep American accent. She blinked against light that felt like ice picks stabbing into her brain and waited as a face came into focus. She frowned. She knew that face. It was attached to the most masculine man she'd ever seen, and she vaguely remembered he was some sort of fighter…

"MMA! Cage fighting," she said with a smile, making him frown.

Wow, she hadn't seen a man pull off a look that brooding since Brando in *A Streetcar Named Desire*. It shot his looks from unconventional straight into panty-melting. And she had to admit, she'd been rather partial to his looks before he went all broody on her.

The man had skin the colour of warm caramel, cheekbones sharp enough to cut paper and hair that was so inky black it was almost blue. His nose had been broken at some point and hadn't set properly. It was a crooked line on a face made up of angled planes.

A white scar cut through his left eyebrow and another curved round his jaw. Thick black lashes outlined exotic almond-shaped eyes with the palest grey irises she'd ever seen. They were hard eyes that betrayed a man who didn't trust easily. Eyes that dared you to challenge him. Eyes that seemed to see through the polite veneer of the world around him straight to the dirt that lay beneath.

No, there was nothing pretty about John Garcia. He was a barbarian dressed in a tailored shirt and five-thousand-dollar watch—an incongruity on a man that had instantly fascinated her with his presence. He'd dominated the room when she was introduced to him earlier that day, after he'd arrived late to the week-long party. His arrival had blown every other man in the room out of the water for Belinda. Yet when he'd looked at her, she'd seen nothing but dismissal in his eyes. He was one of *those* men. The ones who thought she was useless because she spent her life pretending.

Which made it all the more humiliating that she'd ended up in bed with the man. "Please tell me we didn't sleep together?" she said, without thinking it over first—a flaw she had.

His eyes went flat. Like a shark. "Don't worry, Hollywood. You didn't lower your standards that far. We've been kidnapped."

Belinda felt her face flush as his words stung. Either the guy had a chip the size of California on his shoulder, or she'd said something to offend him when she'd been out of it. Oh, she hoped she hadn't been rude. She wasn't usually… Wait— kidnapped? What the hell?

"We've really been kidnapped? Taken? Like the movie? You mean this isn't your room?"

"You thought this dump was my room?" The jaw clenching was back.

Belinda tore her eyes from his and looked around. They were in a shack. That was the only word for it. The walls were made of planks of untreated wood, haphazardly nailed together. Overhead, beyond the torn and grey mosquito net, was a straw roof. Beneath them was a stained mattress, on a bare dirt floor. It was as far away from a hotel room as they could get and still be indoors. It was a hovel.

"No, I don't think this is your room." She looked back at him. "We've really been kidnapped? Both of us? Are you sure?"

He gave her a terse nod, as though he was losing patience. But nothing he said made sense.

"Why would they kidnap you?" she said. "I can understand why someone would kidnap me. I get lots of threats. It's part of being in the public eye. But you're...?"

His jaw became even tighter than it had been before. At this rate, the guy was going to crack the bone. "I'm what?"

Intense? Sexy? Broodingly male? Obviously, a bad-tempered dickhead? "You aren't famous."

The tension in his jaw eased somewhat. "I saw them try to take you and I stepped in to stop it. It didn't go as planned."

Now Belinda felt bad for thinking he was dickhead. "I need to sit up." She put a hand on his chest to push him out of her way.

It was a mistake. A jolt of pure electricity ran through her body as her surroundings disappeared. There was only her awareness of John. It was primal. Her body wanted his. Their chemistry was off the charts, which was not only embarrassing, but also dangerous. Getting physical with a man who barely tolerated her was a recipe for disaster. She snatched her hand away, feeling as though she'd been burned, and sat up. He backed away from her, and she noticed that his hands and feet were tied, but hers were free. It didn't make sense. None of this did.

"Are you sure this is a real kidnapping and not a fake one?" she asked.

"Fake one?" He looked at her like she was several sandwiches short of a picnic. "This is real, Hollywood. Your driver set you up. That's how this happened."

Now it really didn't make sense. "No. Brian wouldn't have done that. He's been with me for years."

His face gave nothing away. "The guy opened the back door of the car for you. While you were smiling at him, someone drugged you and pulled you inside. I was the lucky bastard who stepped in to stop them and ended up going along for the ride."

She stared into his eyes, trying to read the truth in them. She knew subterfuge. She worked in an industry of liars. And John Garcia was telling the truth—or at least he believed he was, which meant he wasn't in on it. Because Belinda was beginning to believe that her kidnapping was nothing more than an elaborate prank.

"They drugged us. We've been out cold for hours," John continued in that flat voice she hated, as though he could barely tolerate talking to her. "It's three in the morning."

She watched him for a couple of minutes, but he didn't even blink. He was definitely being pranked too. Nobody was that good an actor.

"My brother and I talked about this a couple of months ago," Belinda said. "There are security companies who arrange fake kidnappings to teach you how to act if a real one happens. I was going to attend a workshop before I took on a movie role where I played a kidnap victim, but I chickened out at the last minute. My brother thought I was a wimp and threatened to arrange to have me fake-kidnapped when I least expected it. He must have gone ahead with it and roped Brian in to help."

John's eyes went wide, then narrowed to hard little slits. "Listen to me carefully. This is not a joke. It is not a training exercise. You really have been kidnapped."

She reached over and patted his arm, again feeling that strange, tingling awareness when she touched him. This time, she tried not to let it bother her and kept her hand in place.

"I know you believe what you're saying," she said in her most soothing tone, "but think about it carefully. A fake kidnapping is the only logical conclusion. We were in a private resort, miles from anywhere. The resort has its own security staff. At least a third of the guests brought their own security teams to the wedding. On top of that, half the wedding guests work with Benson Security—one of the best security companies in the world. Do you really think, given all that information, that someone could waltz in and snatch us out from under their noses? Does that seem likely to you? I don't think so. The only way it could have happened was if the people at the party were in on the kidnapping plot—ergo, fake kidnapping experience!"

He seemed to be grinding his teeth together, so she gave him another pat. She'd bet her next paycheque that her brother had boasted about his plan to John's friends and they'd jumped at the idea to include him. Probably because John was late getting to the party. Surely his friends would have known he couldn't cope with this sort of joke. She was going to give them a serious talking to once this experience was over.

"Don't worry." She patted him again. "I know what I'm doing. Just follow my lead. I don't think they're expecting expert level acting, anyway. In fact, we could totally ham this up. This is going to be fun."

John opened his mouth, no doubt to argue further, but the door to the hut slammed inwards. A man stepped into the room. He had a lean and hungry look about him that told her he could be cruel and enjoy it. He wore grey jeans and a pale blue dress shirt that had large, dark patches of sweat under the arms. Tucked into his belt was a large machete. In his right hand he held a revolver, and in his left, he held a large mobile phone. Overgrown, greasy hair had been swept back from his forehead, and calculating, beady eyes considered them.

"*Bueno*, you're awake. Now we talk business, no?"

With a smile that chilled her to the bone, he walked towards them.

Belinda stared at him in awe. Here was a man who really knew how to get into character. She could learn a lot from him. Maybe she'd get something out of being pranked after all.

CHAPTER 3

Beast had descended into the ninth circle of hell. Not only had he been kidnapped, but he was with a woman who didn't believe it was happening. A woman who thought they'd have fun. They weren't going to have fun. They were going to die. And he would bet that the asshole in front of him would be the one to pull the trigger.

With bound hands, Beast grabbed Belinda and shoved her behind him.

"Great improvising," she whispered to him, making him growl.

Their captor smirked at the move, thinking he was the one with the power. He didn't know Beast. Even bound, hands and feet, he'd take the guy in a fight. The guns were a problem, though. Fists were no good against bullets.

"Señorita Collins," the kidnapper said.

Beast didn't like his tone. It made his skin crawl. This guy wanted Belinda. And not just for money.

"And"—the kidnapper cocked his head at Beast—"it seems we have an extra guest. One who isn't as famous as the beautiful señorita."

Beast didn't answer. He wasn't giving this guy anything if he could help it. Not even his name. Behind the kidnapper, two more men sauntered into the tiny room, and the tension amped right up. They were both armed with rifles. The two men stood either side of the door, ready to protect their leader. Or to kill the captives. With a knowing smile, the leader turned to the two men behind him and spoke in Spanish, a language Beast spoke fluently.

"See how he protects her still? What a good dog!"

Beast's muscles went taut. But he didn't move. He'd learned the hard way not to react, to bide his time before he struck his foe.

"Señorita Collins, it is a pleasure to have you as our guest." The leader's eyes lazily scanned her body, lingering at her breasts and thighs. Yeah, the asshole definitely had plans for Belinda that didn't involve making money from her.

"Who are you? What do you want?" Belinda sounded terrified. Over-the-top terrified. The airhead was acting. Overacting, in an attempt to have some fun. Beast itched to shake some sense into her, but he didn't move. He had to keep his eyes on the biggest threat in the room—the kidnapper.

"What do I want?" The guy shared a laugh with his colleagues. "I want money."

He crouched down in front them. Beast noticed he made sure to keep out of reach of his feet. It said a lot about their kidnapper, that he realised Beast was dangerous to him, even while bound. Which made Beast even more worried. This was a man who knew violence, who assessed people quickly and wasn't afraid of striking out. In fact, Beast suspected their kidnapper enjoyed making people suffer. He reeked of it. His eyes glowed when Belinda cowered. Yeah, he was definitely their biggest threat.

The kidnapper held a phone out to Belinda. "I need you

to call your very famous father and tell him that he must do as I instruct. If he doesn't, I will feel the need to send his princess back to him in pieces."

His voice was calm, to the point where he could have been discussing the weather, not threatening an A-list actress. Beast felt Belinda still behind him and hoped reality was sinking in for her at last.

"I know I should stay in character," she said cheerily, "but I have to ask. I mean, you're an amazing actor. Right up there with De Niro. You've even got me second-guessing things. This *is* a fake kidnapping, right? Not a real one?"

If this were any other situation, and Beast's life wasn't on the line, he would have groaned. Belinda Collins didn't think like normal people. She was in a world all of her own. One that was most likely populated with Disney princesses, rainbows and unicorns.

The kidnapper looked stunned for a second and then burst out laughing. "*She thinks this is fake. She thinks we're all acting,*" he told his men, who laughed heartily too.

"Oh, señorita," the guy said, "this is very much a *real* kidnapping. And as *real* kidnappers, we want our ransom." He gave her a wide smile that didn't touch his eyes.

There was silence for a second as Belinda processed his answer. "Gotcha, you can't break character. I should have known. You're professionals."

"*She still doesn't believe me,*" he told his men. "*She thinks this is a game. I wonder if she'll think my dick is real when I shove it into her.*"

Beast clenched his fists to stop from lunging for the man. He obviously assumed his captives didn't speak Spanish, or he didn't care if they did. His eyes shot to Beast and he smirked, challenging him to do something about his plans. Beast clenched his teeth hard as he narrowed his eyes at the man. As far as Beast was concerned, his kidnapper was nothing more than a dead man walking.

The kidnapper held the phone out to Belinda. "Make the call," he ordered her, his voice cold and flat.

Belinda took the phone. "And you promise that once you have the money, you'll return us to our families?" She was back to acting.

"But of course." He shrugged, as though he was a reasonable man.

"Unharmed?" She infused the word with trembling fear. If only it had been real caution Beast heard instead of the part she thought she was playing.

"I'm sure we won't hurt her too much while we use her," the kidnapper said to his men, who laughed again.

He turned back to her with a leering smile. "Of course you will be returned in one piece to your family. We are not monsters. We are businessmen."

Yeah, even if he couldn't speak Spanish, Beast wouldn't have believed him.

"What do you want to do about her bodyguard?" one of the men asked.

The leader gave Beast a considering look. *"We keep him for now. We can use him to get her to behave. But once his usefulness is over, get rid of him."*

Beast tensed. He'd known he was useless to the kidnappers. Now he knew his time was already running out.

"Should I get my father to handle John's ransom too?" Belinda said, making the men still. "Or do you want John to speak to his partners at the studio himself?"

What the hell? Beast wanted to turn to her and shake some sense into her. He wasn't a damn character in her delusional game. None of them were.

"Studio?" The leader eyed Beast.

"Oh, yes, studio. Unless it's too expensive to call the States." Belinda had obviously decided that her character should be dumb as dirt. Great. More fun for all.

"Oh, wait," she said as she scooted forward, phone in hand. "That was your agent at the party, right? You could call him instead." She beamed at him, clearly enjoying herself.

Beast stared at her. He couldn't speak. There were actually no words in his head.

"Why would your bodyguard need an agent?" the leader said.

Belinda giggled, and Beast had to fight the urge to shake his head. What the hell was she doing? She was going to get them both killed.

"This isn't my bodyguard," she said. "This is John Favreau. He's one of the best directors in Hollywood. He directed *Iron Man*. He's known for his action movies, and he's going to direct me in my next movie." She lowered her voice as though she was imparting a national secret. "I'm playing the title role in a reboot of *Supergirl*. That's why he was invited to my sister's wedding." She gave Beast a vapid but shaky smile —still playing her part of airheaded kidnap victim. "We're practically best friends, seeing as we'll be working together."

The leader gave her a lecherous grin. "*So pretty and yet you stupid,*" he said.

Beast knew he radiated tense readiness. If their kidnappers bought that he was anything other than a caged animal waiting to pounce, then Belinda was a better actress than he'd given her credit for.

"A movie director?" Their kidnapper was, unsurprisingly, unconvinced.

Beast silently willed Belinda to shut her mouth and stop weaving stories that were going to get them both shot.

She didn't. Instead, her eyes widened and she nodded.

"Oh yes, he started in the business as a stuntman. That's where the muscles come from; he's known for his healthy movie sets. All of his casts are expected to work out and eat, like, salads and stuff."

She'd lost the plot entirely now. Beast wasn't even sure what she was talking about. She was so focused on making the fake kidnapping fun for them both that she was weaving incredible stories. He'd seen photos of the real John Favreau. The guy did not look like he worked out ten hours a day. All their captors had to do was Google the name and they'd know Belinda was lying.

"Stuntman?" The leader was clearly sceptical.

"Oh yes." She nodded, all wide-eyed and breathy with conviction. It was hard to believe she'd been nominated for an Oscar. She looked better suited for the type of acting you found in a porn movie. A comparison that must have occurred to their kidnappers too. They were looking at her as though they were starving and she was steak.

"After a few years getting knocked around doing stunts," Belinda carried on, oblivious to the hole she dug deeper with each crazy word, "John decided he knew more about making action movies than the guys ordering him around, and he made one to prove it. The rest is box office history. Now he makes the best action movies on the planet."

He also made *Elf*. Another fact the kidnappers would find out when they Googled the real John Favreau.

There was a moment's silence before the leader spoke. "I think the *big director* can make his own phone call."

Yeah, that hole was even deeper now.

"You first." The leader motioned to the phone.

Beast kept his eyes on the men as she dialled. "Dad, it's me, Belinda."

There was silence. Belinda smiled. "I knew you were in

on this too! Tell Daniel I'm going to get him back for this." She actually winked at her captor before getting back into character. "Dad, listen, the men who've taken us want me to give you a message." Her voice broke on the last word, and if Beast didn't know she was hamming it up, he'd have thought she was genuinely scared. "John Favreau has been kidnapped too. We're together. John is going to call his agent, Michael Carter, and tell him he needs to pay the ransom. I'm telling you the same thing. Everything will be okay if you pay. The—"

She didn't get to finish, as the phone was snatched from her hand.

"Señor Collins," the leader said to her father, his eyes still on hers and a smirk in place, "I have left a letter for you at reception. Follow the instructions in it and you'll get your daughter back in one piece." He hung up. "Well done, Señorita, we are going be good friends—this I know."

The leader handed the phone to Beast. "Your turn, *big director.*"

Beast had no choice but to play along. He had absolutely no doubt that if he didn't, there would be a bullet lodged between his eyes before he could take another breath. He stabbed Harvard's number into the phone, his eyes never leaving their captor. With bound hands, he held it to his ear. "I've been kidnapped. Pay the ransom." He tossed the phone to the leader, who narrowed his eyes.

The man held the phone up. "Is this the director's agent?" There was a pause. "That depends on you. I didn't plan for two captives. You will follow the instructions given to Señor Collins or your client will die."

Belinda shrank behind Beast and started to sob. Crocodile tears. Great.

"You're going to regret this," Beast told the leader when

he'd finished the call. His voice lacked emotion of any kind. He was imparting fact. Nothing more.

The man stood and turned his back on them. A clear message that the man didn't fear Beast. His threat meant nothing to him. *"What's he going to do?"* he said to his men. *"Go on TV and complain about me? Americans! Always complaining about something."*

No, Beast thought, *I'm going to hold your head and twist until I hear your neck crack. That's how I'm going to make my complaint.*

"Rest," the kidnapper said. "This will be over in the morning." He turned towards the door but looked over his shoulder with a chilling smile. "I wouldn't try to escape. We're in the middle of the jungle. There are no towns for miles. Your chances of making it out alive are non-existent. Trust me, you are better off dealing with me than the jaguar who prowl this area. And to prove I am a businessman and not a monster." He ordered one of his men to give them provisions.

The man reached outside the hut and came back with two bottles of water. He tossed them on the mattress beside Belinda.

"We will bring more in the morning. Now rest. You have had a stressful day, no?" And with that, he was gone.

Beast turned to find Belinda grinning at him, her eyes dry. She reached for the bottles and handed one to Beast. He ignored it.

"You need to drink," she said. "You dehydrate fast in this humidity."

He felt his eye begin to twitch. There was a good chance that if the kidnappers didn't rid the world of Belinda Collins, he might do it himself.

"What the hell did you think you were doing?" he demanded.

She blinked at him with confusion and twisted the lid back onto the bottle. "I was establishing your role. It will be much more fun for you if you're a famous victim too."

Beast was pretty sure a vein popped at his temple. "This. Is. Not. A. Game. This is a real kidnapping. Those were real guns. You are in real danger."

She rolled her eyes. Dramatically. "I'll admit, for a second there, I doubted. That guy was such a good actor. He totally gives me the creeps. Like De Niro in *Cape Fear*. He's wasted in the jungle. He should be in Hollywood; he'd make a fortune. Anyway, I thought it through, and really, this couldn't be anything but fake. Think about it logically. There was too much security at the hotel, Brian would never betray me, and my brother threatened to arrange this experience for me. I'm sorry your friends roped you in too, but you should suck it up and make the best of it. Think of this as training for when you take the job with Benson Security. They do a lot of hostage retrieval work. This way, you get to see things from the victim's side, and it will help you become a more sensitive security specialist."

A rumbling growl was the only answer Beast could give her.

"Do you have to growl at me? How about you use your words instead. Huh?"

Beast could have sworn a blood vessel popped behind his eye, because he was definitely seeing red. "How's this for some words, Hollywood? This is a real kidnapping and we're in a fuckload of trouble, which you just made worse. You put us on a deadline. As soon as you opened your mouth and gave him a name he could look up on the internet, the clock started ticking. Now, we have no option but to escape tonight. Which means hiking through the rainforest with no resources, no idea of our location and no experience in this terrain. Basically, we're up shit creek and I'm your only paddle, because somehow, I don't think you have the skills we need to get out of this alive. So, listen very carefully to what I say—this shit is real."

She stared at him for a long time before she smiled. "That was awesome! I actually had goosebumps. That's some of the best acting I've seen in years."

Beast couldn't help it. He growled again.

CHAPTER 4

Ryan Granger, security specialist and ex-soldier, was on round two of his own private party with a waitress called Esperanza, when the *Batman* theme blared from his dress trouser pocket. The trousers were on the floor, where he'd kicked them off in his rush to get naked. Unfortunately, he'd forgotten to switch off his phone before he'd undressed, hence the very loud and very annoying music.

As the sound grew in volume, Ryan knew he couldn't ignore it. It was the ringtone he'd assigned to his boss. And if he didn't answer, Callum would come find him instead. Reluctantly, Ryan rolled off the gorgeous woman beneath him. Esperanza was made for sex; she had curves in all the right places and inky-black hair that fell in waves to her hips. Separating from her, even for five minutes, was damn hard to do.

She groaned, grabbed his hand and pulled him down for another kiss. Damn, but it was tempting to pretend he didn't hear his phone and instead concentrate on the very needy woman in his bed. After all, he was technically on an enforced vacation. And this was what he did on vacation—he found a willing woman and lost himself in her until it was time to return to reality.

With genuine regret, he extradited himself from Esperanza's arms, rolled to the edge of the bed, put his feet on the ground and reached for his phone. Esperanza sat up behind him, pressing her lush breasts against his back. Ryan mentally cursed his boss and prayed Callum had a genuine reason for interrupting one of the best nights of his life.

"Don't answer it," the temptress said as she kissed Ryan's neck.

She spoke English as though she was born to it, but with the sensual accent of a native South American Spanish speaker. Compared to the flat tones of his London accent, every word Esperanza uttered was an invitation to sin. Just hearing her talk made him hard all over again.

"I have to answer. I wish I didn't, but it's the bat signal."

"You're a superhero?" He felt her smile against his skin.

He smiled back, even though she couldn't see it, as he glanced at his phone's screen. Yep. It was his grumpy-arsed boss, Callum McKay. A text appeared on the screen while he held it: *Answer your bloody phone!* Callum seemed madder than usual, which only happened when Ryan did something particularly dumb. He glanced over his shoulder at Esperanza. Could she be considered a dumb decision?

"You didn't answer my question," she said as she nibbled his shoulder. "Are you a superhero?"

"One of many. I'm on a team of superheroes," he told her. "We're all ex-military, or ex-law enforcement. It's our job to fight the bad guys."

He felt her tense behind him. "I knew you were security, but I thought you installed cameras and made sure shopping malls were safe."

"Nope, baby, we're the real deal. We're the guys the cops call in when their hands are tied. We do a lot of bodyguard work, hostage retrieval and investigative work. Think A-Team rather than mall cop."

Before she could say anything else, Ryan answered his phone. "Yeah?"

"We need you in the ballroom. Belinda and Beast have been kidnapped."

A burst of adrenalin shot through him, and just like that, his mind wasn't on sex any longer. "On my way."

He ended the call and reached for his pants. There was no time to dig around looking for jeans, in the bag he hadn't bothered to unpack. The dress clothes he'd worn to the party would have to do. Belinda and Beast were as much a part of Benson Security as anyone employed by the company. Belinda was the sister of the London office manager, Julia. And Beast was one of Joe's best friends. That made them family.

As he buttoned up his crisp white shirt, Ryan looked at Esperanza. She was kneeling in the middle of the bed; the sheet was pulled up to cover her breasts, and her hair was wild about her shoulders.

"I need to go." Ryan didn't bother tucking in the shirt. "Something's come up. You don't need to leave, but I don't know when I'll be back. This could take a while. Make yourself at home, huh? Have a shower, or there are snacks in the fridge." He leaned over, clasped her nape and pulled her in for a kiss that quickly turned desperate.

With great difficulty, he pulled himself away from her. Damn, he'd never seen anything sexier than this woman. With her kiss-swollen lips and gorgeous golden skin, she was temptation personified.

But she was a temptation he had to resist.

"I really don't want this to be the end of things. I'm here for a few more days, maybe longer. Leave your number on the nightstand, and I promise I'll take you out for a five-star meal." He snorted. "Somewhere where you don't work." His phone beeped and he looked down to see another text from Callum. *Get your arse down here!*

After one last kiss, Ryan headed for the safe in the room's closet. He punched in the code and retrieved his pistol, tucking it into the back of his pants, under his shirt.

"Don't leave here without giving me a way to contact you," he ordered the lust-dazed woman, and then he forced himself out of the door and ran for the little golf cart that would take him back to the main hotel building.

As soon as he was moving, he regretted that he'd ever answered his phone. Leaving Esperanza in his warm bed was tantamount to torture. He actually felt like he was being pulled apart the further he got from her. He was never this soft over a girl. It had to be the wedding. Or the champagne. Or the rainforest. Something was affecting his brain, because he never gave a second thought to a woman after he left her bed. He'd made a fine art out of being carefree when it came to sex.

Why then couldn't he get the sight of her dark eyes watching him leave out of his mind? Why was he thinking about Esperanza when he should have been focused on their missing teammates? Bloody Peru. He hated the country. Every damn time they were in it, things went balls up. And now, instead of enjoying the woman in his bed, he was running off to deal with another South American crisis. He should have stayed in England.

CHAPTER 5

Belinda felt sorry for John. The stress of the situation had to be hard to deal with if you believed it was real. And she was sure it wasn't. What else could it be other than the fake kidnapping her brother had threatened her with? There was just too much evidence against it being real. Although she would have been a tad more confident if the kidnapping guy had broken character for a couple of minutes to reassure her things were fake.

"Don't worry, John, everything is going to be fine," she said to the man who was glaring at her.

"Don't call me John."

She blinked several times. That was not what she was expecting him to say. "Why shouldn't I call you John? It's your name. Did the drugs they gave us affect your memory? Have you forgotten your name? How many fingers am I holding up?" She held up two.

He did that annoying growling thing again. "I'm not concussed. I know who I am. What I'm telling you is simple. See if you can follow along. Don't call me John. Call me Beast. Or nothing at all."

Belinda gaped at him. "Call you what?"

He held out his bound hands and made a fist with the right one. Sure enough, tattooed on each knuckle were letters that made up *Beast*.

"B.E.A.S.T. Beast," he said. "You memorise lines for a living; one word shouldn't be too hard to remember."

She opened and closed her mouth a couple of times. "Beast? You want to be called Beast?"

"This isn't hard, Hollywood. Say it with me—Beast."

This was just too, too funny. Belinda grinned at him. "This is priceless. My name is Belinda, but people call me Belle...and you're Beast!"

He stared at her. "Are you one of those actors who takes a pill to get through the day, and another one to get to sleep at night? Did you miss some meds?"

Belinda started to giggle. "Don't you get it?" She burst into the theme from *Beauty and the Beast*, which was hard because she was still laughing.

Beast didn't even crack a smile as Belinda wiped tears from her eyes. This was too good not to share. As soon as she was done being kidnapped, this was going on Instagram.

"Just use the name," he snapped. "Now, stop laughing and untie me. We need to get out of here."

She shook her head as she struggled for composure. "We can't."

His eye twitched and his jaw clenched and unclenched. "Why not?"

She pointed at the tiny, glassless window. "It's dark o'clock. Didn't you hear him? We're in the middle of the rainforest, and you don't want to be out in the jungle at night. Especially when you don't have a clue where you are. Don't you watch the Natural History channel? Didn't you see the movie Daniel Radcliffe made? Four men got lost in the jungle; only two of them made it out. Daniel was one of them. That's how bad it is out there. Everything can kill you in the jungle at night. Everything."

He gave her a look that made her think *he* might turn out to be one of the things that could kill her.

"Untie me," he said very slowly. "I have a plan."

"Oh." Her eyes went wide. "I get it. You think we should do what kidnap victims would actually do. I agree. We should definitely escape. We should make this as hard on them as possible."

"Then untie me."

She considered him. He was a loose cannon. He could get himself hurt if he freaked out and ran off half-cocked. "Tell me the plan first, and if it makes sense, I'll untie you."

Yeah, he was definitely going to kill her. It was there in his eyes.

"Hollywood, you wouldn't recognise a good plan if it bit you in the ass."

She shrugged. "Then I guess you stay tied up until someone comes to rescue us." A rescue had to be part of the package Daniel paid for? Surely, she wasn't expected to rescue herself? That seemed like way too much work.

They waited in silence. She folded her arms over the silver dress that was little more than a long T-shirt and wished she'd been kidnapped when she'd been wearing jeans and sneakers.

The silence stretched, and it became clear that Beast had a stubborn streak to match hers, which was impressive.

"Fine," he snapped at last. "I was going to get you to put your acting *skills* to good use and send you outside to see what their camp looks like."

"I'm going to ignore the fact you sneered the word *skills* and say that's a great idea."

Before he could say anything else, she was on her feet and

thumping at the door. "Hello, anybody, I need to use the bathroom. *Hola, tengo el baño.*"

"I wasn't finished detailing the plan," Beast snarled at her.

"What's to finish? I agreed with this stage. If it looks like we might be able to escape, we'll discuss the next step. First, we need to see what we're up against. Right? And I can totally do this. I have kidnap victim experience. Although the woman I played was kept in an apartment in Manhattan. But I can adapt. Don't worry. I've got this."

She beamed at him. Beast leaned back and hit his head on the wall. Repeatedly. She would have told him to stop before he hurt himself, but the door opened and a man with a gun appeared.

"*Baño?*" Belinda flashed her movie-star smile.

"*Vamos.*" He motioned for her to follow.

"Oh wait, my shoes." She ran for her silver high-heeled sandals as the guy followed her into the room. He sneered at Beast as Belinda tugged her shoes on. Then the two men watched in bewildered wonder as she fluffed her hair and adjusted the strap of her tiny cross-body bag. "I'm ready."

Both Beast and the guy with the gun just stared at her.

"What?" she said as she tottered towards the door on four-inch heels.

She heard Beast groan as the door closed behind them.

CHAPTER 6

Ryan jogged down the long corridors of the overpriced resort and slammed through the ballroom doors. The party was well and truly over. The lights were on full and the tables had been pulled into the centre of the room to form a makeshift command centre. His team were at the tables. Elle Roberts, their IT expert, was busy tapping at her laptop. She'd dyed her hair lavender to match her party dress, rather than the usual electric blue she preferred.

"Any word?" Ryan asked her as he pulled up a seat beside her.

"The kidnapper called and spoke with Belinda's parents and then Harvard." She pointed at the giant black man who was one of Joe Barone's childhood friends and, if rumours were right, ex-CIA and about to become part of the Benson Security London team. "Her dad said Belinda wasn't making any sense. He thought she was drugged. I'm trying to pinpoint the location the call came from, or at least narrow it down."

"Why'd they talk to Harvard?" And what was it with Americans and nicknames? On Joe's side of the wedding party, there was a Grunt, a Beast and a Harvard. Ryan felt sorry for the fifth guy, Noah, and wondered why he didn't have a nickname too.

Elle let out a tense sigh. "Belinda told her captors that Beast was really John Favreau, the movie director, and that Harvard was his agent."

Ryan let out a low whistle. "Rookie move. Now all they have to do is Google him to see if she's lying. A made-up name would have bought slightly more time than a real one."

"Yep, she put them under pressure."

"Listen up." Lake Benson, the original owner of the company, raised his voice to cut through the chatter, and all eyes turned to him. "The clock is ticking here. The ransom is supposed to be transferred to the kidnappers' account by midday. Seeing as it's past three now, that doesn't give us much time to find them. The Collinses are insistent on paying the ransom by the deadline. Delaying payment would have bought us more time. As it is, we have nine hours to get to them."

As an ex-SAS soldier, Lake was experienced with these situations. The man was still lean and muscled well into his forties, and there was barely any grey in his blonde hair. He stood at the end of their makeshift war area, with two of his partners, Callum McKay and Rachel Ford-Talbot, flanking him. The fourth partner, Harry, was a silent partner. Ryan had never actually met the guy. As far as he knew, he had very little to do with the business.

"Elle," Lake said. "What can you tell us?"

Elle's fingers stilled over the keys as she looked up at her team. "I'm not sure yet, but I think I may have narrowed down the search area—and it isn't good news. It looks like they're being held in the middle of the Peruvian jungle. As far as I can tell, they're nowhere near a road, or a town."

Callum did that rumbling thing he liked to do when stuck

in an enclosed space with other human beings. "Harvard, what are the chances your man will try to escape with Belinda?"

"Pretty damn high." Harvard ran a hand over his bald head, sounding as grim as everyone else felt. "I don't see him sitting around waiting for the ransom to be paid. Even if we had the money to pay it. Beast might have squirrelled some cash away, but it sure as hell isn't anywhere close to the ten million they're asking."

Callum let out a huff. "Tell me your guy has experience in the jungle."

"Wish I could. He's city, all the way. There's no better man to have at your back, but he doesn't have any experience with this terrain. Don't underestimate him, though. He's a mean son of a bitch. When he isn't touring the MMA circuit, he works as a bodyguard. He knows how to fight, and he's street smart."

"They aren't in the street," Callum said.

The rest of the team fell silent for a minute.

"What about Belinda?" Lake turned to Belinda's brother, Daniel. "Has she got any experience in the jungle, any survival or outdoor skills?"

Daniel had paled to the point of being unrecognisable as his action-hero persona. "She made a movie once where she lived in a cabin in the Canadian wilderness."

"That's a no, then," Lake said.

"They are so stuffed," Ryan whispered to Elle, who nodded.

"Looks like we have to get to them before they start hiking out of there," Lake said. "Elle, can you narrow the search area down further?"

"Working on it." Elle's eyes didn't leave her screen. "The satellite phone signal is easier to trace than I expected it to be. They obviously didn't expect anyone to follow the call back to them,"

"Any word on the missing driver?" Lake said.

"He's involved," Elle whispered to Ryan, bringing him up to speed. "Witnesses saw him disable Beast and shove him in the car. Then the coward made a run for it."

Ryan was furious. It was people like that who gave their whole business a bad name.

"Aye, I've heard something," Callum growled in his thick Scottish brogue. "I got a text from Violet. I sent her and Noah to the airport, and they hit the jackpot. They found the bastard trying to make a run for it." Callum's eyes narrowed and he got that look his team liked to call Killer-Callum. It meant someone was about to get hurt. "They're on their way back with him. Give me five minutes alone with the guy and I'll get the information we need."

Lake nodded and turned to Dimitri, yet another American on their London team. Ryan was beginning to feel outnumbered. "Belinda's bodyguards?"

Dimitri shook his head. His wife and partner, Megan, stood beside him. The blonde Scot looked more like a Barbie wannabe than a security specialist, but Ryan knew exactly how deadly she could be—sometimes totally by accident. Megan had recently finished her trainee period and was now considered a full member of the team—something that made everyone nervous.

"Let me answer this one, babe," she said. "The guys are morons. They're drunk. They didn't even see their charge leave the room. But they could rate the racks of every woman present. I'm an eight." She frowned at Dimitri. "Told you they were bloody idiots. My boobs are a solid ten."

"At least," Dimitri said, making Megan beam at him before she turned back to Lake.

"They insist they had nothing to do with the kidnapping," she said.

"Yeah, right," Rachel said with a snort, her eyes on her phone rather than on the group.

"I'm with Rachel—" Harvard started.

"You wish," Rachel muttered.

He grinned in her direction. "They've worked as a team for years. Seems suspicious that the night their driver decides to sell out their charge, they're otherwise occupied."

"They're always like that," Daniel said. "That's why Julia wanted her to fire them and take on a Benson Security team instead."

The kid's face was ashen and his hands trembled. Ryan gave him credit for the fact he was still standing, but he was totally out of his depth.

"He doesn't need to be here for this," Ryan whispered to Elle.

"He's the family representative. His mother was hysterical and his dad took her up to their room. They left him behind to keep them informed."

Ryan's eyes were drawn to movement behind the bar. The shadows seemed to solidify, and Grunt appeared. The man mountain was Joe's best friend, best man at his wedding and the most taciturn guy Ryan had ever met. Grunt worked out of the Scottish office with Lake and was married to Megan's twin sister, Claire. Claire didn't have anything to do with security work. As far as Ryan could tell, her main function was to soothe her husband and make sure he didn't go on a rampage.

Sure enough, as Grunt stalked further into the room, a small blonde trailed in his wake. She was heavily pregnant with baby number three, the first two being twins, and was eating her way through a plate piled high with sandwiches.

Ryan's stomach grumbled, and he checked his watch. It had been over an hour since he'd last had a snack.

"I'm calling Joe," Grunt said.

"Not a good idea," Lake said. "Wait until we have more information."

"I think Julia should know about her sister," Claire said around a mouthful of food. "She'll be upset if she finds out her sister was in danger while they were on honeymoon. I know I would have been if Megan had been kidnapped during my honeymoon."

"We wait," Lake said, in that tone that brooked no argument. "We need more information first."

"They're out of contact right now anyway." Rachel held her ever-present iPhone in front of her as her red talons tapped at the screen. "Their flight to Brazil is in the air. They won't land for another four hours."

"Then you have four hours before I tell Joe," Grunt said.

Everyone in the room, bar Harvard, looked at Grunt. The man was huge and built like the Hulk on steroids. He rarely spoke, and when he did, he generally could not be moved. Ryan noticed that even Callum and Lake were leery of arguing with him. There was an uncomfortable silence.

Megan let out an exasperated sigh. "Claire, you want to deal with this?"

Claire looked up at her husband with suspiciously convenient tear-filled eyes. "Baby, this is upsetting me. And the baby. I agree we should tell Joe, but a few more hours won't hurt. Will it? Can't we wait until the team knows more? For me?" She pouted as she rubbed a hand over her swollen belly.

Ryan felt his jaw drop. There was no way Grunt would fall for that act. She wasn't even trying to be believable. He watched in awe as Grunt wrapped an arm around his wife and pulled her into his side. "Don't cry, baby. I hate it when you cry."

"What the hell?" Ryan whispered to Elle.

"Love is a mysterious thing," Elle whispered back before she grinned.

Grunt grunted. "Ransom time," he told Lake. "You have until midday."

"Thank you." Claire pressed a kiss to his chest while she gave her sister a thumbs-up.

Everyone else looked on with bewilderment.

"Elle," Lake said, "you keep working, narrow down a search grid. Dimitri and Megan, arrange transport. If we're going into the rainforest to get them, we'll need a helicopter, a boat, and a guide we can trust."

"That's asking a lot," Dimitri said. "We don't know who's taken them, and we don't know who to trust."

Elle's fingers stilled on her keyboard. "We *do* know someone we can trust. Someone who knows Peru inside out."

Ryan groaned. It didn't take a genius to figure out who she meant. David was one of Lake's shady contacts. He had skills that very few men on the planet had, which meant some government somewhere had put a whole lot of time into training him. The thing was, they didn't know for sure which government he worked for, although Elle had been obsessed with finding out ever since they'd met in Peru.

"I'll call him," Lake said. "See if he's close enough to help out."

Elle actually blushed as she went back to tapping her keyboard. Women? Who knew what they were thinking? Ryan's thoughts turned to the one in his bed. Maybe she'd be there when he got back and they could pick up where they'd left off. Yeah, that would be perfect. He shifted in his chair and hoped no one would notice that his mind wasn't on the operation.

"Ryan, Harvard," Lake said. "We need weapons, comm equipment and jungle gear. I don't know how long we'll be in that terrain. You also need to assemble supplies for Belinda and Beast."

Ryan nodded. They had contacts in Peru who could help them out. They'd made sure to establish them after their last mission in the country had gone balls up.

"Rachel," Lake said. "You run interference with the authorities, act as project coordinator, seeing as Julia's on honeymoon."

"Seriously? Rachel?" Callum was outraged.

"Like you're more tactful," Rachel scoffed.

"I don't offend everyone I talk to," Callum snapped.

"No, you punch them."

"Mummy and Daddy are fighting again," Ryan whispered to Elle, who smothered a laugh.

Callum opened his mouth to argue, but was distracted when the ballroom doors crashed open. A man flew through them. He landed in a groaning heap on the floor. Two seconds later, one of their newest team members strode in after him. Violet Lee, a miniature Scot with Chinese ancestry, stood over the man. Her hands were on her hips and there was a look of disgust on her face. When she realised everyone was staring at her, she cocked an eyebrow.

"What happened?" Callum barked.

"Nothing to worry about," Violet said. "The driver and I had a little talk on the way here. He was reluctant to tell me what he knew. I helped him to get over it."

"Damn it," Callum shouted. "I wanted to hit him."

"You snooze, you lose," Violet said.

It had become clear about ten seconds after Rachel had hired the woman that Violet showed no fear of anyone on the team. Ryan wondered if she'd been introduced to Grunt yet. Now that was a meeting he'd like to witness.

Noah, another of Joe's childhood friends—and an Atlantic City cop—rushed into the room, looking harried and slightly shell-shocked. He glanced at the driver on the floor, then looked over at Callum. "If I take the job with Benson Security, I want your word that you will never partner me with her again. You hear me? If you do, I'll quit and move the family back to the States."

"Drama queen." Violet strode towards the rest of the team, stepping on the driver's hand as she passed him. She didn't even look back as he wailed and curled into a ball.

Elle leaned in to Ryan and whispered, "You know what they say about her in Glasgow?"

"No." Ryan kept his eyes on Violet, just in case the woman decided to take out her gun and massacre the lot of them.

"Before she was kicked off the police force, there were incidents where suspects under her care were mysteriously hurt. If one of them disappeared, never to be found, the rumour was that they'd died *Violent-Lee*. Violently. Get it?"

"Yeah, Elle, I got it." Violet scared the crap out of him. He could totally understand why Noah looked like he needed some up close and personal contact with a bottle of whisky.

Violet came to a halt beside Callum. "I know who the kidnappers are."

"Who?" Callum snapped.

"The Martinez family."

The tension went up a notch. The fledgling cartel was fast gaining a reputation for their kidnapping for ransom efforts and their willingness to run drugs where others feared to tread.

"But"—Violet reached into her pocket, pulled out a wet wipe and calmly proceeded to clean the blood from her hands—"it wasn't the gang's idea to snatch the actress. Someone hired them." She cocked a thumb behind her. "Tiny dick over there doesn't know who. He just took the money they offered him and tried to run." She reached into another pocket and tossed a piece of paper onto the table in front of

Elle. "That's his bank account number. Maybe you can trace the money back to the source." She turned to glare at the driver. "Now what do you want to do about him?"

"Don't let her near me," the driver begged. "Please, somebody, keep her away from me."

The smile that crept over Violet's face was chilling.

"We'll secure him for the cops," Lake said. "No more damage unless it's necessary." Violet opened her mouth, but Lake held up a hand. "Unless *I* deem it necessary."

She frowned, clearly in disagreement with that edict.

After another terse command to reconvene half an hour before dawn, Lake dismissed the team to their tasks. Ryan wondered if Harvard would give him a minute to run to his room and see if his girl was still there before they went about assembling the team's gear. One look at the big man's stony face told him no. Guess he'd have to be happy with chasing her down when this was over. He was due a proper vacation. Maybe he'd take some time and hang around after everyone else had gone home. Yeah, he liked that idea a lot. For some reason, he knew it would take a lot more than one night to get Esperanza out of his system.

CHAPTER 7

The kidnappers' toilet turned out to be a ratty wooden cubicle built over a hole in the ground. Belinda thought it was taking the whole experience a step too far. Would the kidnapping have felt less authentic if they had a proper toilet? She didn't think so.

Someone had strung some storm lamps throughout the camp, and the dull yellow glow gave barely enough light inside the toilet hut. She looked in the hole. Eyes shone out at her. Oh no. Just no. There was no way she was baring her backside to whatever was down there. She would just hold it until the rescue, because seriously, how long would it take? They already knew where she was being held.

After a suitable amount of time had passed to make him think she'd used the facilities, Belinda called for the guard. With a bored jerk of his head, he motioned for her to follow him back across the compound to her cell. She desperately wanted to question him about his role in the fake kidnapping, but she knew she couldn't break character. She'd done that enough already, and it was clear it wasn't allowed.

The setup of the camp was impressive. If she didn't know

it was fake, she would have totally believed it. In fact, it was so authentic that a niggling thought started jabbing at her brain, telling her it was real. Could John be right? Had they really been kidnapped?

Walking across the uneven ground was tough in her party shoes. Her four-inch heels weren't designed for traversing the outdoors. Actually, she was pretty sure they weren't designed for anything other than standing still and looking pretty. Each step was agony, and she worried she'd roll her ankle and John would have to carry her back to the resort. Not John, *Beast*. She rolled her eyes. It was the kind of nickname a kid picked for himself, not a full-grown man. But whatever, she'd play along. It was what she did best.

Belinda slowed her walk to give her time to see as much as possible. There were five shack-like cabins dotted around the clearing. The voices of several men could be heard coming from the largest one. A radio blared and people laughed. It was another clear sign that this was all fake, because surely if it were real they wouldn't be hanging around partying.

The camp was surrounded by the dense foliage of the Amazon rainforest. The faint light didn't let her see much beyond the huts, but she could still make out a wall of trees and plants. Nothing else. Just trees and plants. There was no sound of rushing water, which meant they were nowhere near one of the many rivers running through the rainforest. Instead, she noticed a dirt track behind the main cabin. The path to a boat? She wasn't sure.

"I speak English," the man beside her announced.

"That's nice." Belinda smiled at him. No point in being moody with the cast.

The guard smiled, revealing stained and crooked teeth. As far as Belinda was concerned, that was taking a role a step too far. "After we get the money, I'm going to rip that dress off your body, force you to your knees and shove my dick down your throat. You'll like that, no? You actresses are all the same. Whores. Expensive whores. But instead of paying you, I'm the one that will get paid for using you. Are you worth ten million dollars?"

Belinda's stomach surged and she fought the urge to vomit. It was so real. The look on his face, the malice behind his words, the sweat-stained clothes and rotten teeth. Had she been wrong? Was this real? Or was he saying these things to make her think it was real? Sweat trickled down her spine and her hands began to shake. A door to one of the huts crashed open and a man staggered out. Drunk. He was fastening his pants. Behind him, a topless woman, wearing a ripped skirt, sobbed as she watched him leave. Her eye was black and there were bruises on her breast. The world shifted beneath Belinda's feet.

The man fastening his trousers shouted something in Spanish to her guard, who laughed. He turned back to Belinda, who was frozen in place.

He reached out, took her hand and pressed it against the front of his jeans. He was hard. Belinda tried to tug her hand away, but he held her tight, grinding her palm into him and laughing while he did it. "As soon as we get the money, we're going to play. I'm going to take that perfect mouth, and my friend over there, he's going to come in behind you and shove himself in your backside." He reached out with his other hand and grabbed a lock of her hair. He brought it to his nose and sniffed.

Belinda couldn't move. Couldn't breathe. She just stood there, watching him, horrified by his words and the images he'd put in her head. Horrified by his obvious erection. Horrified by the sobbing woman who cowered on the bed inside the cabin.

Another man sauntered across the open area and into the

cabin with the woman. The door slammed shut. There was a scream. Belinda felt tears run down her cheek. This wasn't happening. It wasn't. It was fake. Designed to make her believe the experience was real.

"You're all actors," she said, her voice hoarse. "This is all fake. My brother paid for this. It's kidnap training."

The man laughed. It was vile.

"You really are blonde and stupid. Once we get the ransom, you'll learn how real this is. And you'll like everything we do to you, won't you? Because you're nothing but a whore. You'll like it when we tie you to the table and take turns fucking you. You'll like the other men watching. Yes, I can see you'll like that very much." He pressed her hand tight against him. "Maybe I should give you a taste of what's to come now, no?"

"Miguel!" someone barked, making the man drop his hold on her hand and step back from her.

Belinda rubbed her hand against her dress, trying to get rid of the memory of touching him. The leader was standing outside the largest hut, scowling at them. From the look on his face, he knew exactly what had been said. He snapped an order in Spanish, and her guard shouted back.

The leader gave her a look of pure speculation and licked his lips. Belinda didn't understand what he'd told her guard, but he walked back into the main building.

"He says," the guard told her, "that once we have the money, I can take your mouth first."

Belinda took a step back, wishing she'd never put on the bloody shoes, so she could run if she needed to.

"*Vamos.*" Miguel put a hand on her shoulder and shoved her towards the cabin.

Belinda didn't have to be told twice; she rushed for it, grateful when the door swung open and she could step inside.

"Not long to wait," Miguel said as he started closing the door behind her. "Then you're mine."

Belinda turned towards John, who was sitting exactly as she'd left him. Her whole body was shaking and her knees gave way. She landed with a thud on her backside and pressed her back against the door.

"What the hell?" John was up on his knees, but the ropes made it hard for him to get to her. "What is it? What happened?"

"I was wrong. I was so wrong. I'm such an idiot. How could I be such an idiot?" Belinda rocked as she muttered. She ran her palm over the ground beside her, rubbing it back and forth, trying to get rid of the feel of that man pressed against her.

"Belinda." John's voice seeped through the noise in her head. "What happened?"

"It's real. It's all real. We need to get out of here." Belinda could barely get the words out. "Now. We need to go now. Now. Right now."

Her hand still felt dirty. She remembered the antibacterial wipes in her tiny bag and fumbled for them.

"Belinda?" John said. "Come over her. Come to me."

"Can't." She was shaking so hard she couldn't move. She crumpled the wet wipe up into a ball and held it fast. "We need to go, John. We need to go now. This is real. It's isn't fake. I was wrong. So wrong. I am such an idiot."

"You're not an idiot, Hollywood. You were confused. You were right, there was a lot of evidence towards this being fake."

"Don't patronise me. I know you thought I was nuts." She looked over at him as tears fell. "You were right. I am so sorry. So, so sorry."

She rocked back and forth. This was a nightmare. She was stuck in a nightmare. She could cope with make-believe.

She could channel whatever feeling a script called for. It was her gift. But this? This sort of brutal reality? This was way too much to handle.

"Come over here, Belinda. You can do it. Come to me now." John's voice was firm, calm, solid. It tempted her to obey. "I want to make sure you're okay. I have to check you over." His voice wavered, and the sound snapped Belinda out of the panic that consumed her.

"He didn't hurt me." She had to reassure him.

"Come here," John said softly. "Come to me. Tell me what he did."

"He just…he just said…things." She clutched the wipe tightly in her hand at the memory.

"Come on, baby, come over here." He made that growling noise again. "I'd come to you, but it would mean rolling over there, and that wouldn't look good."

She forced a tremulous smile. His words, his strength and even his poor attempt at humour calmed her. On shaky hands and knees, she crawled to him. He sat back, his legs out in front of him, and Belinda climbed straight into his lap. She didn't care for one second what that said about her or what he thought. He was big and strong. He had muscles and he knew how to fight. He was her only safe place in this whole terrifying mess. And she needed to be close to him. As close as possible. Just for a minute. Just until she calmed down and her heart stopped racing, and the urge to scream passed.

John lifted his arms over her head and wrapped her in the circle made by his tethered wrists. "It's okay. You're okay. I've got you."

She felt his cheek against her hair as she absorbed his heat. She pressed her ear to his chest, above his heart, and listened to the rhythm, letting it soothe her.

"We need to leave." Her voice was hoarse.

"We will leave." He rubbed his hands up and down her arm. "I should never have let you go out there. I knew you thought this was all an act and I let you walk out of here ill-prepared. I'm sorry, Hollywood."

"No." She wiped her cheeks. "It was the right thing to do. We had to know. *I* had to know. I'm okay. It was just… I just… Damn it!"

"What did the bastard say?"

She hiccupped, the memory of Miguel's words crawling over her skin. "He told me how…how he'd rape me…how they would all…"

"Fuck." John pulled her tighter.

"There was a woman. Crying in a cabin. The men were using her." She sobbed.

"I'm sorry, baby. For her and for you." He rubbed at her back.

"They're really going to do it, aren't they?" Belinda whispered. "They're going to rape me."

"No. I won't let them." John's voice was steel.

And in that moment, she believed him. He was her only point of reality in a situation she didn't understand.

And she held on tight.

CHAPTER 8

Beast listened to Belinda's breathing as she slept at his side. After she'd untied him, and he'd told her they were leaving at first light, the drugs in her system and the stress of the situation had knocked her out. She lay there, pressed against his side on the stinking mattress, trusting him to watch over her. And damn if her trust didn't do something for him. Something that Belinda probably never intended. It cracked open the wall around his heart and let the woman seep inside. Just a little. But still…

He'd spent the hours she'd been asleep planning their escape, while he listened to their captors drink themselves unconscious. After Belinda had filled him in on what she'd seen around the camp, he knew their only chance of getting out of there was by boat. He'd been out cold for the trip into the camp, but there was no other way the kidnappers could have transported them. A large part of him wanted to get his hands on a gun and rid the world of these men. The more sensible, restrained part of him knew he couldn't do anything that would put Belinda in even more danger. That meant sneaking out. Into the fucking jungle.

He mentally groaned. What the hell did he know about the jungle? He knew how to survive on the street. He'd spent more than a year living rough as a kid, rather than taking the risk with another foster home. He'd had several. Some good. Some bad. But the last one had been hell. After that, living on the street had been a breeze.

But this wasn't the street. It wasn't even Atlantic City. And he was also the only chance that Belinda had of getting out of there alive. Or, at least, untouched. His stomach contracted as he thought of the things their guard had told her. The look on her face once the cabin door had closed behind the man was something he would never forget. He'd wanted her to believe they'd really been kidnapped, but he hadn't wanted reality to hit her like that. He hadn't wanted her to be terrified, shocked and broken.

He kept his eyes on the tiny window and watched as the sky began to lighten. It was time to go. Gently, he cupped Belinda's cheek and looked down at her. She took his breath away. So beautiful. So full of life. So fucking innocent. She'd lived her life in a privileged bubble, being adored by family and friends, never wanting for anything. Never hurting. Never even conceiving that their situation was real and something terrible was happening to them. He'd resented that about her, but now, after last night, he found the resentment had gone, and a deep desire to preserve her bubble was driving him now. So, she didn't have the experience of life that he did? Maybe that was a good thing.

"Hollywood," he said gently. "You gotta wake up. It's time to go."

She stirred and snuggled deeper into him. "Five more minutes," she muttered, her eyes still closed.

Beast couldn't help the smile that broke free. She was cute. Like a kitten in a den full of pit bulls. "Belinda. We need to go."

Her eyes fluttered open and the bluest of blues hit him like lasers. "Joh—Beast?" She blinked and looked around. He knew the moment she woke fully and realised where she was —her body lost its fluid softness and became stiff with tension.

She sat up straight. "It's time to go?"

"Yeah, it's time."

"Good." She nodded to herself. "That's really good." She scrambled away from him, embarrassed that she'd been wedged against him. Beast fought the urge to pull her back. It didn't feel right to have distance between them. And what the hell did that mean?

"I'm, uh, sorry for, you know, clinging to you earlier." Her cheeks were red as she scrambled to her feet. "And for falling asleep. I was…I was…upset. I'm sorry. And I'm sorry for not believing you." She shook her head. "I can't believe I got it so wrong."

She backed away from him with each word, until she was against the wall. Beast was on his feet and striding towards her before he could second-guess his actions. He held her chin and angled her face up at him, to make her look him in the eye. Her eyes were wide with vulnerability, and he almost missed the Belinda who'd thought their kidnapping would be a fun experience.

"There's nothing to be sorry about. Nothing. We're in this together. Right?"

She seemed to be searching his eyes for the truth. He hoped she saw it. They had to rely on each other or they weren't going to get out of this alive.

"Right?" he said again.

"Right." She let out a breath.

"Good." He nodded and stepped away from her, again aware at how much effort that action took. He wanted to hold her. He wanted to wrap himself around her. He wanted her in every single way a man could want a woman. It was a primal need. It had nothing to do with who they were, but lots to do with the situation they were in. He was a protector. That's how he was wired. And she needed protection. It was nothing more. Nothing. She wasn't his type. They didn't walk in the same world. Logic told him that the draw between them was based on circumstances. And he could handle that. He had to.

He put as much distance between them as the cabin would allow and ran a hand through his hair. He needed to get a grip. The drugs they'd pumped into him had obviously screwed with his ability to function. He looked at Belinda, whose shoulders had straightened, and she seemed to be giving herself a silent pep talk. Good. That was good. They needed to focus.

He cleared his throat, wishing they hadn't already finished the water they'd been given. "I've been listening. They partied until they fell asleep. With any luck, they're out cold. It's lighter outside, but not full light." He glanced at his watch. "It's five. This is the best time to leave. You ready?" Like she had a choice.

Her chin went up. "Absolutely."

He nodded, unreasonably proud of her resolve. "I need you to call for the guard. Tell him you need to use the restroom again. Get him to step inside. I'll be ready for him."

He watched her swallow hard and knew her mind was going over what happened the last time she dealt with their guard.

"Belinda?" Beast hated the anxiety he saw on her face. "You up for this?"

"Yes." She sounded far more certain than she looked. "Yes. I can do this. I was born to do this."

He strode to stand behind the door. "You get him in. I'll deal with the rest."

She nodded and reached for the door. There was no sign of the nerves or fear from earlier. She was acting, pretending that everything was fine. Pretending she hadn't been scared out of her mind not two hours earlier. Beast knew she was doing exactly what he'd asked her to do, but still, it rankled. He felt a cold chill run down his spine at the sight of her donning her mask. And then she looked up at him, and he saw it. The trace of fear, the hesitant vulnerability that said she more than remembered her earlier experience. At the sight, Beast felt like dirt. His hand shot out, curling around the satin-soft skin of her wrist. Wide eyes looked up at him.

"I won't let him touch you or say anything to you."

Her shoulders relaxed slightly. "I know," she whispered.

Two words that shot straight to his soul. A tether between them.

Belinda reached out and knocked the door. "*Hola*," she called. "I need *el baño*."

There was a scraping noise and the door swung open. Beast couldn't see who was there, but the relief Belinda tried to mask made him think it wasn't the same guard as earlier.

"*El baño?*" the guard snapped.

"*Si.*"

"*Vamos.*"

Belinda took a step towards the open door and then stopped. She flashed a smile at the man. "Shoes." She pointed to her feet.

Before the guy could object, she turned and ran over to where her ridiculous shoes sat beside the mattress. With a grunt, the guy followed her inside. He wasn't the same guard. But that didn't mean he was a good guy. Beast didn't hesitate. He swung the door shut and slammed his fist into the man's jaw. One punch. That was all it took to make him crumple to the floor.

"Glass jaw. Lucky," Beast said. "Get the ropes."

He searched the guy's pockets and took what might be useful: a book of matches and a cheap mobile phone with a dead battery. They wouldn't be able to use it to call for help, but maybe there would be information on it that would help track these bastards down later.

Belinda handed him the same rope that had been used to bind him. "Before you tie him, I need his jeans and his shoes."

He stilled. "What?"

"I can't run in my shoes. Plus, I don't want my toes to be naked, waving around like a tasty treat for anything that wants to take a bite. Trust me, I don't want to put my feet into his shoes. I mean, can you imagine how much sweat has pooled in them?" She shuddered. "But I want to live more than I care about his sweat. I can always bathe in antibacterial wash once we get out of this place. Right?"

And she was back. The mouthy, fluffy-headed woman that drove him nuts. Who was the real Belinda? The woman who curled into his arms and needed him, or the woman who chattered like a chimpanzee? He honestly didn't know, and that was what disturbed him the most. Would be ever know if the woman Belinda presented to him was real? Was everything just an act?

He pulled the guy's sneakers off, while Belinda unfastened his jeans.

"Why do we need the jeans?" Beast asked as he tossed the shoes beside her.

"If I don't cover up, I'm going to get eaten alive." She grinned at him. "That's a relief. He's wearing underpants. If he'd gone commando, I was planning on taking my chances with the bugs. Because wearing jeans his dick had touched—Ew!"

Seriously? "You're worried about mosquito bites? There are guys who want to rape you and you're worried about mosquito bites?"

"It isn't only mosquito bites. There's the bot fly, too. It lays its eggs under your skin. You break out in pustules that erupt with maggots. You want to deal with that, be my guest. I'd rather be covered."

With a grumble, Beast stripped the jeans off the guy and handed them to her. He tied the guard's feet while Belinda shimmied into the jeans. They didn't quite fasten over her hips, so she reached into that tiny bag of hers, produced an elastic hair tie and used it to loop the button and the hole together to keep the jeans in place. A second later, she was sitting on the floor, tugging on the shoes.

"This guy has tiny feet," Belinda said as she struggled to wedge her foot into the shoe. "Made it. They'll have to do. I've worn worse to a premiere, only this time there's no stylist armed with Botox injections to numb my feet so I can walk."

Botox? For her feet? Belinda definitely lived in an entirely different world to the one Beast lived in. He ripped off a strip of the guy's T-shirt and used it to gag him. Then he slung the rifle over his shoulder and slipped the machete into his belt. He was good to go. He turned to Belinda, to find her busy stripping the stained sheet off the bed. She spotted him watching her and pointed at the torn mosquito net.

"Can you get that down? It's a mess, but it's better than nothing."

He didn't even bother to ask what she was doing now; it would only waste time. He grabbed the net, scrunched it into a ball and thrust it at her. She put it under her arm with the sheet and the two empty plastic bottles that they could, hopefully, refill with water.

"Ready now? You sure you don't need to fix your hair before we run for our lives?" He sounded irritated, because he felt irritated. She was wasting time.

Her hand flew to her head, and she patted at her hair. "What's wrong with my hair?"

Beast pinched the bridge of his nose and reminded himself that after this little adventure, he never had to see Belinda Collins ever again. It didn't help.

"There's nothing wrong with your hair. It's paparazzi perfect. I'm sure our kidnappers will appreciate how great your hair looks as they chase us through the forest."

Her eyes went wide. "They're going to chase us? I thought we were sneaking out. I thought they wouldn't follow."

Yeah, he was sure that in Belinda's world, the kidnappers found that their captives had escaped, looked at each other and went, "Oh well, at least we tried." He glared at her. "I'll ask again, are you ready?"

"Ready." She strode towards the door. "No, wait, I lied. I forgot my shoes." She ran back for the stupid, sexy sandals.

"Leave them," Beast said. "They're useless."

She gave him an incredulous look. "These are weapons. Didn't you see *Single White Female*? Jennifer Jason Leigh killed a man by whacking a stiletto heel through his eyeball."

For a second, Beast was lost for words. Then he remembered they had to run. He grabbed her wrist, removed the shoes and tossed them into the corner, before dragging her out of the hut.

"I hated those shoes anyway," she muttered. "They're no good for walking or dancing. But I thought I'd get my money's worth if I could use them to kill somebody."

Beast pretended he couldn't hear her. It was for the best. For both of them.

He stuck to the shadows against the building walls, keeping an arm in front of Belinda to ensure she kept behind him and out of sight.

"We're clear," he whispered, and signalled for her to follow him across the clearing.

He figured they would expect them to take the shortest route of escape possible and run into the jungle behind their hut. So, he headed for the opposite side of camp, the one farthest away from their hut and the track leading out of the clearing. He wasn't sure if going in the direction he chose would take them further into the jungle, or closer to civilisation, but it was the best he could come up with. In hours, they would kill him and rape Belinda. It was too risky to sit around waiting to be rescued. The faster they got out of camp and put as much distance as possible between them and their kidnappers, the better.

The camp was eerily quiet. The only sound of life was the occasional snore from one of the cabins. There was no security, an indication that the kidnappers thought they were invulnerable. Belinda curled a hand into the back of his shirt, and he felt her touch zing through his body. He wanted her close. He wanted to keep her safe. But she didn't have to touch. It was distracting. He glanced over his shoulder at her with a frown. She smiled and shrugged, but didn't let go.

He reached behind him, grabbed Belinda and thrust her in front of him. If there was going to be shooting, they could aim at him. She gave him a quizzical look but kept on running. As they reached the thick wall of greenery, Beast looked back. Nothing. No movement. No sound. Nothing. A feeling of elation rushed through him, but they weren't out of the woods yet—literally.

They ran as quickly and as quietly as they could. Every sense Beast possessed was working overtime. He hated that his back was facing the camp. He half expected a shot to ring out and their escape to end with a bullet in his spine.

"If someone shoots me," he said, "keep running. Don't stop for me."

She looked back at him in shock. "Don't be an idiot. If someone shoots you, I'm staying beside you to keep you alive. We're in this together. Remember?"

Beast wasn't sure what use she would be if he were shot, but he kept that to himself.

Once they were hidden by the dense plant life, Beast reached for Belinda's arm. "I'll go in front now, clear the way. We're going fast. Keep up."

She moved behind him, staying close. "How long do you think we have before they wake up?"

"Depends how drunk they were."

The rainforest closed in around them, and Beast fought the feeling of disorientation it caused. This was nothing like the city. Everywhere he looked, there was dense foliage in every shade of green imaginable. There was so much of it that it was hard to find a place for the eyes to rest, to focus. Tall tree trunks stretched up high into the dense canopy, where their branches spread. Above them, the blue sky was replaced by green. Every now and then, the canopy broke and early morning sunlight streamed through to the forest floor. They were boxed in on all sides, green all around them, green above and green underfoot. It was claustrophobic.

And everywhere he looked, there was chaos. Long vines wrapped around branchless trunks, plants crept up the vines, hitching a ride up to the canopy and the sun above it. The ground was littered with leaves and dense with spindly young trees, bamboo and palms. It was impossible to see more than a few feet in any direction, and anywhere he did focus seemed to be alive with insects and birds. As far as he could see, the Amazon forest was literally covered with ants. Then there were the flying insects that buzzed around the trees. And the mosquitoes who'd made a beeline for them as soon as they were out of the hut. Everything moved. The ground. The trees. The plants. Everywhere he looked, something looked back at him.

They clambered over a fallen tree, which was covered in moss and vines, before moving deeper into the mass of green and further away from their captors.

"I don't think we need to worry about them hearing us," Belinda said. "I never realised the rainforest was this noisy."

Beast didn't reply, just held the leaves of a large palm out of her way to let her pass.

"There must be about a billion cicadas in this part of the forest alone."

He didn't answer because she didn't seem to need one.

"And the birds. Have you ever heard so many different calls? I haven't. I'm sure that's monkeys I can hear." She paused. "Yep, there are definitely monkeys overhead. Did you know that scientists don't know how many species of monkeys there are in the Amazon? They're still discovering new ones." There was a loud screeching sound, and Belinda's hand curled into the back of his shirt. "Oh, did you hear that? It's a howler monkey. They're the loudest monkeys in the world. The baddies will never hear us over that."

Baddies? And seriously? Where did she get this crap? "Let me guess, you learned all this from Daniel Radcliffe's movie."

She let go of his shirt, and he almost regretted the loss of her touch. "Wow, you really have a low opinion of me, don't you? What do you think I do all day? Hang out at the spa, get facials and watch gossip TV?"

That was exactly what he thought, so he kept his mouth shut.

"Guess there's no need to get to know me, then, huh? Seeing as you've already made your mind up about who I am. I'm the frivolous airhead who doesn't do anything of use with her life. I can't possibly know anything of value. Poor, poor you, you're stuck with me in the middle of the jungle.

I'm such a weight around your neck. Oh, how ever will you cope?"

"I didn't say that." It was a lame argument. He sure as hell had been thinking it. And to be fair, she hadn't exactly done anything to prove him wrong.

"Well, let me know when you want to say something of value, John. It would be nice to hear from the man instead of the chip on your shoulder."

They were running for their lives. He didn't have time for this shit. "Don't call me John."

"No, of course not. You're Beast. Big. Bad. Beast. The scary, tattooed wonder of the MMA world."

He spun to face her, and she walked right into his chest. He grasped her shoulders.

"Woman, you need to shut the hell up before you get us both in trouble."

She waved a hand around to indicate their surroundings. "They can't hear us. I can barely hear you over the damn monkeys."

"Well, I have no problem hearing the crap you're spouting, and you're driving me nuts."

"Oh, get over it. I talk when I'm nervous. Guess what, I'm not perfect. And neither are you…"

She paused and her eyes gleamed, and he knew she was going to do it. He willed her not to. His jaw clenched, his eyes narrowed and he willed her not to taunt him. But he could almost feel the emotion bursting from her. She was wired, looking for an outlet, looking for a confrontation to release the pressure inside her that fear and anxiety had caused. And she chose to pick a fight with him. Beast understood. He did. It was one of the reasons he still climbed into a ring.

But this wasn't the time.

Because the need to let off steam was riding him hard too.

"Don't do it." His voice had dropped an octave, and he willed her to heed the warning in it.

Her eyes sparked. Her cheeks flushed. She took a breath and with a tilt of her chin that challenged him she said, "No, you aren't perfect either, are you, *John*?"

She folded her arms, cocked her hip and smirked at him with those pouty lips of hers, daring him to do something about it, pushing him over the edge on which the two of them were so precariously balanced. He felt himself fall as he reached for her. And then he did what he'd been wanting to do since he'd first set eyes on her. He shut her up the only way he knew how, by slamming his mouth over hers.

It was electric.

Static charges shot through his body, making his skin sizzle with need.

Because of her.

Because of how she tasted, and felt, and moved against him.

She moaned as her lips opened. He clasped her head. His tongue surged into her mouth. There was a second when the world around them seemed to stop, when silence engulfed them as the rainforest disappeared. There was only the two of them, sharing the desperate need to release everything within them. To let the other person take it all. To find some relief.

CHAPTER 9

It had been two hours since their last meeting, and now the Benson Security team assembled in the ballroom once again. Ryan noted that this time, the family members who weren't part of the team were missing. Coffee was flowing freely, and a buffet table had been set up near the bar, laden with finger food. Ryan had helped himself to a plate full of sandwiches, pastries and cake. He planned to go back for seconds.

"They have fruit, too," Elle pointed out as he sat back down beside her.

"Fruit doesn't fill you. You need stodge for that."

She shook her head. The programming genius had changed out of her party dress and into a pair of purple shorts that sported a vintage Minnie Mouse pattern, and a yellow T-shirt with 'Ka Pow!' in a jagged cartoon bubble, printed across her chest.

"See you took the time to get back into your work clothes," Ryan said around a mouthful of food.

She answered him with a hand gesture before she went back to typing.

"You managed to narrow the location down?" Ryan

nodded with thanks when a waitress refilled his mug with coffee. She made him think of Esperanza, and he wondered if she was still in his bed, waiting for him. He hadn't had a minute to check. He'd been running around with Harvard trying to sort out supplies for the rescue effort. Man, he hoped she was still in his bed. And he wished he was back there with her.

"Yes," Elle said. "It's still a large area, but I called in some favours, and we should be getting satellite imagery through soon. Maybe we can see a settlement, or some buildings, to give us a clue where they're keeping our people."

Ryan let out a whistle before taking a sip of coffee. Caffeine. Just what the doctor ordered. "What kind of favours did you do that gives you access to satellites? And whose satellites are we talking about?"

She smiled, her eyes still on her computer screen. "That's need-to-know. And you don't. Plus, I didn't say they were favours I was owed. I just said someone at Benson Security was owed favours. Big favours. Satellite-sized favours."

Ryan bet he knew who it was. Benson Security's silent partner, Harry Boyle. The guy was an IT genius, who'd written security programs for the British government, among others. He wasn't involved in the day-to-day business at Benson—he spent his time helping his wife run a charity that worked for greater literacy in Africa—but that didn't mean he didn't have fingers in pies that could be useful. Speaking of pies... Ryan picked up a tiny meat one and popped it in his mouth.

"Listen up," Lake called, and all talk stopped instantly. Every eye in the room turned to him as he looked at the waitstaff. "Please leave us."

They didn't have to be told twice. The group of men and women scurried from the room.

As they went out, a tall South American guy, dressed in

jeans and a T-shirt, sauntered into the room. He headed straight for Lake and took up a position at his side. Lake waited until the doors closed behind the waitstaff before he started speaking again. "This is Rodrigo De la Cruz. I have it on good authority that he's the best tracker and guide in South America."

"That would be *my* authority," De la Cruz said with a grin.

Lake didn't smile. "David sent him."

Elle's head jerked up on hearing the name of the man she'd been hunting for online for months. Even using the DNA sample David had taunted her with, Ryan knew she was no closer to finding out who the mysterious man really was, or which government he worked for. When Elle realised that David hadn't accompanied De la Cruz, her shoulders slumped. Ryan wasn't sure what was going on with David and Elle, but he knew he'd sneaked into her bedroom in Scotland months earlier and warned her to stop hunting him —by securing her with pink fluffy handcuffs, no less.

Ryan leaned in and whispered, "Maybe he'll turn up later."

She shrugged. It was forced. "No biggie."

Yeah, right.

"Elle," Lake said. "You got anything else for us?"

"I have satellite pictures coming in right now," she replied. "Give me a minute to go through them. I might be able to narrow this location down even further."

"Impressive," De la Cruz said. He spoke English with an American accent, but Ryan would guess it wasn't his first language. It was his mannerisms more than anything. Americans weren't generally as expressive when they spoke.

Megan plopped into seat on the other side of Elle. "At least David sent some eye candy in his place. Damn, that man is hot!"

Her husband, who stood behind her, tugged her hair.

"What?" she demanded as she looked up at him. "He's the

sexiest Latino guy I've seen since Ricky Martin. And I'm still upset that he plays for the other team. In fact, women everywhere are still upset about that."

Dimitri smiled and shook his head, leaving Ryan to wonder, once again, why any man would take Megan on.

"Megan," Lake said with a long-suffering sigh. Sometimes, Ryan forgot that, living in the same small town in Scotland, Lake had watched Megan grow up.

"What?" Megan said.

"Want to keep your voice down? Nobody cares how hot De la Cruz is."

"I do," De la Cruz said. He winked at Megan.

Dimitri let out a threatening rumble, and Megan looked up at him. "Don't worry, baby. Nobody is hotter than you."

"And this is why we shouldn't let couples on the team," Callum said. "It's distracting and unprofessional." He shook his head. "I wish I was back in the army," he said at the same time as everyone from the London office.

He glared at them as laughter broke out.

"Okay, settle down," Lake said with a grin. "It's good to let off steam, but we need to focus. Elle?"

She was studying the photos on her screen. "Can the new guy come look at this?"

De la Cruz didn't wait for permission—he strode around the table and came to stand behind Elle. He peered over her shoulder and tensed. "What's the location?"

She tapped her keyboard and brought up a map. He nodded.

"Go back to that photo," he said. An aerial view of an encampment surrounded by jungle appeared on the screen.

It seemed like everyone present was holding their breath while they waited to hear what the man had to say.

"Zoom in, *bonita*," he muttered. "Scroll left. Zoom again." He stiffened before standing straight. "It's the Martinez family for sure. I recognise their setup. All of their jungle camps look exactly like this one. Each camp is isolated and rigged to blow if it's penetrated by the enemy. The only access in or out is by boat, and usually the river is a hike from the camp." He looked at the photo again. "This one is closer to the water than most. But still a good few hours on foot—if you take the shortest route. Days if you head in the other direction."

"Aren't they making it hard for themselves to get out of there, if there's only one way in and out?" Megan said. "If we take their path in, it will be like shooting fish in a barrel."

De la Cruz shook his head. "They grew up in the jungle. They know the area inside and out. They'll just scatter into the trees if they're attacked, and meet up at another encampment later. It's one of the reasons they've been so difficult to eliminate. That and the fact they are merciless in making a name for themselves." He looked back at Lake. "You know what they do to their kidnap victims?"

"Yeah," Lake said, but didn't elaborate.

"I don't," Ryan said.

De la Cruz looked down at him, his brown eyes turning black. "They cut and brand the men. They gang rape the women. It's their way of putting their stamp on their victims and increasing the fear people feel for them. They want people to be terrified of being taken by them. They want to be able to ask for more ransom each time."

"Shit," Ryan muttered.

"Yeah," De la Cruz said.

Lake cleared his throat. "You know where this camp is?"

"With the map and the photos, I can find it."

Lake nodded. "Then we leave now. Everybody get ready. Gather your gear."

"Wait." Rachel Ford-Talbot held up a hand. Ryan noted that Harvard was hovering close to her again. The guy had it bad. "The local chief of police wants to ride along—with a couple of his men. He pointed out that the last time Benson Security was in Peru, there was a bloodbath. He insists his presence will stop that from happening again."

"That isn't good," De la Cruz said. "The local police force is full of guys who're on the take with the cartels. There's no way to tell who you can trust."

Rachel gave him a cool look. She hadn't bothered changing out of her sparkly red gown, but her clothes didn't soften her demeanour any. "The police chief says that he will arrest us, shut this retrieval operation down and take over himself, if we don't comply." She turned to Lake. "I suggest we comply."

"He wants the glory," Callum spat. "He wants to be the one who can say he rescued Belinda Collins."

"That was my assessment too," Rachel said. "He's an unctuous little man. But, as they say in America, he's the law in these parts. If we want to do our job, we have to play nice."

"We don't say that in America," Harvard said. "Not since the time of the wild west."

She didn't even look at him. Instead, she shared a look with her business partners, Callum and Lake. "We don't have a choice. Not unless you want this to be another international incident. And Benson Security can't afford another one of those. It took a lot of money and playing nice to get rid of the last one."

The last one being when they'd accidentally blown up a plane in Peru and massacred a cartel who was trying to kill them. Yeah, the authorities had *not* been pleased about that.

"The police chief comes along for the ride," Lake said, but he clearly wasn't happy about it.

"That's a mistake," De la Cruz said.

"This whole thing is a mistake," Callum said. "We should have ended this wedding celebration in Scotland. Why we had to come here, I don't have a bloody clue. Rich people are nuts."

Ryan couldn't agree more. He watched as the team dispersed. They were wired. Eager for action. Eager to succeed. Determined to bring their people home.

Beside him, De la Cruz dug into his jeans pocket. He brought out a piece of paper and handed it to Elle. "From David," he said with a smile.

She fell on it like a starved dog before she realised how much she was giving away, and calmed her actions down. She opened the paper, and Ryan made no effort to hide that he was reading over her shoulder.

Ellie, what did I tell you about hunting me? Stop. You're putting us both at risk. D. P.S. I like the lavender hair better.

Her head jerked up and she looked around the room, as though he was hiding in the shadows somewhere, watching her. When she realised he wasn't, her shoulders slumped slightly and she grinned at the note.

"Did he wear gloves when he handled this?"

De la Cruz had a smile on his face. "He said you'd ask that. The answer is no." With a shake of his head, he walked away.

"Hot damn!" Elle shrieked. "I have his prints. I am so going to track his backside down."

"Uh, Elle?" Ryan felt someone should be the voice of reason. "That's exactly what the note said not to do."

She snorted. "Like he meant it." Then she was tapping away, her focus firmly on her laptop and the rescue effort.

Ryan stood and followed the rest of his team out the door. The sun was rising over the rainforest, and the sound of birds calling to one another had reached cacophonous levels. The heat hit him as soon as he stepped outside the air-conditioned interior of the hotel, and he started to sweat instantly. Even this early in the morning, the humidity was killer.

He glanced in the direction of his cabin and wondered again if there was a beautiful woman waiting for his return. His feet took a step in that direction without him even realising he'd done it. He was that desperate to get back to her. The need driving him was unusual and disconcerting. He never reacted like this with women. Usually, he had a great time and then walked away. He rarely, if ever, wanted to go back. In his experience, repeat performances made women think there was more going on than a few hours of shared pleasure.

Yet here he was, hungry to get back to Esperanza. What was it about her that made her different? He honestly didn't know. All he was sure of was that he wanted to get back and investigate the power she had over him.

"You coming?" Dimitri called.

Ryan let out a sigh. There was no going back to his woman right now. He turned and followed his team towards their helicopter, hoping Esperanza would be there when he returned.

CHAPTER 10

Belinda gasped when John's lips covered hers. For a second, she was frozen in shock, and then a delicious awareness set in and all she wanted was more. More of John's touch. More of his lips against hers. More of his engulfing strength surrounding her and pressing into her. Oh, how she wanted him pressing into her. She tightened her grip on his shirt and pulled him closer.

His kiss was dark and dangerous, like the man. There had been no preamble. No gentle touch. This was a taking. A desperate, wonderful taking. And she was just as eager to let him have anything, and everything, he wanted. He kissed her deep, plundering her with his tongue. Nipping at her lips. Sucking on her. He tasted like sin. But it was his strength that undid her, the feeling of his hands on her jaw, holding her in place. The flex of his muscles under her touch. The sheer overwhelming power of the man, channelled into one blistering kiss.

She pressed her tender, swollen breasts against him, seeking relief. She wanted him to release his strength. To let loose. To let her have it all. She wanted to feel all of that contained passion and power that rippled through every movement he made. She wanted his control destroyed. Because of her. For her. She wanted to be overwhelmed by him. She wanted to lose herself in him. She'd never felt anything like it before. Never. He was raw in his maleness. Raw. Powerful. Commanding. And she was desperate for him.

Suddenly, he ripped his mouth from hers, his hands fell to his sides and he staggered back. Belinda swayed, fighting to stand without him to lean against. She felt dazed, desperate. She stumbled towards him. Just one step before she could stop herself.

"What the hell?" His words stopped her in her tracks.

He was breathing hard. His hands were fisted at his sides. His cheeks were flushed, and his lips, those amazing lips, were parted and swollen. She'd done that. Her. And she needed more. Although her feet didn't move, her body leaned towards him. All she could see, all she could feel, was him. It was as though he'd wrapped her in a cocoon. A place where all of her senses were heightened and her only focus was on pleasure, on him. And now, he'd cast her out in the cold.

"That was a mistake." Harsh words that jerked her back to reality.

She blinked several times as her environment came crashing into focus. She suddenly saw the jungle, heard the animals, and felt the humidity coat her body. For a moment, while John had been touching her, she'd been somewhere else. A place where only the two of them existed.

"What…?" she whispered as her fingertips touched her lips.

He ran a hand through his short hair. "That was a mistake," he said again.

Belinda started to shake and wrapped her arms around herself. "What happened?"

"Damned if I know." He took another step back and ran a hand over his mouth to his jaw. "Adrenalin?" He let out a heavy breath. "Had to be adrenalin. Yeah. We were working off adrenalin." He nodded to himself. "It can't happen again. We need to focus. We weren't focused."

She watched his jaw harden and knew what he meant. Anyone could have sneaked up on them. Anything could have approached. They'd made themselves vulnerable.

"That's never happened before..." She'd lost herself in him. And part of her yearned to do it again.

For a heartbeat, they stared into each other's eyes. She saw the same desperate need in his eyes that must have been in hers.

"It was an anomaly," he whispered, his eyes still trapped on hers. "Too much adrenalin. Not enough sleep." He cleared his throat and tore his gaze from hers. He nodded as though that explained the way they'd combusted together—with just one kiss.

"Yeah, adrenalin..." Belinda wasn't so sure, but she was equally desperate to cling to any viable reason that excused their reaction to each other.

"Adrenalin." He looked back at her, sounding firm. In control again. Unlike her.

"Yeah..."

"We don't do that again." It was a decree that might have carried more weight if his eyes weren't glued to her lips while he made it.

"Yeah."

"Come on. We need to keep moving." He looked at his watch. "We've only been out of camp for an hour. We need to put as much distance between them and us as possible."

"Yeah."

His lips twitched and his eyes sparkled. "Worked, though. The chatter has stopped."

"Yeah."

"Come on, Hollywood. Let's get out of here."

She almost reached for him. Instinct told her to hold him tight, that he shouldn't be walking away from her. Her hand was up, reaching, when shots rang out. Rapid fire. An automatic weapon. Birds shrieked and scattered. Belinda swallowed a scream and dived for the ground, only to find Beast beside her.

"Where's it coming from?" Belinda said. "Are they close?"

He shook his head. Unlike her, Beast hadn't sprawled on his belly—he was crouched, eyes on the forest, searching for a clue as to how much danger they were in.

"It sounded like it came from a distance away. Maybe even back at the camp," Beast whispered.

The jungle was eerily silent for a minute before monkeys started hollering in the canopy above them, warning each other that danger was coming.

"How far are we from camp?" Belinda whispered.

"Not far. We haven't been walking long, and we can't move fast in this terrain."

Another couple of shots rang out, and Belinda flinched, even though this time she knew they were coming from a distance away. Beast's hand curled round her arm.

"Come on. We need to get moving." He pointed into the bush. "I think it's coming from that direction, but I'm not sure. Sound gets muffled and bounces around in here." He stood, pulling her to her feet, and then glanced at his watch. "We're going that way." He pointed. "Start running, Hollywood."

Belinda didn't need to be told twice.

"Gunfire," Ryan reported over the comm system that linked the Benson Security team with the local chief of police and the two officers he'd insisted accompany him. "South side of camp."

He signalled to his teammates, Harvard and Violet, indicating that they should up the pace. Together, they ran as silently as possible through the forest, aware that Dimitri and his team were doing exactly the same on the other side of the camp. They'd been flown in to a clearing not far from the cartel's base, but not so close that the noise from the chopper would tip them off that they had company. From there, they'd cut through the jungle on foot.

De la Cruz had stayed with the chopper. He'd been impressive on the flight over the jungle canopy, handling the chopper deftly and spotting landmarks that none of them would have seen. Ryan wasn't sure what his background was, but he would bet there was time in the military in there somewhere. De la Cruz fit in easily with the Benson Security team, making it hard to remember that they barely knew the guy.

Lake and Callum had taken the local police along with their team and were following the path from the river into the compound. Ryan knew that Callum's job wasn't to watch for the kidnappers, but to keep an eye on the chief of police and his men, to make sure they didn't go rogue on them.

There was silence as Ryan's team jogged towards the kidnappers' encampment. No one wanted to think about what the gunfire might mean. Their focus was on the mission. There was no time to speculate.

Two more shots rang out, followed by shouting. It was too far away for Ryan to make out what was being said— even if he had understood more than basic Spanish.

"I will go in first, with my men," the police chief said over the comm unit tucked into Ryan's ear. "This is our turf, our people. You will take orders from—"

Ryan didn't hear the rest, because Lake's voice cut in. "Frequency Delta."

Everyone on the team changed comm frequency, effectively cutting the police chief and his men out of the loop and leaving them to deal with Callum's sunny disposition.

"Coming up on the camp," Dimitri said.

"Roger that," Lake said. "Check for explosives."

"Roger," Dimitri answered.

It was a reminder to all that the kidnappers were known for rigging their camps to blow.

"We have visual," Ryan whispered, knowing the throat mic would easily pick up his voice. His eyes were on the small, badly built shack visible through the trees.

"Roger that," Lake said.

Ryan signalled for Harvard and Violet to eyeball the building, while he held back to cover them. Someone shouted. An engine revved.

"Team one," Dimitri said to Lake. "Two on dirt bikes, coming at you fast."

"Roger," Lake said.

Ryan kept low and covered Violet as she peeked through the cabin window.

"Empty." Violet's voice was loud in his ear.

"Proceed with caution," Ryan told them.

Gun in hand, they moved forward, using the foliage for cover as they swept for any sight of their targets.

A shot rang out. Someone in the camp shouted orders. There was the sound of running.

"Anyone get that?" Ryan wished like hell he'd learned to speak Spanish after their last mission in Peru.

"He's telling them to scatter," Harvard said, his voice flat and even. "To find the captives and bring them back." He paused as more shouted orders rang out. "He's telling them to search the jungle for Beast and Belinda. And he's got some inventive threats going on if they fail."

Ryan felt his stomach settle. "Did everyone get that? The targets are not in the camp. I repeat—the targets are not in the camp."

"Roger that," Lake said. "We've secured the drivers of the two bikes."

"Another one heading your way," Dimitri said as an engine was gunned.

"I'm on it," Callum rumbled. "Keep as many alive as you can. I have questions for them." Callum did love a good interrogation. It was stress relief for him.

Slowly, Ryan inched forward, ignoring the flies and mosquitoes that buzzed around him, until he had a clear view of the small camp. A small gecko ran over the toe of his boot, but Ryan didn't move. His eyes were on the camp. Men were disappearing in all directions into the jungle. One man stood at the edge of the treeline opposite Ryan. Fury radiated from him. There was another man beside him, crouching, studying the ground. As Ryan watched, the man stood and pointed to the ground then into the forest.

"Guess they think Belinda and Beast went that away," Ryan muttered.

"You heard Callum—round them up," Lake said. "We need information."

"Roger," Ryan said, and signalled to his team that they were going in, confident that Dimitri was dealing with the explosives.

Two steps into the clearing, a kidnapper ran out from behind a hut—straight into Harvard. The kidnapper screeched to a halt, lifted his gun and fired. Harvard dived for him, disabling him in a second, but not before the gun went off. The man on the other side of the clearing, the one Ryan would have bet was the leader, turned back from the edge of the forest. It took a second for him to realise what was happening, and then he held up his phone. He didn't take his eyes off the Benson Security team while he dialled, and Ryan's heartbeat shot through the roof.

A slow, thin smile spread across the kidnapper's face. A smug smirk. And Ryan knew absolutely, with every instinct he possessed, that the guy wasn't making a call.

"He's triggering the explosives," Ryan snapped as he turned to run. "Get out of the camp. Repeat—get the hell out."

His team turned and ran. A blast hit them from behind, making them stumble. They kept on running. Several more blasts followed before the hut closest to Ryan exploded. The blast took him off his feet and propelled him into the jungle. He crashed, shoulder first, into a tree. The crunching noise told him he'd broken something, long before the pain hit.

"Count off," Lake ordered them.

One by one, the team stated their designations, letting their leader know they were alive. Ryan pulled himself up to sitting and leaned back against the tree. Black spots appeared in front of his eyes and he couldn't move his right arm.

"Team leader three?" Lake barked.

It took a second for Ryan to remember that was him. "I'm here." He forced the words through clenched teeth as the pain hit him hard and fast. "I'm gonna need a medic."

"Status?" Lake's calm voice was a lifeline.

The bushes shook beside Ryan as Violet and Harvard crashed through them. They screeched to a halt in front of him.

"I can tell you the status," Violet said. "Looks like his shoulder bone lives outside of his body now."

"Oh crap," Ryan said.

And with those words, the world went black for Ryan.

CHAPTER 11

Beast and Belinda were making their way around a mammoth kapok tree when the world abruptly exploded. He grabbed Belinda and pulled her into the shelter of the tree as the ground shook. Around them, insects stilled. Above them, birds took to the air in droves, squawking their fear as they did so. Monkeys went crazy and ran through the branches above them, making a shower of leaves fall like snow.

"What was that?" Belinda whispered as she clung to him.

"Explosions." Five, if he wasn't mistaken. The same as the number of buildings in the clearing the kidnappers had made.

"What blew up?" Belinda whispered.

"I think it was the camp." But it didn't make sense. Not unless the search team had gone in, guns blazing, to find them. No, even then, it didn't make sense. Benson Security had a rep for being the best. And being the best meant they *didn't* blow up the people they were trying to rescue.

"Does this mean they're all dead and they won't chase us?" Belinda sounded so hopeful that he was almost loath to burst her bubble.

"No. The kidnappers could have blown the camp themselves, to cover their tracks after they discovered we were gone."

"Will they still try to find us?"

"Can we take a chance on thinking they won't?"

Her whole body seemed to deflate. "No, I guess we can't."

"We need to keep going. Get some more distance between us and the camp. Head that way." He pointed. "I'll bring up the rear."

He swung the gun that was across his back to his front, ready to use. It bothered Beast that the natural noise of the jungle covered any sound their captors might make. If someone was close by, he honestly wasn't sure he would notice until they were right on top of them. He wished this fight were happening back on his home turf. Buildings and alleys he knew; trees and rivers—not so much.

They ran, uncaring about leaving a trail or making noise. The most important thing was to get as far away as possible, as fast as possible. They crashed through bushes, shoving palms out of the way and feeling them slap against them as they passed. They stumbled over roots, grass and fallen trees, all the while batting at the insects hovering in a cloud around their heads.

Belinda started and detoured to the left. "Snake." She pointed at the long reptile curled around a vine, watching them with yellow eyes.

Beast was glad she'd spotted it, as he wasn't sure he would have. Tiny yellow frogs with large black eyes jumped along branches, singing to them.

"Don't touch anything red. Red is bad. Everything red can kill you," Belinda called over her shoulder. "And don't touch any frogs. Most of them have excretions on their skin that can kill you or make you hallucinate. Neither of which would be good right now."

She sounded out of breath. Beast noted that her dress was clinging to her back and sweat made her hair stick to her neck. As if thinking exactly the same thing, Belinda reached into her tiny bag, came out with a hair tie and pulled her hair in a ponytail. For some reason, the sight of her bare neck made Beast want to lean in and take a bite out of the woman. He shook his head to clear it. He had to stay focused on their problems, not on Belinda. And the biggest of their problems was water. They were losing too much fluid and would have to make finding water a priority.

They broke through a thicket of bushes and found a muddy bog on the other side. Belinda put a hand out to stop him walking straight into it. "We don't know how deep it is."

She headed off on a path that would take them around the muddy area. The sound of something large crashing through the bushes made them stop dead. Belinda reached back and placed a hand on his arm. He covered her hand and squeezed it before holding the rifle out in front of them. They stood unmoving, barely breathing, afraid of making any noise at all; anxious they'd been found, and ready to defend themselves.

The palms wavered and shook. There were moaning noises, followed by clacking sounds. Belinda shot Beast a querying look and he said, "Shh," to make sure she maintained silence. And then the smell hit them. Belinda covered her mouth with her hand and gagged. She looked at Beast, clearly asking what it was. He shrugged. Damned if he knew. It smelled like skunk. Lots and lots of skunk.

Suddenly the grass parted and a small, pig-like animal ran out. It crossed in front of them, about six feet from where Belinda and Beast stood frozen. The noise increased as several more of the same animals crashed into the tiny clearing. They were built like pigs, with white snouts and spiky black hair covering their bodies. Beast watched stunned, as they kept on coming. There were hundreds of them, ranging from babies the size of domestic cats, right up to adults the size of wild boars. The herd rushed past them and headed straight for the mud pool. And the smell was overwhelming, to the point where Belinda's eyes were watering and his were stinging.

Once the last of the animals were frolicking in the mud, Belinda tugged on his hand and signalled for him to move out. He nodded, and they slowly made their way around the mud. It took a few minutes to get far enough away from the animals for the smell to fade. Belinda dropped her hand and gasped for air.

"That was gross." She pulled at her dress, lifting it up to sniff at it. "Does the smell cling? Do I smell like white-lipped peccaries?"

"White what?"

"Peccaries. They're like pigs. Only way smellier." She looked up at him. "Can you sniff me and tell me if the smell lingered?"

"No. I'm not going to sniff you. How the hell do you know what they are?"

She shrugged. "Must have picked it up somewhere. Weren't they cute? That wild, bristly hair standing on end and those tiny, wee eyes. I could totally have cuddled one—if it wasn't for the smell. I don't even think they're vicious. Though I'm not sure. Apparently, they snap their teeth together to make a kind of clacking sound when they're cornered. They probably bite, too."

Beast stared at her. His main thought had been whether the herd would overwhelm them and eat them alive. Hers had been whether it was safe to cuddle them or not. He looked at his watch.

"Get moving," he said, because he didn't know what else to say.

"Do you think we're going in a circle and we'll end up back at the camp?" Belinda said. "I've heard that most people naturally veer to the left when they choose a direction. We could be doing exactly that."

"I have a compass built into my wristwatch."

"Oh." That took the wind out of her sails. "Did you take into account there's so much iron in the Amazon basin that compasses have been known not to work in the rainforest? You might think you've chosen a direction to keep us going in a straight line, and really we might as well have been following the second hand on your watch."

"How the hell do you know this stuff?" Beast urged her forward as he spoke. "You recognise pig species, you know about iron deposits. Are you making this stuff up?"

"Yes. That's what I *must* be doing. There can't *possibly* be any other explanation."

"How about we drop the sarcasm and focus on getting out of here alive."

"You can if you want. I like my sarcasm. I'm quite attached to it."

"Get moving," he ordered her again.

He held the stolen rifle in front of him and hoped like hell their captors were far, far away. If they weren't, he was prepared to strike first and ask questions later. But he'd have to make every shot count. Their ammunition was sorely limited. For the first time in his life, he wished he were as deadly with a gun as he was with his fists. Not that his aim was bad, but he hadn't practised as much as his friends. There was no need for it. It was a decision he had come to regret.

"Can you fire a gun?" he asked Belinda, suddenly aware that if something happened to him, she would have to survive on her own.

"Sure. I've had to do it for several movies."

He felt his ire rise every time she mentioned her profession. It was totally unreasonable. But he still couldn't seem to stop the reaction. Actors were liars by trade. And Beast hated liars. "Can you fire a real gun?"

"They were real guns." Now she sounded irritated.

"Can you hit anything you fire at?"

"Well, I don't know that part. I only ever fired blanks."

Beast looked heavenwards and asked for patience.

"I'm good with a bow and arrow, though. I had to learn archery for a movie once."

"We don't have a bow and arrow. We have a gun."

"I wonder if we could make a bow and arrow," Belinda said. "I mean, how hard can it be?"

Beast deeply regretted bringing up the subject of weapons. It was clear that when it came to defending them, he was on his own.

"I'm good with throwing stars, too," Belinda told him as she pushed a palm out of her way.

"Are you good with anything we have on us?"

There was a long pause while her little airhead mulled that over. "No." She let out a heavy sigh. "We should have kept the shoes. I'm sure I could have taken someone out with a four-inch pair of Jimmy Choos."

Beast bit back a groan.

BELINDA WAS sure she smelled like a herd of white-lipped peccaries. That kind of stink had a tendency to cling to everything it touched. They'd been going steadily uphill for hours, and Belinda felt her thigh muscles ache. She looked up but saw only green above her. The trees reached high into the sky and then exploded with lush, dense foliage. She wondered if there were rain clouds beyond those leaves. She could use the shower. It felt like they had been trekking through mud for hours. It came up to her knees and had gotten into her shoes; her toes squelched with each step she took. There were mud streaks on her hands, in her hair, on her face. The only bonus to being covered in mud was that it acted as a barrier between her and the mosquitoes who thought she was a tasty treat.

And she was thirsty. So darn thirsty. How was it possible to be surrounded by so much mud, but not one drop of clear, cool water? There was no sound of a flowing stream or rush of a river. No tell-tale pitter-patter of raindrops falling. This was the *rain*forest, and she was going to die of thirst.

"I need to drink." She hated that her words came out as a whine, but she was dying of thirst *and* exhaustion.

"We'll find water soon." He didn't sound convinced.

Neither was Belinda. They'd been walking for hours and the only water they'd seen was filled with dirt. She scanned the area again, hoping there was a source of water she'd missed. All she saw was a bunch of ants making a trail down the tree and across the ground. Each one carried a perfectly cut piece of leaf. Because the ants were so tiny and the leaf pieces so big, it looked like the leaves were walking away from the tree all on their own. She stopped to watch, fascinated by the sight.

"The leaves are walking." She couldn't help but smile as she watched the thousands of pieces of leaf move up and down the tree.

"But you aren't." Beast prodded her shoulder to make her keep walking.

"You know, when I played a kidnap victim, it was a whole lot more fun than this."

"Do I have to explain the difference between reality and make-believe to you again?"

"I'm still not sure this is real," she said. "You could be in on it. The stuff that happened back at the camp could have been an elaborate act." She looked up at him. "I've heard they make those fake kidnappings as real as possible."

"The kidnapping is real. I'm not in on it."

"Ah, but you would say that if you were playing the part. Heck, even the guy who pressed my hand to his dick could have been lying. It could have been a bratwurst he shoved down the front of his jeans."

A hand clamped on her arm and Beast turned her to look at him. "The guard made you touch his dick?"

"Or his bratwurst?" From the crazy jaw clenching and the eye-twitch thing he had going, she maybe shouldn't have mentioned that part.

"If I see him again, I'm going to kill him."

Belinda patted his arm and felt that familiar awareness burst into life. Only now, it was worse. Because now she knew how it felt to kiss Beast.

"Okay," she said to appease him. "I give you permission to kill him next time you see him." She turned away and kept walking. "If he's real and the two of you aren't playacting," she muttered.

"I'm also going to punch your brother the next time I see him. It's his fault I have to listen to this crap about being in the middle of a fake kidnapping."

"I am totally fine with that." As far as she was concerned, Daniel could use having someone knock some sense into him. "But seriously, this whole thing is messing with my head. Is it real or is it just an elaborate setup? It's like that episode of *Buffy*, in series six. The one called 'Normal Life,' where they show Buffy as a psych patient and she's just been dreaming about being the slayer for six years. At the end of the show you aren't sure if the whole series is a lie, or if her being in the asylum is a lie. Really brave of Joss Whedon. He could have lost a lot of fans pulling a stunt like that."

"I have absolutely no idea what you're talking about." Beast sounded weary.

Belinda was outraged. "How can you not know about *Buffy the Vampire Slayer*? It's seminal TV. It shaped a genre and changed the television landscape."

"Never heard of it. Don't care about it. Now move faster."

"Heathen," Belinda muttered as she lifted the bottom of her dress and used it to wipe her brow, uncaring that she was giving Beast a show. Her body was coated in perspiration, but her mouth was dry. How was that even possible? Surely if she was dehydrated, she'd stop sweating too?

"I really need some water. I don't know how long I can go on without it. There has to be something around here somewhere." She was back to studying the jungle, hoping some water presented itself to her.

"I don't see anything," Beast said. "Our best bet is to keep moving and hope we find something further on."

Belinda had stopped listening. Her heart raced and she felt lightheaded—because she'd spotted their salvation. She grabbed Beast's shirt and pointed. "There!"

She rushed straight towards her prize, tripping over tree roots and getting smacked in the face by a palm as she did so.

"Slow down," Beast snapped. "I don't want to lose sight of you. I don't see any water. Are you having one of those delusions people get when they're dehydrated?"

"It's not a mirage." No, she was seeing something way better. She screeched to a halt, put her hands on her hips and beamed at him. "Our prayers have been answered."

"Hollywood," Beast said, voice gentle, as though he was afraid to push her over the edge, "that isn't water. It's bamboo."

"I know it's bamboo. Give me your machete." She held out a hand.

"Yeah, there's no way I'm arming you when you're hallucinating. Why don't you sit down on that log and take a deep breath?"

"Honestly!" She let out an exasperated sigh. "Fine, you do it."

"Do what?"

She stomped over to the bamboo and pointed at it. "Chop here. Cut a V into the bamboo and we'll get water."

"Belinda…" It was clear from the set of his jaw that he was going to argue with her.

"I'm not making this up. This isn't some weird hallucination. I know this is bamboo. And bamboo is hollow. It stores water in each of its segments. Give me the machete and I'll prove it."

He frowned at her, thinking. She wondered if it hurt. With a grunt of annoyance, he pulled the knife from his belt and sliced diagonally into the bamboo. He changed angle and sliced upwards, taking a wedge out of the stalk.

"See, no water." He stepped back and glared at her.

"Do it again," she ordered as she unscrewed the tops of their bottles. "You need to keep going until you make a hole that goes through to the centre."

"This is a huge waste of time."

"I hear lots of whining but no chopping."

With an irritated grunt, he hit the bamboo stalk again. A hole appeared and water started to trickle down. Beast stood there, gaping at it. Belinda elbowed him out of the way. If he wanted to think he was seeing things, then that was fine— she wanted a drink. She put the empty bottle under the flow and let it fill. Once it was full, she handed it to him and put the other bottle under it. She didn't even bother to throw an 'I told you so' at him. It wasn't worth the effort.

"How?" Beast stared at the water in his bottle.

The *crystal-clear* water that Belinda had found for them, *thank you very much.*

"Each segment of bamboo contains a couple of litres of water. Well, bamboo this big does. Drink up and we'll refill." She brought the bottle to her mouth and took a long swallow. The water was cooler than she'd expected it to be, and it tasted better than the finest champagne. She gulped until her bottle was empty. Better. So much better. She grinned at Beast, who was staring at her like she'd suddenly grown an extra head.

She didn't have time for his disbelief. She had water to mine. "Do you have any condoms on you?" Belinda asked him.

He choked, sputtering water everywhere. He bent over as he coughed, holding a hand up to stop her when she moved towards him to helpfully thump him on the back.

"What the hell?" he snapped at her when he'd finished coughing.

She knew exactly what he'd been thinking, and it was so far from reality that it was laughable. "We can use them as water containers. I have a couple. I was wondering if you had more. You didn't think I meant something else, did you?" She batted her eyelashes at him.

"You have an evil streak a mile wide, Hollywood," he told her as he fished his wallet out of his back pocket. "I have two condoms." He tossed them to her.

Surprise, surprise, they were extra-large. "Do you think any man, on the face of the planet, ever walks into a pharmacy and buys extra-small condoms?"

"I can't talk for other men. I buy what fits."

She snorted. "Sure you do."

He ignored her, obviously confident that he had nothing to prove. Which in itself was intriguing. Belinda shook her head to clear it. That wasn't a safe direction for her thoughts to follow.

Beast cleared his throat, as though he knew what she was

thinking. "I'm not sure I like the thought of drinking water out of something that usually goes on my dick."

"I like the thought of dying of dehydration less." She pointed at the bamboo and arched an eyebrow at him.

With a shake of his head, he clutched the machete and set about getting the water out of some more bamboo segments. It didn't take long to repeat the process and refill the bottles before filling the condoms Beast had given her.

She reached into her tiny bag and pulled out the two she carried.

Beast winced when he saw them. "Green?"

"Mint-flavoured, too."

"But green?" Seriously, what guy wants to walk around with a green dick?

She shrugged. "A girl has to get her fun wherever she can. Now fill the minty green condoms with life-giving water."

Watching Beast cringe while they filled the green condoms turned out to be even more fun than Belinda had thought she'd have with them. A few minutes later, they had two full water bottles and four water balloons. Belinda made a cross-body bag out of the sheet she'd nabbed and put the water balloons into it.

"I'll carry them," Beast said.

"I was going to suggest exactly that, caveman. With those excessively large muscles of yours, you won't even notice the extra weight. Now turn around and bend so I can strap this on you."

He did as he was told, crouching in front of her, to allow her to tie the sheet diagonally across his body and over one shoulder. Belinda fought not to notice the way his muscles rippled and tensed when she touched him. She had a vision of the two of them topless and her pressing her breasts against his back as she tried to wrap her arms around him. The urge to act out the pictures in her mind was almost overwhelming, and her hands shook with the effort it took not to succumb.

"Done." Belinda stood back and found her eyes drifting down to his beautifully round backside. Something else she shouldn't be thinking about. Or touching. Her fingers itched, and she took a step back. *No. Touching.*

"Now we have water." Her voice was low and husky, giving her thoughts away. She cleared her throat, but it didn't help. "Try not to pop the condoms."

"I'll try." He smirked at her, making her think he could read her mind. Belinda felt her cheeks burn and looked away.

"Let's get going," she said.

"How did you know to do that trick with the bamboo?"

She wiped the back of her mouth with their hand. "Maybe, just maybe, I'm not as dumb as I look."

"I never said you were dumb. I said you were dramatic. An actress. Everything is an act. It's hard to tell what's real."

"The water feels pretty darn real to me."

"Seriously, what movie did you see that in?"

"Of course, because I only know movies. Come on, we need to get going," she said as she walked past him and headed into the jungle.

She left him staring after her, his tiny mind trying to figure out how she could know something that wasn't movie trivia. Infuriating man. She should have kept the water to herself.

John—*Beast,* ah to hell with it, she could think of him as John if she wanted to. He'd never know. All she had to do was make certain she didn't call him it to his face. Not unless she wanted a repeat of their earlier kiss—and Belinda wasn't exactly sure that was a deterrent. Anyway, she had more important things than their explosive chemistry to think about—like where they were going to sleep.

John had called a welcome halt to their trek into the jungle, saying they had a couple of hours before the sun set. They had enough water to last the night, but finding more would be their first priority in the morning.

Belinda's feet ached, and she was sure there were at least a couple of blisters from where her borrowed shoes rubbed. She was still grateful. They were a whole lot better than trying to walk in her heels. Her skin was dry from the caked mud covering it, she itched all over from mosquito bites and she was sure there were ants in her hair. To say she would have killed for a shower would be to put it mildly.

She watched as John kicked the rocks from the tiny

clearing he'd found, trying to make the ground smoother for them to lie on.

"Don't bother," Belinda said. "We can't sleep on the ground. Every insect and creature that comes out at night will be all over us."

He stopped and put his hands on his hips. "What are we supposed to do, then? Climb a tree?" He cocked an eyebrow at her, which implied he would be able to climb the tree but she wouldn't have a hope in hell. Or maybe she was inventing conversations again. It had become a habit over the last few hours because *John* rarely answered her when she spoke to him.

She shook out the stained sheet she'd taken from their hut. "We make a hammock. It will be cosy, but it's our safest option."

"Okay. Timeout. Who do you think you are? Bear Grylls?"

"Oooh, I love that guy. He is so cute. I did a UK chat show with him and he was adorable. But he has a weird obsession with drinking urine. I mean, he filters it through his socks first, but it's still all kinds of wrong." She shuddered.

John pinched the bridge of his nose. "Seriously? What are you doing? Where is this all coming from? The bamboo water, the hammock, the white-faced pig things, the flies who lay eggs under your skin? Every time I turn around, you have another piece of information to throw at me. Tell me the truth, right now—where's this all coming from?"

"Does it matter?" She pointed to one of the many rope-like lianas hanging from a nearby tree. "Cut some of those and test them for strength, will you?"

With an irritated grunt, he did as he was told. Meanwhile, Belinda shook out the sheet, inspected it to ensure it was hole free and folded it in half, lengthwise. By the time she was done, John was back, holding out the jungle ropes. She scrunched the end of the sheet together, wrapped the rope around it, then folded the end of the sheet over the rope coils and wrapped it again to make a tight loop. The last thing they needed was for the sheet to slip free during the night and for them to land on the forest floor.

"Tie this tight." She handed it to him. "You're stronger than I am."

Without a word, he did as she instructed while she repeated the process with the other end of the folded sheet. The resulting hammock wasn't wide, but it would work. Belinda tried not to think about just how familiar she was about to become with John's body. She already salivated just looking at the man. How she was supposed to sleep plastered against him, she didn't know.

Together, they strung the makeshift hammock up between two trees, making sure it was well off the ground but not so high that they couldn't get into it. The light was fading fast, and Belinda worked faster.

"Cut more ropes, will you?" She pointed to the length of the hammock. "We need one to tie above the hammock, for us to drape the mosquito net over."

They tied a rope between the trees a couple of feet above their bed, and Belinda threw the tatty mosquito net over it to make a tent. The net was big, covering the hammock with enough spare material for her to tie knots over the tears.

She stepped back to look at her efforts. Ugly, smelly and probably full of germs. But it was practical.

"What about these?" John handed her the last of the lianas.

"Tie those two above the rope with the netting, side by side, but about a foot apart. Then if you could grab some palm leaves to rest on top of them, that would be great. It will give us a little shelter if it starts to rain."

With a shake of his head—in awe at her genius, she presumed—he helped her tie off the ropes. The light was dim now, and the noise of the forest had amped up several notches. Belinda heard animal sounds she hadn't heard before the birds fell silent. Owls called to each other; small creatures began to scratch their way along the forest floor; bats squawked above them. The forest had turned sinister with the fading light.

"Better go use the facilities before it gets too dark to see," John said with a hint of amusement in his voice.

She didn't see what was funny about it. Belinda didn't like using the facilities in the jungle. Peeing behind a tree meant baring her bum to the wildlife. Unfortunately, she'd drunk a lot of water and there was no way she could sleep on a full bladder. Still, the forest was looking pretty darn dark. Earlier in the day, John had gone behind another tree at a distance from her, but she didn't like the thought of losing sight of him in the dark.

"Will you guard me?" Yes. She was that pathetic.

"From what?" His lips twitched. He was playing with her. Teasing her. So *now* it was okay *not* to be serious and focused on their mission.

"I'd really like it if you stood in front of me, with your back to me. You can put your fingers in your ears, so you don't hear anything, but keep your eyes peeled in case something decides to take a bite out of my backside." There. That should be clear enough for him.

His eyes crinkled and his lips went suspiciously tight. She could have sworn he was trying not to laugh at her. "Put my fingers in my ears?"

"I'd really rather you didn't listen to me do my business."

His lips twitched again.

"And don't look. At me, I mean. Look at the forest."

He turned from her, but she caught his grin before he managed to hide it again. "Come on. We wait any longer and we'll both get eaten." He swatted at his neck. "By more than the mosquitoes."

They walked behind a giant kapok tree, with its strange roots. The buttress root "walls" were taller than she was and came out from the tree at an angle, making wedge-shaped spaces between them. Belinda pointed to one of the cubicle shapes made by the buttress roots. "I'll go there. You stand at the entrance."

"With my fingers in my ears. I know."

She watched him until he turned his back on her. He made no move to put his fingers in his ears. "Joh—*Beast!*"

"Fine." He lifted his hands to his ears.

There was no time to lose. Belinda undid her stolen jeans and, with her back to the tree and her front to John, squatted. And nothing happened. Her bladder was full, but it didn't want to cooperate. Not while she knew he could be listening. There was only one thing for it. She started to sing. Loudly. And the only song she could remember in that second, was "Row, Row, Row Your Boat."

John started to turn back towards her. "What the—"

"Don't look!" she screeched.

He jerked back around. "Why are you singing?"

"I don't want you to hear. I need cover noise. Put your fingers in your ears and let me get on with it!"

He stuck his fingers in his ears as she began to sing again, but she could have sworn that his shoulders were shaking. Once she was finished, she took a tissue out of her tiny bag and thanked the Lord that she didn't have to use a leaf to clean up. Then she used a wet wipe to wash up her hands. She was done.

She took a few steps forward and tapped John on the shoulder. He didn't jump, which made her think he hadn't blocked his hearing after all.

"I'm done."

"What a relief."

"Do you want me to guard you?" Belinda felt it was only polite to offer.

His grin was wide. "I think I'll manage, Hollywood." And he sauntered towards another partitioned area under the tree.

Belinda grumbled about men under her breath as she stomped the few feet back to their tiny camp. It wasn't fair that they could do their business standing and didn't have to bare their backsides to the world. Belinda had long thought that men would be a whole lot more sympathetic if they were the ones who had to sit down to pee. Let them sit on a public toilet seat and deal with the trauma. That kind of experience softened a person.

While John was gone, Belinda toed off her shoes and shrugged out of her jeans and dress. She hung everything, shoes included, over the rope above the hammock, but under the mosquito net. The last thing she wanted was to wake up to shoes full of bugs.

Wearing only her underwear, she sat in the hammock, under the netting, and used a precious wet wipe to clean off as much dirt as possible while she waited for John. Fortunately, a lot of the mud had dried and was easy to brush off. The rest, the stuff she couldn't remove with one measly wet wipe, she would have to live with.

Night was falling fast now, and Belinda double-checked that everything of importance was stored safely under the mosquito net. Their makeshift water bottles, or balloons, were hanging off the rope above her, along with her handbag and the plastic water bottles. The rifle was wedged into the ropes holding one end of the hammock up, allowing for easy access should they need it. It was the best she could do. It was cosy, some would say claustrophobically crowded, but she had never been more grateful for her shelter than for anything in her life.

Night hadn't dropped the temperature any. Her whole body felt clammy with perspiration. She almost wished it would rain so that she could stand in it and wash the salt off her skin. It wouldn't make a bit of difference, though, because as soon as she was clean, the humidity would make sure she was sweating all over again. Even now, when it was almost fully dark and she could barely see, the heat was stifling, making each breath she took thick with moisture.

She made out the shape of John as he walked towards her, and instantly felt reassured by having him closer. He might be annoying, he might even think she was dumb, but he was still a mountain standing between her and trouble.

"Take your shoes off and I'll hang them over the rope inside the netting. Your clothes, too. Hopefully they'll dry out a little before the morning." She didn't think so, but she was keeping her fingers crossed. Wearing sweat-soaked clothes was no fun at all.

The shadowed outline that was John stopped dead. "You got undressed?"

"Well, duh. It's about four hundred degrees and I'd really like my clothes to air out before I put them on again tomorrow. If the mud dried, so I could shake it off, that would be a bonus too."

"You're naked?" He sounded strangled.

"I kept my underwear on and my feet are caked in mud, so I'm practically wearing socks."

He definitely made a strangled noise. "I think it's best if I sleep out here."

"J—*Beast*." Damn it, she could not get used to calling him Beast. "You can't sleep out there. It isn't safe."

"I'm not sure how safe it is in there with you, either," he muttered.

And it hit her. She almost laughed. John was worried about sex, when she felt less sexy than she'd ever felt in her life. Even after her valiant effort to clean up, she was streaked with mud and sticky with perspiration. There were bites on every piece of skin that had been exposed to the elements, and leaves in her hair, and in place of brushing her teeth, she'd chewed a piece of gum she'd had stashed in her bag. Yeah, sex was *totally* on her mind.

"I hate to disappoint you," Belinda said drolly, "seeing as you are obviously so desperate to get your hands on me, but there's no way we can have sex in this hammock—even if we wanted to. And trust me, I don't. Now, if you were offering a shower, that I'd take you up on. But sex, no. Apart from the fact I feel gross, there's no room in the hammock to get physical. Plus, we'd probably break it if we tried. So, get your backside in here before a jaguar gets you. I promise to keep my hands to myself as best I can, given that we'll be sleeping squashed together."

"This is a bad idea."

"This is a bad situation. We're making the best of it. Now stop screwing around. You need to get your clothes off or they'll rub all night and cause you more pain tomorrow. You can't sleep in clothes that stick to you."

He muttered a whole string of things she couldn't catch, but she heard the rustle of material and knew he was undressing. A minute later, something was thrust at her. "Here. My clothes and shoes."

"I wish we had a flashlight." Belinda felt her way as she hung his things over the rope above her. "Tomorrow, if we're still out here, we need to make camp earlier so we can do everything before the sun sets and we can't see. And we need food. I'm hungry."

"I want the gun where I can reach it," John said.

"I put it above us at the head end of the hammock. Please tell me the safety's on?"

The answer was stony silence, which she took as an affirmative. Once everything was stored, she turned in the blackness, to face the edge of the hammock where John stood. Their surroundings had disappeared in the inky night and the volume of the jungle seemed to have been turned up. There were noises she hadn't heard during daylight, deeper calls that seemed far more sinister in the dark.

"Come closer," she ordered him. "Give me your hand and help me get out of here. If you climb on top of me, I'll suffocate. It's a better idea if I get out, then you get in and I climb on top of you."

She heard a strangled groan, which she ignored. The air shifted and his hand landed on her arm. She moved it so she could take hold of his hand. It didn't take long to get out of the hammock. She held up the net to let John under, showing him where to go with their joined hands.

"Don't move around too much. I'm worried the thing won't hold us."

He muttered some more.

"That muttering is a really bad habit. You should work on that."

He muttered even more, and Belinda found herself grinning.

There was the sound of material shifting and trees creaking as the hammock took his weight.

"I'm in." His voice was a deep growl that made it clear he was not happy with the situation.

"Good." She didn't wait for him to have second thoughts. Instead, she scooted under the net and climbed into the hammock—right on top of a solid bed of hot muscle.

She stilled, not quite sure where to put her hands or legs.

He let out a strangled groan.

"To hell with it," he said. "If we're going to do this thing, we might as well stop screwing around."

She felt his hands at her waist, and he lifted her, shifting her to suit himself. When he was done, she found herself lying plastered to his side with one arm over his waist and her head on his shoulder. Their bodies were wedged tight together, his arm wrapped around her and their feet tangled. It was as intimate as two people could get without making love.

"Comfortable?" he said in that deep, rough voice of his.

Belinda cleared her throat. "Yes."

Comfortable wasn't the word for it. She was insanely aware of her breasts pressed against him and his thigh wedged between hers. The heat of his body, coupled with his solid muscles, made her want to wriggle against him. If she'd been hot on her own, she was now in a furnace.

They lay stiffly together, listening to the noises of the forest growing louder around them. Strangely, she felt secure in their tiny hammock, with John at her side—secure and hyperaware of every inch of her skin that touched him. This was a new kind of agony. The man made her want to touch and taste and tease. Instead, she had to lie still and pretend his presence wasn't turning her on more than other men had managed when they were putting the effort in. It was a sensory hell that she both loved and hated at the same time.

"This is awkward, isn't it?" she said into the silence.

John froze and then burst out laughing. He laughed long and hard. Belinda pressed her ear to his chest and let the sound rumble through her as she relaxed, safe in his arms.

CHAPTER 13

Ryan woke up in a hospital bed. One glance at the window told him it was night. Apart from that, there was no other information in his fog-filled head.

"What happened?" It felt like he was pushing the words past a mouth full of cotton balls.

"Hey, you." Elle's purple hair came into view. She held a plastic beaker with a straw to his lips. "You broke your shoulder and they had to operate. Drink."

He didn't have to be told twice. As he drank, he began to notice his surroundings. There was an IV line in his left arm, and his right shoulder had a thick dressing and was strapped up tight.

"Better?" Elle put the beaker on the table beside his bed.

"Where am I?" Before she could explain that he was in hospital, he added, "Which town?"

"Cusco. That was the nearest hospital. De la Cruz flew you in on the chopper a few hours ago. It will take another few hours for the anaesthetic to work its way out of your system. Until then, you'll feel groggy." She smoothed his hair back from his forehead in a sisterly gesture.

"What's this for?" He lifted his left arm to indicate the IV line.

"Antibiotics. You'll need them for a few days."

A surge of panic ran through Ryan as he struggled to sit up. "I can't stay here for days."

"Hey, don't go nuts on me." Elle gently pressed his chest to push him back down. "You won't even be able to stand right now. And where, exactly, do you think you need to be?"

"Belinda. Beast." It was hard to think when his eyes felt so heavy. "Esperanza." A vision of a mass of wavy black hair framing a heart-shaped face and large hazel eyes filled his mind. "Got to get back to Esperanza."

"Who's Esperanza?" Elle tucked the sheet in around him.

"She's an angel." Ryan smiled as his eyes closed. "Gonna marry her…"

And then the world faded as he sank back into sleep.

"It's the drugs talking," De la Cruz said as he sauntered into the room.

Elle was pleased to see he was armed with coffee. She gratefully took a cup from him.

"I once declared love to my dentist after getting my wisdom teeth out under anaesthetic. Proposed, too." De la Cruz grinned widely, making her agree with Megan that he was one seriously good-looking man. "Mr Donahue was flattered, but seeing as he already had a wife and eight grandkids, he decided to pass."

"I had my appendix out when I was a kid," Elle said. "Woke up singing the *Teletubbies* theme song."

De la Cruz threw back his head and laughed. The man was too attractive for his own good.

"Where's Mrs De la Cruz?" Elle asked, before she could stop herself.

He cocked an eyebrow at her. "You want to audition for the part, *bonita*?"

Her cheeks flushed. "Just curious. Mrs De la Cruz?" She gave him a cheeky smile.

"She's somewhere out there, waiting for me to find her."

"Ah, a romantic." She sipped her coffee.

"Something like that." He pointed at Ryan. "What about him? Is Esperanza real?"

"Who knows. Ryan goes through women like…" She looked up at him. "I can't think of any analogies that aren't rude."

"Don't spare me, *bonita,* I like a woman who knows how to get down and dirty."

She snorted. "You should be so lucky."

He leaned back against the windowsill, the lights over the red roofs of Cusco acting as his backdrop. "Does that mean you're spoken for?"

Elle hesitated, because the answer was complicated. She wasn't dating anyone, but her thoughts were consumed by one man alone. He was her obsession and she wasn't entirely sure why.

"Ah, you pine for my friend David."

Elle bristled. Even the sight of De la Cruz's disappointed smile didn't appease her. "I wouldn't say pine. That makes me sound like a puppy waiting for its owner to return."

His eyes went wide. "He owns you? This is much more serious than I thought."

She answered him with a gesture that made him chortle. "Shouldn't you be back at the resort helping search for Beast and Belinda?"

"It's dark. There's no searching the jungle in the dark."

"I can't imagine being lost out there," Elle said. "It's beautiful, but terrifying."

He shrugged. "I grew up out there. We lived on the edge of Maldonado. The Amazon was my backyard."

"But you spent time in the U.S." His accent testified to that. "Is that where you met David?"

He gave her a teasing grin. "You can't wheedle information out of me about our friend. David's secrets are his own. But me, I'm an open book."

"Fine, explain the American accent, then." She was mildly curious; mainly she wanted to know about his relationship with David. Did they both work for the same government? Would he tell her if they did? No, one look at the man told her he wouldn't. He might ooze charm, but he had a spine of steel.

"It's no mystery," he said. "My father was Peruvian, my mother American. She was a scientist, researching in the jungle. He was a river rat, running supplies up and down the Amazon. They fell in love, got married, had kids, split up and Mom took us back with her to the States."

"That must have been tough." She couldn't imagine her parents living so far apart. How would they argue?

"It is what it is. I got to spend summers down here, on the river with my dad. We had good times. It wasn't a bad life."

"Now you work for the Peruvian government? Or is it the U.S. government?" She tried to keep her tone light, but could tell from the amusement in his eyes that she'd failed miserably.

"I'm a free agent, *bonita*. I have skills and I hire them out."

"Is that how you met David?"

He laughed hard, making Elle smile. There would be no getting information out of the man.

"Tell me this," he said, when he'd stopped laughing. "Once you figure out who David is, and you catch him, what then?"

Elle stopped with her coffee cup halfway to her mouth. "I

honestly don't know." And now she was wondering why she hadn't thought that far ahead.

"Maybe you want to think about that, *bonita*. David isn't a man you play with."

There was a groan from the bed and Ryan's eyes flickered open. "What happened?" he said.

"Here we go again," Elle muttered. "I really hope the anaesthetic gets out of his system soon. I'm fed up repeating myself."

She put the coffee down and went to tell Ryan all over again that he was just out of surgery. It was going to be a long night.

BEAST WOKE to the sound of something large moving around, and he didn't think it was human. For a start, they were enveloped in absolute blackness and there was no sign of a flashlight. Slowly, he inched his wrist up in front of his face. The faintly illuminated watch dial told him it was one a.m. He'd managed to sleep for a good few hours, which was a miracle in itself.

Sometime, while he'd been asleep, they'd shifted position. Now, instead of Belinda lying curled at his side, she was draped over him. Her knees were either side of his thighs, her arms were tucked in at his sides and her nose was nestled in the crook of his neck. One of his hands was tangled in her hair; the other had been resting in the small of her back—before he'd looked at this watch. Beast couldn't help but notice that she moulded to his body perfectly. Her soft curves were a foil to his hard muscles, and the little mewing sounds she made when he moved reminded him of a kitten.

As he listened to the creature move around the clearing near their bed, he gently stroked Belinda's back, soothing her

—or maybe himself. Her skin was satin smooth under his touch, and he was deeply aware of the heat coming from between her legs as she straddled him. Against his will, he grew hard. It was a sweet agony lying there, with temptation in his arms, unable to do anything about it.

He shifted his hips slightly, trying to angle them so that his hard length wasn't pressing against her mound. It was impossible; there was nowhere to move and no way to turn his body without waking Belinda and letting the animal outside their hammock know they were there.

She gave a little moan and shifted against him, rubbing against his painfully hard cock and making him swallow a groan. Reflexively, his hand tightened in her hair and he felt the moment she woke. She sucked in a breath and started to lift her head, ready to move away from him.

He turned towards her and whispered in her ear, "Don't move—there's something out there."

She froze. And now the two of them were painfully aware of the condition he was in. She lifted her hips slightly, trying to put some distance between them. The sensation of her body dragging against his cock was almost too much to bear.

"No! Don't move."

They heard a snuffling sound, very close to their bed.

Belinda pressed her lips to his ear and whispered, "What is it?"

He bit back the answer that almost burst from him. She was talking about the animal, not his desperate dick.

"Jaguar?" Belinda whispered.

"Don't know."

A large form passed under their hammock, lifting them up and making them rock. Beast pressed Belinda's face into his neck to stop her from crying out. The animal didn't seem to notice them; it carried on walking, and they heard it crash through the brush and into the jungle, leaving them to sway in the darkness.

For minutes, they lay there, afraid to move. Eventually, Beast relaxed. The jungle noises were back to normal. Whatever it was had gone.

"I think it was a tapir," Belinda whispered. "They're nocturnal. They're big like that. They're related to the hippo. It felt like something big and wide under us, didn't it? Not like the sleek back of a cat. And a cat would have scented us, wouldn't it? Tapirs are herbivores. It wouldn't have cared how we smell. Unless it *was* a jaguar and the smell from the white-lipped peccary is still clinging to us and put him off. What do you think?"

What did he think? He thought the animal, whatever the hell it was, wasn't the only big and wide thing that wanted to move under her. He squeezed his eyes shut and tried hard to get his mind out of the gutter. It was tough.

"It's gone now," was all he could manage to say.

They lay tense against each other, painfully aware of every single thing they could feel.

Belinda cleared her throat. "I should, um, get off."

"Hollywood, you're killing me here."

"I mean get off your body!" She groaned. "Never mind. I'm moving."

He didn't object. Having her straddle him was agonising, and he was close to breaking point. With some awkward manoeuvres that made the hammock swing, and a near-miss between her knee and his balls, Belinda ended up where she'd started—curled against his side.

For a few minutes, they lay there, listening to the night. Beast wasn't a nature buff, but even he could tell that the majority of the calls going out through the forest belonged to bats and owls. Night predators searching for prey.

"I know I should pretend to be all tough and everything," Belinda said softly, "but I want you to know I'm scared out of my mind."

He tightened his arms around her. "We both are, Hollywood."

"Really? You are too?"

He almost smiled at the incredulous tone. "They're blowing stuff up and firing machine guns. We're lost in the middle of the jungle and I'm a city boy. This is not in my realm of expertise." Hand-to-hand combat—*that* he was good at. Give him one opponent, in a ring, and he'd turn him into hamburger. But this? This was something else entirely. "You going to tell me where all your jungle skills come from?"

"You won't laugh?" She sounded vulnerable, and Beast hated it.

"I won't laugh." Even if she told him it was another Daniel Radcliffe movie.

"There's a lot of downtime on movie sets, and I spend it watching the natural history channel or reading books on the military, survival, bush craft, that kind of thing."

She paused, waiting for him to laugh. Mainly, he felt a little confused at her choice of subject matter, and grateful he was benefiting from it.

"Why those topics?" He couldn't stop from curling his hand back into her silky hair as they talked. He missed having her weight, as light as it was, on top of him. Even with her wedged against his side, it somehow didn't feel close enough.

"It was Bear Grylls. I told you I'd met him on a chat show?"

He nodded.

"Well, he was fascinating. He'd done all this exciting life-and-death stuff—things I'd only pretended to do for movies. I went away and read his biography, then the biographies of other explorers and adventurers, then I moved on to how-to books and became obsessed with wilderness shows."

She stopped talking, and from the tension in her body, he got the impression she was debating whether to tell him something more. She waited so long to speak that he almost believed she'd fallen asleep again.

"I'm not smart like my sister," she said at last. "Julia is practically a genius. I have a good memory and I can act. I love to act. Not because of the attention, but because I get to *be* someone else for a little while. It's like living lots of different lives in one. You know? But sometimes, I wonder about packing it all in. Giving up the dresses and the shoes, and the senseless interviews where I answer bubble-gum questions about my hair and what it's like to kiss Leo."

Beast stiffened at the thought of her kissing anybody at all. Other than him. He wasn't sure who this Leo guy was, but he had the sudden urge to introduce him to his fist.

"I sometimes wish I could be anonymous and travel the world having adventures, pitting my wits against nature, taking hours, days, months to watch all the fascinating things out there," she said in a rush, as though making a confession, one whispered into the small, still hours of the night when people say things they would never say in daylight. "I'm grateful for my success. I worked hard for it. But sometimes, I'd like to be nobody famous, living life by the seat of my pants and hoping for the best."

"Like now." Beast felt shame that he'd never taken into consideration what it must be like to constantly live your life in the limelight. The pressure of being available for everyone. The constant scrutiny. The endless, mind-numbing ques-tions and desperate pleas from people who only wanted a piece of you. "You act in your interviews too, don't you?" Of course she did. She wouldn't survive otherwise.

"I have a celebrity persona. It's my brand. Imagine that

I'm a company. The company of Belinda Collins is always bright, happy, funny, a little bit shallow and eager to talk about nothing at all. I'm the non-threatening girl at the party who guys want to dance with and girls want to gossip with. That's my brand. But it isn't who I am. Do you understand?"

"I'm beginning to."

They lay in silence, listening to the night. The overwhelming sounds were a wall of white noise that wrapped around them. Beast knew they were exposed, with only a shabby net and a thin sheet between them and the rest of the jungle, but he didn't feel that way. With the darkness, the blanket of sound and the sheet wrapping him and Belinda tightly together, he felt hidden. Secure. Apart. As though they'd stepped off the world for a moment and it was only the two of them in this place together.

"Can I ask you something, without you getting mad?" she whispered as she traced circles through the dusting of hair in the middle of his chest.

"Not sure." He wanted to be honest with her. There, in that place together, it felt like there should only be honesty. "But I'll try."

He felt her take in a shaky breath. "Why do you hate being called John?"

Yeah, that wasn't the question he'd wanted to hear. He took a minute to control his reaction, aware that his fingers had tightened in her hair. He let out a long, slow breath.

"You don't have to tell me," she said. "I shouldn't have asked. I'm sorry."

His arm tightened reflexively and he cleared his throat. He'd never told anyone the story behind his name, but for some reason—maybe the intimacy of their predicament—he wanted to tell Belinda. He stared out into the blackness, but the images he saw in his mind were clear as day. Memories. A childhood no kid should experience.

"My mom was a street worker." His jaw clenched and he swallowed hard. "A hooker."

Belinda stopped playing with the hair on his chest and wrapped her arm around him, holding him tight.

"She was young," he said, "a teenager, when she had me. I don't know how long she'd been on the street before I was born. Her name was Ria Green. I always thought that was the wrong name for a hooker, but she never went by anything else. I don't know where her family came from, or where she grew up. She rented a room in a run-down building not far from the boardwalk in Atlantic City. The woman who owned the boarding house, Miss Mabel, was about five hundred years old, smoked a pipe all day long and would look out for me while Ria worked the alleys around the casinos. We were there until I was seven. I pretty much raised myself."

He didn't bother describing the overwhelming loneliness of those years. The clawing hunger. The constant fear. Belinda didn't need to know any of it. He cleared his throat. "One day, Ria went to work and never came home."

He fell silent, seeing images from those years flash through his mind, like a movie montage: Miss Mabel, with skin the colour of liquorice, opening the door to his room and calling out to ask if he was okay before she went back to her daytime soaps; him stealing food from the grocery store, and hiding terrified in a closet because Ria had brought one of her clients home; trying to shake his mother awake when she was high on crack and lying in her own vomit...

"What happened to her?" Belinda's soft question snapped him back to the present.

"She OD'd."

Belinda stroked his chest as though to soothe him. He didn't need it. It had happened a lifetime ago. He barely remembered her.

"What happened to you?"

"Foster care." He'd wanted to stay with Miss Mabel, had begged, but she hadn't wanted him any more than his mother had.

"You don't need to tell me anything else," Belinda said, as though she somehow knew how truly crappy things had been.

But Beast had started now, and somehow that made it easier to go on. "Ria didn't know who my father was. She thought he might have been a Mexican-American guy who used her often during the right time frame."

"That's why she called you Garcia?"

"Not quite." He felt the words solidify in his throat. The full, ugly truth about his start in life. The truth he carried with him every day. The one his mother had been kind enough to put on his birth certificate to remind him. "My full name is A. John Garcia," Beast said.

Belinda gasped, and he knew she got it straight away.

"Yeah, she named me after my father—*a john*. And she used Garcia because she thought it sounded like *gracias*. It was sarcastic. She liked to laugh about it. A final thank you to the unknown man for his unwelcome gift."

Belinda held him tight. "That was unbelievably cruel."

That made him smile. Belinda Collins, darling of Hollywood, was outraged for him—a bastard mutt from the wrong side of the tracks. Who would have thought?

"I know she was your mum, Beast, but if she were here right now, I would be sorely tempted to slap her."

He couldn't help it. The thought of the delicate British celebrity taking on his street-toughened mother was just plain funny. He let out a bark of laughter that surprised them both and wrapped his arms around her, pulling her over his chest.

"She would have eaten you alive, Hollywood."

"Not before I got a good smack in. Your mother was an irresponsible…terrible…person."

He laughed again. "You can say bitch. Trust me, I get it."

She stilled then reached up to cup his cheek. "I wish it had been different for you. I wish you could hear the name John and feel pride, because when I think of you as John, I think of a strong, honourable, accomplished, sexy man. It's the name of presidents, of apostles, of musicians and actors. It's an amazing name. And you fit it. If I were you, I'd claim the John and make it yours. Then I'd punch anyone who didn't use it."

Beast laughed again and pressed a kiss to her hair. "You think I'm sexy?"

She huffed. "*That* was your takeaway?"

"You think I'm sexy." He grinned against her hair.

"I also think you're annoying. Focus on that."

"Belinda Collins, world-famous actress who's worked with some of the sexiest men alive, thinks little old me is sexy."

She pushed back from him with a frustrated grunt. "Trust me. On my list of sexy men, you are right at the bottom."

"But I'm on the list," he said smugly.

"I'm going to sleep, *John*."

For once, the name didn't make him angry. Instead, it made him laugh. Belinda was trying to twist around, to give him her back. Beast was having none of it. He pulled her into his side, took her hand, placed it back on his chest and kissed her hair.

"Sleep, Hollywood. You need your rest."

"You need some too," she grumbled, but she didn't try to pull away from him again.

His heart clenched at her protest. His life hadn't exactly been overflowing with people looking out for him.

"We'll both go to sleep," he said through a throat that felt tight.

As he felt her muscles relax and sleep take her over, Beast smiled into the darkness.

CHAPTER 14

They woke with the birds. Belinda opened her eyes to see the trees around her filled with colour. A flock of noisy, screeching macaws had taken up residence. The large red and blue parrots didn't care that Belinda and Beast were asleep. All they cared about was breakfast.

The warm early morning light filtered through the canopy above, giving their tiny clearing a hazy glow. The upbeat singing of the waking birds and the all-encompassing hum of the crickets had replaced the threatening sounds of the night hunters. Already the day's heat was building, and the glasshouse scent of the plants surrounding them was heady, a perfume to tease the senses.

"Stunning," she whispered.

"Yeah." Beast's word rumbled through her body, making her realise that she was, once again, draped all over the man. When she glanced up at him, he wasn't watching the birds—he was watching her. Everything within Belinda stilled. Their surroundings faded as she became acutely aware of the man beneath her.

"Sorry." She tensed her arms, ready to push away from him. "I'll get off you. Guess it's just more comfortable sleeping on top of you."

"Isn't like we have a lot of space."

"No." The sheet hammock wrapped tightly around them, making it difficult to move.

She struggled and wobbled, brushing her body over his, feeling every hard inch of him. At last, she was up on her hands and knees over him as the hammock swung gently from the trees. Beast's jaw clenched tight and his pale grey eyes had turned dark.

"I'm sorry," she said. "I'm trying to get off you as quick as I can." She moved again, rocking their bed.

John grasped her hips and she stilled. They were face to face, their bodies barely an inch apart. Everything within Belinda paused as the world faded to the man beneath her.

"You're killing me here, Hollywood." The husky rumble of words went right through her, making her blood fizz and bubble in its wake.

Her gaze slid from his eyes, over the masculine planes of his face—complete with a day's growth of hair—to his soft, sensual lips. Her breath stuttered as the memory of their kiss slammed into her. Suddenly, all she wanted to do was feel his lips on hers again.

"Belinda?"

She shivered as his tone went lower still. All night long, she'd lain beside him, their bodies entwined. She'd listened to his heart and felt the ripple of his muscles under her touch. All night long, she'd pretended she wasn't hyperaware of how he felt against her. Pretended she wasn't desperate to let her fingers explore, caress, tease.

All.

Night.

Long.

"This is a bad idea," he mumbled, making her look back into his eyes.

What she saw there robbed her of any reason that remained. Because Beast wanted her, just as much as she wanted him. Her thoughts stilled and narrowed. The jungle faded around them. The anxiety and fear from being kidnapped and hunted was wrestled into submission under the stark awareness of the man in front of her. There was only one thought in Belinda's head—*want*.

"Belinda?"

She shivered. His fingers were a brand on her hips. His thigh muscles flexed against hers. His chest was a hard wall beneath her, tempting her to press her aching breasts against him, seeking relief. Even this early in the morning, the heat and humidity meant there was a sheen to his skin. A tempting sheen that seduced her to touch.

"This is a *brilliant* idea," she whispered as her eyes rested on his lips again.

His reply was a pained groan that made her smile slightly. His fingers flexed on her hips, and slowly, Belinda lowered her mouth to his. Electricity shot between them, increasing in intensity the closer she came to his lips. They sparked. Sizzled together. One touch would ignite them. Anticipation made her heady as she prolonged her journey towards him.

"The hammock," he whispered, and she felt the words against her lips. His air became her air in a teasing intimacy. "You said be careful."

"Mmm, let's make it swing."

She closed the distance, and her lips touched his. It was an explosion of sensation, one that overwhelmed her rational mind. There was no thinking anymore. Only feeling. And what she felt was out of this world.

Beast splayed a hand on the small of her back and pressed her against him, joining them. Skin to skin. Body to body. Heart to heart. She felt his heart beat right through to hers. An intimate joining. She gasped into his mouth as she felt his hard length press against her. It wasn't close enough. She needed to feel him inside her. No barrier between them.

The kiss was ferocious, a meeting of intense need. Of overwhelming desire. She wanted him deep and hard. She wanted to taste all of him. She wanted to lose herself in his strength and in the animal longing he built within her.

He growled against her lips, wrapped his fingers in the hair at the back of her head and angled her mouth to suit his desire. Belinda's nails dug into his shoulders as she moaned into his mouth. More. She needed more. Her tongue went searching for his until they tangled together, dancing around one another, tasting and teasing and tormenting each other.

She felt Beast's hand slide from her back, over her hip, to cup her behind.

Yes!

She pressed back into his touch, delighting when he massaged her flesh. She pressed her needy core against his erection, seeking relief. Her hips moved, rocking against his length, making her whine with desperation.

His kiss turned feral. Desperate. Commanding. He was taking her over with his desire, making her fly out of control in a fierce tornado of bliss. She felt a touch at her back, and her bra fell loose. She shivered as his hands ran up and down her spine. The rough callouses and scars on his hands, presumably from fighting, set her nerves on fire wherever they went. She undulated under his touch, following the heat of his hands. Wanting more. Needing more.

It was almost too much. Her head was spinning and she could barely breathe. She broke their kiss, digging her fingers into his shoulders as she threw her head back, gasping for air. Her whole world had become his hands, as they caressed her behind and followed the line of her panties down to her wet and needy core. She arched her back, lifting her hips in invitation, silently asking him to touch her where she needed it most.

He didn't leave her wanting. She felt fingers trail down towards her clit, brushing back and forth over her damp panties, making her moan with longing. One strong hand held her tightly in place, while the other brushed her most sensitive flesh with the barest of touches.

"You already wet for me, baby?"

Her only reply was a moan as his finger slipped under the leg of her panties. He teased her tender flesh, stroking in long circles, but never touching her desperate clit. She looked down, dazed and desperate, to see John's head lift. His dark gaze captured hers as his mouth latched on to her oh-so-sensitive nipple. He sucked hard. The contrast between his brutal suction and the teasing soft touch of his fingers was almost too much to bear.

"Yes," she moaned. "Please, John, please."

He stilled for a second, leaving her dazed. And then his hand captured her nape and he made her look him in the eyes.

"To you, I'm always John. You hear me? You don't call me anything else."

His intensity made the words cut through the fog in her brain. This was serious. He was serious. She nodded as she pressed her breasts into his chest. Oh, yes, that was good. So, so good.

He let out a dark chuckle and his mouth was on her throat. She felt his teeth nip, and she shivered. Her body wasn't her own anymore. He owned her. With each touch, he wove a spell around her, until she was lost in a maelstrom of sensation. There was no thought. There was only need. Only John. The centre of her universe was now the desperate teasing touch of his fingers on her swollen folds. He teased her, dipping inside her only to retreat just as fast, to lazily circle around the tiny bundle of nerves that needed him so desperately.

"John," she gasped.

He chuckled against her breast, and she felt the sound vibrate throughout her body. She writhed against him, pleading for relief with every move. A thick finger slipped inside her, while his other hand cupped her nape and pulled her mouth to him for a punishing kiss.

She couldn't stop moving. She was desperate for him. His hard length was a tease, promising paradise that was just out of reach. The whole world moved with his touch as the hammock swung with their passion. The added sensation of flying built the pressure within her until she was a bundle of oversensitive, desperate nerves.

"Please, please, please…" she chanted against his mouth.

She needed him inside her. She needed him to stop the ache that was a tidal wave pulling her under. She needed the release that only he could give.

He withdrew his finger from her, making her wail her objection. He circled her clit. Once. Twice. And then he pinched it. Belinda's world stopped entirely. One second. Two years. A lifetime. And then it exploded. A keening wail escaped her as her whole body clenched and spasmed. The earth was moving. Swirling, swinging, shifting as she clenched on nothing when she desperately wanted to clench on him. She was empty. Needy. Desperate to be filled. Soaring without him when she needed him closer. As close as he could get.

"John," she moaned against his neck as she came back down, "need you. Need you now."

He growled, low and rough. His hand slid down her stomach as it moved between them. And there was a loud ripping noise. Belinda smiled, knowing he was desperate enough to rip off his underwear, to get rid of the barrier between them. There was another rip, louder this time, and Belinda's dazed brain began to register that something was wrong.

John let out a low curse and his arms wrapped tight around her, pulling her flat against him. With one last ripping sound, the soft sheet gave way beneath them and they were falling. They landed with a thud and a groan on the jungle floor.

"What the…" Belinda was still dazed, her body shaking from the high she'd experienced. It took her a few long seconds to realise what had happened. She looked up. The underside of their hammock was swinging above them and had split in two.

All around them, screeching birds flapped, taking to the air en masse, jarred into flight by the noise Belinda and Beast had made. Slowly, Belinda looked down at the man beneath her. She was still straddling him, only her knees had hit the earth. John had taken the brunt of the fall.

He lay there, his eyes closed, not moving an inch. Belinda scrambled off him.

"John?" She pulled up her bra and fought to hook it behind her back as she leaned over him. "Beast? Are you okay? Did you break anything? Please, don't let it be your back!"

His eyes cracked open. "I should have cleared the damn ground last night."

Her gaze shot to the clearing, which, on reflection, wasn't

that clear. There were a few branches scattered beneath them, some rocks and lots of twigs. That had to have hurt.

"Have you broken your back?" She needed an answer to that question before she dealt with anything else. She was panicking. How was she supposed to transport him out of the jungle if he was injured? The guy was a massive block of solid muscle. He had to weigh as much as a small car.

"No, but I'm probably bruised to hell." He frowned at her. "What did you say? Don't bother clearing the area. It won't affect us."

"Are you blaming me for this?" She couldn't believe her ears. She glared down at him.

"Hollywood, your exact words were 'let's make it swing.'"

She frowned as she racked her brain. Nope. Nothing. "I didn't say that."

"Yeah, you did. It came right before 'Please, John, please.'"

Her face burned, and not in a good way this time. "You're making this up, because I don't remember telling you to make the hammock swing. I do remember telling you to be careful. That the sheet might rip."

"You didn't tell me that I'd end up on my ass on the ground."

"That part was a given!"

"One sheet for a hammock," he grumbled. "I shouldn't have listened to you. There was no way that thing was going to hold both of us."

"That *thing*?" Now she wanted to stomp on his stomach. How could one man make her desperate to caress him one minute and desperate to hurt him the next? "That *thing* kept us safe all night long. If we hadn't been in that *thing*, then you would have been trampled by a tapir in the middle of the night. And who knows what else would have crawled all over you. You should be grateful I thought of making a hammock. And you should have respected the damn thing. Now look at it. Where are we going to sleep tonight?"

"Yeah, because this is my fault. You jumped me. I was being a gentleman. I kept my hands to myself. But you just had to crawl all over me."

"Crawl all over you?" She wanted to kick him now. Sure, he was sore and grumpy, but did he have to be an arsehole about it? "It takes two to tango, mister."

"But I didn't *tango*, did I? Only you *tangoed*. I got dropped on top of a tree trunk."

She put her hands on her hips and glared at him. "Is that what this tantrum is all about? You're upset because you didn't get off?"

"No, Hollywood, I'm upset because I fell through your *brilliant idea* and landed on my back in the middle of the jungle."

He looked from side to side, proving that at least his neck wasn't broken. "Looks fine down here. Might even have been comfortable, if I'd been allowed to clear it. And guess what? There would have been no falling if we'd been asleep on the ground."

Belinda had opened her mouth to tell him what she thought of his comment, when something big and black caught her eye. She froze in awe. A Goliath birdeater—the biggest spider on the planet. It was the size of a small cat and it was making its way across the log beside them—straight for John's head.

"Uh, John?" Belinda pointed to the spider.

"I don't want to hear any more excuses, Hollywood. We both know you were happy to risk the hammock while you were having fun. Now you're done, you're looking for some-where to put the blame."

Belinda watched the spider stomp its eight huge, hairy legs towards John. It seemed mad. The kind of mad you get when your neighbour is still partying at two a.m. and you have work at six.

"John, there's—"

"What?" John snapped.

It was too late to warn him. The spider launched itself straight off the log and right into the middle of his chest. He let out a roar that shook the trees. A split second later, he was on his feet. He moved so fast that Belinda wasn't even sure how he went from lying flat to standing. She watched in stunned horror as he danced around the clearing, as though the ground were a bed of hot coals. The spider clung to his chest hair, holding on for far longer than Belinda would have thought possible. Maybe it was disorientated with the way Beast was spinning and jumping. Maybe it was scared of the lunatic man who was slapping at it. Maybe the way he squealed like a baby pig was confusing for the creature. Eventually, it fell to the ground and scurried for the underside of the log.

John stood, rubbing his chest in the spot where the spider had clung. His hands shook as he backed away from the log with the spider under it. His eyes were continuously scanning the ground, looking for more man-eating insects that were waiting to jump out on him. Belinda watched, openmouthed, as he fought to get himself under control. His jaw was tight, his naturally tanned skin was pale and she could have sworn his hair was standing on end.

When he caught sight of her staring at him, his shoulders went back and his hands dropped to his sides. Although, she noticed the hands became fists and his eyes moved restlessly, keeping a lookout.

"That was a Goliath birdeater spider," Belinda said. "They're nocturnal and tend to stay in their burrows during the day. I think you pissed it off when you fell on its house. They're big but harmless, and they don't actually eat birds.

They eat frogs and grubs. As far as I know, they've never eaten a human."

He pointed a finger at her. "We will never speak of this again."

She gave him an angelic smile. "Of course. How about we talk about the hammock being a bad idea instead?"

He let out a strangled growl and stomped over to the hammock. He pulled out his clothes and got dressed in record time as he kept scanning the area around them.

CHAPTER 15

"Bloody hell," Callum barked when Ryan walked into the ballroom just after dawn. "What are you doing out of hospital?"

"I'm doing my job, old man." Ryan wasn't in the mood for dealing with Callum. His shoulder was killing him, but he refused to take anything stronger than ibuprofen, because it made his head feel fuzzy.

Callum folded his arms over one of his regulation grey Henleys, his self-imposed uniform since getting a medical discharge from the SAS. "What job are you going to do, *son*? This is a search and rescue operation—with a side serving of arse kicking for any kidnappers we find. You're in a sling and you're supposed to be on intravenous antibiotics."

"Still am." Ryan held up his free arm to show Callum the cannula still in it. "I brought the antibiotics with me. I'll hook them up to the vent later. I know I can't go out in the field, but there's nothing to stop me helping out here. Is there?"

Callum glared at him, but Ryan was more interested in the fact there was a buffet table set up near the bar. He headed for it and grabbed a plate, piling it high with everything in sight before going back to take a seat at the table.

"Nice to see your appetite isn't affected," Callum said.

"Takes a helluva lot more than a broken shoulder to put me off my food." Ryan looked around. "Is there any coffee?"

"Here, doofus." Megan set a mug on the table in front of him before plopping into the vacant seat on his right. "How long until you're fixed?"

Callum snorted. "Never."

Again, Ryan ignored him. "Six weeks, give or take."

"You're right-handed." Megan helped herself to one of the mini-pastries from his plate.

Ryan smacked her hand. "Get your own. I can still shoot better than you using my left hand."

Her eyes narrowed. "You might have to prove that."

"Okay, enough of this crap!" Callum called the meeting to order with his usual lack of charm.

Lake's lips twitched in his version of a smile. "Rachel, what happened to the men we detained?"

Rachel had changed into a black trouser suit and crisp white shirt, with black-widow stiletto heels to match. Ryan glanced around the table, noting that everyone else was in jeans and T-shirts. Guess a designer suit was Rachel's idea of casual. He shrugged then clenched his teeth as a wave of pain washed over him.

"You okay?" Elle whispered to him. "You turned grey."

"Forgot not to shrug." He squeezed the words out as the pain passed.

She winced and gave him a sympathetic smile.

Meanwhile, Rachel had consulted her phone. Whether it was to check on notes she'd made or take a selfie, Ryan wasn't sure.

"For those who managed to get broken and miss some of the action," she said to Ryan, "the police chief insisted in taking the men we apprehended into custody." She tossed her head, sending her poker-straight, dark brown hair over her shoulder. "That meant Callum didn't get a chance to *talk* to the men, which means we have nothing. They clammed up as soon as they went into custody. They now have lawyers and are eating a gourmet breakfast in the local jail." Her eyes went hard. "And I do mean gourmet. It was ordered from a local five-star hotel."

Eyebrows went up around the room. Dimitri let out a low whistle. "Looks like you were right, De la Cruz. The gang have the local police in their pocket."

Ryan shook his head in disgust. "We won't get anything out of them now."

"No." Lake was about as pleased as everyone else in the room. "We don't even know how many kidnappers are still out there."

"I saw two head into the jungle," Ryan said around a mouthful of food. His plate was empty already. He turned to Elle and gave her his best charming smile. "Elle, honey, would you top up my plate? I didn't get anything to eat in the hospital and I'm starving here."

"You're always starving." She rolled her eyes and took his plate. "Maybe if you'd stayed in long enough for the meals to come around, you wouldn't be so desperate to eat right now."

"Thanks, *Ellie*." He used the name David had written on her note and earned a glare.

"Ryan," Callum snapped. "Focus on something other than your stomach for a minute. What else did you see?"

Ryan became deadly serious. "Two men. One was checking tracks on the clearing floor. He pointed into the jungle. I got the impression he was telling the other guy which way Belinda and Beast had run. The other guy seemed to be in charge. He was the one who triggered the explosives with his cell phone."

"What did the guy with the cell phone look like?" De la Cruz was perched on the bar. One glance at the man would lead you to assume he was perfectly relaxed. It was deceptive. Ryan had used that trick himself on more than one occasion. He'd bet, if pressed, that De la Cruz could tell them where everyone was positioned, what weapons they were carrying and what the biggest threat in the room was. It was Lake. It was always Lake. He might not have been the biggest—or most gregarious—of the team, but he was by far the deadliest.

"He was average height. Overgrown black hair. He had jeans and a blue shirt on. He was thin, but not hungry thin, mean thin. Long nose. Scar on his throat." Ryan closed his eyes, bringing up the images of the man he'd seen for only a few seconds. "The scar was horizontal. Maybe somebody tried to cut his throat sometime?" He opened his eyes. "That's all I've got."

De la Cruz wasn't pleased. "It's enough. The guy is Angel Martinez. One of two brothers who run the baby cartel. He's mean as they come. Smart, too."

"Will he hunt Belinda and Beast?" Lake said.

"Yeah." De la Cruz gave Lake a dark look. "He won't stop until he has them. And they'll suffer when he does."

A ripple went around the room. Beast and Belinda were running in the jungle, unprepared, ill-equipped, and with no idea where they were or which way to head. Martinez, on the other hand, knew the jungle and was used to negotiating it. He had all the advantages over the pair. And he had a head start on the team when it came to searching for them.

"Can you pinpoint where Martinez and his man headed into the jungle?" Lake said.

Ryan nodded as Elle put another fully loaded plate in front of him. "I think so."

"Elle?" Lake said.

"On it." She tapped at her laptop, and the aerial image of the kidnappers' encampment appeared on the screen—taken before the place had blown sky high.

De la Cruz and Lake came to stand behind Elle and Ryan. Ryan studied the image. The dirt track into the camp was on one side of the clearing, and he was sure the Martinez men had gone into the jungle on the opposite side.

"There." He pointed.

"Elle, can you zoom out?" De la Cruz said.

A few keystrokes and the camp became small dots, as the vast green of the Amazon rainforest filled the screen. A red snaking line cut through the green, marking one of the many tributaries of the Amazon River. This river was called Madre de Dios—Mother of God. There were large yellow patches beside the river in one area, and Ryan wondered if they were massive sandbanks.

De la Cruz leaned forward, between Ryan and Elle, pointing at the screen. "That isn't good."

"What isn't?" Callum said. "Elle, do your bloody magic and project the image for us all to see."

"It isn't magic, Mr Dinosaur, it's a tiny projector you can buy on the internet." She pointed the cube at one of the walls and tapped a command into her laptop. The wall filled with the aerial image of the jungle.

De la Cruz walked over and pointed at the yellow patches Ryan had noticed. "See those? That's the damage caused when miners dig into the riverbank looking for gold. It pollutes the water, poisons the fish and erodes the rainforest." His demeanour was grim. "It's also illegal. These miners are dangerous. They don't want to get caught, and they don't take kindly to anyone showing an interest in their business. They're violent, often deadly—especially with strangers."

"Surely, if we can see where the mines are located, the authorities can too," Megan said. "Why don't they go in and shut the operation down? Maybe they have already. How do we know those mines aren't abandoned?"

"Elle," De la Cruz said, "zoom out until we can see most of the Madre de Dios River."

The screen shifted and the red lines of the river shot off in all directions, curving and winding through the green. There were a lot of yellow patches dotted along the river. Far too many for any authorities to police. "See how big the operation is? If they shut down one mining site, another pops up. Then they wait a few days and go back to the first. These guys don't care about the damage they're doing. They want the money and they're not afraid to kill to make it."

"Surely the locals want rid of them if they're causing that much damage to the environment?" Megan said.

"Who do you think works for the mining companies?" De la Cruz said. "The local villagers are in a tight spot. If they don't work for the companies, they're in danger from them, because they see too much. If they do work for them, they get much-needed money coming into the local economy. Many of these people live subsistence lives. The money is tempting. They want a better standard of living, just like the rest of us."

"Okay," Callum said. "What happens if Belinda and Beast walk in on the mining operation?"

De la Cruz ran his fingers through his hair. "Hard to say. But a lot of the mines in this area are run by the Martinez family."

"That isn't good," Elle muttered.

"Elle, go back to the search area, will you?" De la Cruz said, and the image on the wall immediately changed. "Here's the camp." He pointed to the small clearing. "Here are the river mining operations." He pointed again. "This is the direction Beast and Belinda went in." He drew an invisible line with his hand. "If they stay on that line and don't wander off, they're heading straight for the mines. I'd say it's at least two, three days' walk to get there. Maybe more, seeing as they aren't used to the forest."

"They managed to exit on the side of the camp that was furthest from the river," Dimitri said. "It's like they were trying to make it hard for us."

"At least they will eventually hit the river," Megan said. "It goes two-thirds of the way around the camp."

"That's a typical setup for the Martinez gang," De la Cruz said. "They like to make camp in the horseshoe bends of the river. It means they have fast access to transport in several different directions, if they need it. There is another option. If Belinda and Beast got turned around entirely, then they're headed away from the river and deeper into the jungle."

The atmosphere in the room turned thick. No one needed to say what would happen if Beast and Belinda kept walking into the rainforest. The chances of finding them in countless acres of jungle were slim to none.

"Search options?" Lake said.

De la Cruz rubbed a hand over his face, suddenly looking weary. "There's very little chance of finding them from the air. You can't see through the canopy. Our best bet is that they find a small clearing and somehow signal when a helicopter goes overhead."

"Searching from the river is out," Callum said.

De la Cruz nodded. "If you take a boat up past the mining sites, they will most likely fire first and ask questions later. You could do it. But it's risky."

"Then we go in on foot," Lake said.

"It's the only option," De la Cruz agreed. "Especially if they're being hunted by Martinez. Won't be easy, though. In jungle that dense, you could pass within a couple of feet of someone and not know they're there." He looked around at the Benson Security team, all of whom had the same sombre expressions. "We'd could use more people if we're going in on foot."

"Which means more targets for Martinez," Megan said. "I don't want to be a target. I've done that. It wasn't any fun."

Dimitri smiled and stroked his wife's golden hair. "Nobody's gonna be a target, baby."

"How else will we find them if we don't go play hide-and-seek with the baddies in the jungle?" Megan asked with a pout.

Lake shared a look with his two partners. They seemed to be able to speak telepathically. Lake gave a short nod before turning back to the rest of the team. "We'll split into teams. Rodrigo in the chopper, scouring for signs from the air. Callum on the river. You can focus on the stretch of river leading up to the mining operation, but keep your distance from it. We don't want the Martinez brothers to get wind that we're there."

Callum nodded grimly.

"Two teams in the jungle," Lake said as he looked over at Grunt, who was standing, arms folded and frowning. "You staying here or coming?"

Grunt didn't want to leave his pregnant wife unprotected, and with Ryan in a sling and Elle's notoriously bad aim, they would be if Grunt left.

"Do you have jungle experience, big man?" Violet asked.

Grunt grunted.

Violet nodded. Apparently, she spoke Grunt. "Then I'll stay here. You go. I don't have jungle experience, but I can guard everyone who stays here."

Grunt studied her for a moment before looking at Lake, who read the unasked question in his frown. "Ex-police. Commendations. Expert marksman. Mean as hell. She'll get the job done."

"No one will get past me to anyone here," Violet said.

"Eh, hello?" Ryan called. "Remember me? I may be injured, but I'm not dead. I can fight and shoot left-handed."

"If he isn't using it to eat," Elle said, and Ryan gave her a dirty look.

"Okay. I'll go," Grunt said to Lake, and then looked at Violet, who was about a quarter of his size. "If anything happens to Claire, you pay."

"Fair enough." Violet shrugged, not in the least intimidated by the man mountain.

"Right, meet out at the helicopter pad in an hour," Lake said. "Elle, mark a grid of the area and coordinate the search from here. Use our GPS signals to maintain search parameters. That way there won't be any duplication of areas searched. Dimitri, Grunt, you're jungle team one. Harvard and I will be jungle two. Megan, you're on air lookout with Rodrigo. Ryan, Violet and Elle are coordination and cover back here at base. Rachel…"

She raised a perfectly manicured eyebrow at him, as though daring him to give her a job.

Lake's lips twitched. "You're liaison with local law enforcement. Keep them off our back. We can't trust them, and I don't want them anywhere near this search."

"Consider it done." She inclined her head as though she were a queen deigning to listen to a commoner.

"Any questions?" Lake looked at each of them, but there was silence. "Good. Gather your gear. Make sure each team has a satphone and plenty of water on them. We meet in an hour."

The team dispersed, hurrying to get ready for a long day searching the Amazon forest.

"I have a couple of questions," Ryan said to Elle, who was busy overlaying an aerial map of the search area with a grid outlining its coordinates. "Did Grunt tell Joe about the kidnapping?"

"Yeah," Elle said. "Joe decided to keep the news from Julia for a while longer."

"At least it was his call and not one of the bosses'." Although Ryan wouldn't like being in Joe's shoes if the final news he had to give his new wife was bad.

"What's the other question?" Elle said.

"I don't suppose anyone asked for me while I was in the hospital?"

She cast him a sideways glance. "You mean like the million people here who all love and worry about you?"

"Apart from them." He waved a hand. "Never mind." He pushed back his chair. "I'm going to my cabin. I need to get changed and get my weapons out of the safe."

"Mm-mm," Elle said with a knowing smile. "Make sure all you get while you're in there is your weapons. We've no time for you to *get* anything else."

With a smile, Ryan hurried out of the ballroom and straight for his cabin, where he hoped Esperanza had made herself at home and was, somehow, miraculously, still waiting for him. Or had at least left a note telling him how to get in contact. Because he very much wanted contact with her. Full body contact.

CHAPTER 16

"I'm starving." Belinda placed a hand on her rumbling stomach. "How long can people go without food, anyway?"

Beast strode through the jungle in front of Belinda, keeping his eyes open for anything that looked like it might jump out at him. He wasn't proud of losing it when the spider landed on him. But, in his defence, it had been big enough to eat his head.

"Forty days. That's how long you can go without food. You ate at the reception dinner. You aren't starving."

"It feels like I'm starving. I've been hungry before. Usually before a premiere or a red carpet event. But I've never felt like I might die if we don't eat within the next five minutes."

"That still isn't starvation. When you've gone a week with nothing in your stomach, talk to me then."

She muttered something, but he couldn't catch it over the noise of the insects swarming around them, and the monkeys in the trees overhead. He had a suspicion that they were being followed by a troop of monkeys. Obviously, Belinda's constant chatter wasn't a deterrent to the animals. But then, the monkeys never shut up either.

"I think it's too dangerous to eat the fruit," Belinda said. "I don't recognise half of this stuff, and I don't know what's poisonous and what isn't."

"Didn't they cover that in the many books you read when you weren't making movies?" And yeah, he sounded sarcastic.

"Yes, they did, but I was more interested in the stories about animals and how to make shelter. Which, might I remind you, we don't have because your oversized body broke the hammock."

He wasn't going into it again. They were hot, tired and running on adrenalin. It was natural to want to relieve pressure by arguing. Or by having sex. Nope. He wasn't going to think about that either. He reached down to adjust the confining crotch of his pants.

"Can't you catch us some fish and cook it over an open fire?" Belinda said.

Beast stopped and turned to face her. Her focus was on the ground, not on him, and she ran straight into him. Wide blue eyes looked up at him.

"What?"

"Catch some fish? Cook it? Hollywood, didn't you hear me when I told you about my childhood? I didn't spend my formative years camping out with the Boy Scouts. If you want to know how to dumpster-dive, I'm your man. Catching and cooking food ain't in my bag of tricks."

Her face softened and she placed a hand on his shoulder. He felt her touch burn through his body, raising his temperature in an environment where it was already perilously high. For the first time in his life, he almost understood why his mother had lost herself to crack cocaine, because the woman in front of him could easily become his addiction. As soon as he was within reaching distance of her, he wanted to forget all about their circumstances and the danger they were in, and spend his time with her beneath him. When he was around her, he became someone else. Someone who could only think of Belinda Collins and his need for her. It was a disturbing realisation.

"I'm sorry you know that stuff," she said. "No kid should know how to go through bins for food."

He shrugged the comment off. He knew a whole lot worse than that. Dumpster-diving was the least of his down-and-dirty skills. The year he'd spent on the streets as a teen taught him all sorts of things that would freak the life out of a Hollywood princess.

She took a deep breath and her hand dropped to her side, making him itch to snatch it back up and return it to his shoulder. "I think fish is the way to go. You can't really get poisoned from eating well-cooked fish, and I hear piranha is tasty."

His eyebrows shot up. "You want me to catch fish that eat people? You want to eat them?"

She rolled her eyes, like he was somehow being overly dramatic. "Piranha don't eat people. That's been blown all out of proportion. They're attracted to blood. There are lots of them in the river. Just don't bleed and it will be fine."

She said it like she was telling him to walk to the grocery store and pick up some milk.

"Okay, assuming we even find a river, which"—he made a pointed show of looking around—"doesn't look like it's gonna happen soon, what do we do when we catch this man-eating fish?"

"You cook it, John." Her voice softened on his name, and she licked her lips as though waiting for him to lose it again.

The funny thing was that he had no desire to tell her not to call him John. On her lips, in that sexy English accent of hers, it sounded like nothing he'd ever heard before. It was as though she made it new, somehow. The memories he associated with his name were gone. But only for her. Only from her lips.

Damn, he was losing his mind when it came to this woman.

"Hollywood, I don't know how to cook."

"You've never barbecued? You've never slapped some steaks on a grill?"

"No. I eat out."

"I thought grilling was genetic. I thought men were born knowing how to set fire to food."

"Why don't *you* cook this mythical fish?"

Her eyelashes lowered. "I can't cook either. I have a chef."

And there it was. The ever-present proof that they lived in completely different worlds. "Of course you have a chef. You probably only drink water out of gold-plated goblets as well."

Her eyes narrowed. "I save the gold-plated goblets for wine. And here I was, thinking I was talking to the man, but I'm right back talking to that chip on your shoulder. Yes, I was born wealthy. Yes, I make a lot of money and I'm wealthy in my own right now. Yes, I employ people. I'm a business." She waved a hand down her body. "The brand is Belinda Collins. I have employees. Don't tell me you wouldn't employ household staff if you had money. There isn't a sane person in the world who wants to do their own cleaning."

"Listen to yourself." Beast felt his ire rise. "Who says stuff like 'household staff'?"

"Normal people who can afford to employ them." She glared up at him. "You really need to deal with that chip, John, or you're going to end up a sad and lonely old man."

"Just the way I want it, baby." He turned and stalked away.

The parting shot would have been more effective if a piece of mystery fruit hadn't flown out of the canopy and hit him square in the back. He stilled as the monkeys overhead hollered. Beast just knew they were laughing at him.

He glared back at Belinda, who was looking suspiciously innocent. "I'm sure they didn't mean to do that."

He grumbled and turned back to the direction they were heading. And another piece of fruit hit his head. The monkeys went wild, and he could hear Belinda smother a laugh. Beast hated the damn jungle. There was no end to his humiliation. Insects, spiders, monkeys—they were all out to get him. He squared his shoulders, gritted his teeth and charged forward. The sooner he got out of the Amazon, the better.

He hoped to hell the monkeys would get fed up and leave him alone. He didn't need to deal with any more wildlife. He already had his hands full with Belinda. Nobody on the planet made him madder, with her superior, entitled, privileged world-view. She didn't have a clue how the other half lived. None. *Household staff!* He smacked a large palm leaf out of the way and strode past it.

And the world disappeared from under him.

ONE SECOND JOHN was stomping along in front of her grumbling to himself, shrugging off monkey fruit attacks and nurturing the black mood he'd been in ever since he'd fallen through the hammock. The next, he was gone. With a startled yelp, Belinda rushed forward to see what'd happened—and screeched to a halt at the edge of a ravine.

She stared down the steep incline in utter shock as John slid on his back, over plants and bushes. He bounced off trees, like a pinball in a machine, all the way down to the edge of the lake beneath them. Belinda covered her mouth and winced every time he hit something hard. That had to hurt.

At last, he slid to a halt at the bottom of the ravine, with his feet in the water in front of him. And then things got infinitely worse. Because the heads of several giant otters bobbed out of the water to watch him.

Belinda's eyes shot to John. He hadn't seen them yet. He was focused on sitting up, ready to stand.

"Don't move!" Belinda called, hoping it was loud enough for him to hear, but not so loud that it freaked the otters out further.

John stilled. Belinda let out a breath as the otters started calling to each other. John's head came up and he stared at the animals, who stared back at him.

"Back off slowly. Really slowly. If you can get up a tree, that would be best."

At six feet in length, the giant river otters of South America, with their powerful limbs, sharp claws and razor-sharp teeth, could easily take on a caiman. If they saw John as a threat, he didn't stand a chance.

"I'll distract them." Belinda kept her voice low and even. "You move slowly. There's a tree behind you to your right. Get up it."

He crab-walked back towards the tree, moving as slowly as possible.

The noise level from the otters increased and the adults headed towards the shore. They were moving straight at him. Belinda didn't know if they were curious, or if they saw John as a threat to their babies, and she didn't want to wait to find out.

"Over here!" she shouted, in the hope of getting their attention off John. "Hey you! Over here! Look at me!"

The animals' heads rose, and Belinda inched her way down from the lip of the ravine, holding on to tree trunks for stability, moving at an angle to force their gaze from John.

"Everybody watch me," she shouted. "John, get to that

tree. Don't make any sudden moves. Don't stand up. Keep your appearance small and non-threatening."

With only their heads visible as they bobbed in the water, they looked more like seals than the otters she'd seen in a zoo. A twig snapped under John, and their heads shot back around.

"No! Over here!" She waved her arms again, but they were watching the two of them now. She needed a bigger distraction. She looked around for one and her very shiny dress caught her attention. She whipped it over her head and started waving it around. Then, to add to the spectacle, she started singing Adele songs at the top of her voice. Singing them badly. Although, she didn't think the otters cared if she was in tune or not.

Slowly, drawing as much attention as possible, Belinda made it halfway down the incline, glancing at John frequently to gauge his progress. Relief swamped her when she saw him step behind the large tree and start climbing. She kept singing and swinging her sparkly dress until he was high in the tree, sitting on one of the wide branches.

His attention was on her now, and she suddenly became aware that she was prancing around in her bra. For once, Belinda was more worried about her exposed skin attracting insect bites than the critical eye of a man. Now that John was safe, she turned her dress inside out, to minimise the glare from the sequins, and shrugged back into it. Then she silently sat down on a grassy ridge behind her to wait for the otters to lose interest in them.

She wrapped her arms around her knees and kept her eyes on the otters. Now that the danger had passed, and they were both far enough away from them to be safe, it was amazing to watch the animals. They gave up watching Belinda and John after a few minutes and went back to frolicking and playing in the water.

She wasn't sure how long she sat there, but eventually the otters became bored with playing, climbed out of the lake on the far shore and disappeared into the forest. Belinda waited a few minutes to make sure they were gone, before she carefully made her way to the tree where John sat high in the branches.

"Wasn't that amazing?" She grinned up at him.

"Hollywood, I nearly got eaten." He shook his head as though she were a mystery to him.

"They wouldn't have eaten you." She wasn't so sure, but the topic of otters eating humans hadn't been covered in any of the books she'd read. "They eat fish. And"—she practically bounced with glee—"they only gad about in fresh water. That means the lake is clean and safe and we can have a bath. Isn't that cool?"

His lips twitched as though he was fighting the urge to smile.

"Go on, John, you can do it. I know you can. Give me a smile."

He shook his head, as the smile broke free. It was dazzling. The man was born to smile. It took her breath away and made her shiver with warmth.

"You're nuts, you know that?" he said as he started to climb down the tree.

"A nut who's going to have a bath!" Nothing could take away that joy. She felt like she'd been dirty for a year. "While we're having a bath and washing our clothes," Belinda said, mesmerised by the sight of his firm, round backside making its way down the tree, "maybe we can use the mosquito net to catch some fish."

John landed with a thump at her feet. His shirt was ripped across the arm and down the back, and there was a piece missing from the bottom of his trouser leg.

"You okay?" Belinda said. "That looked rough."

"Let's just say what was left of my ego after the spider attack took a beating on the slide from hell."

She winced. "Yeah, you aren't doing very well on this trip, are you?"

"Hollywood," he said with a sigh. "This isn't a trip. It's an escape."

"Oh, yeah." She knew that. Of course she did. It wasn't her fault that there were parts of her escape she found exciting. Like seeing the white-lipped peccaries, the macaws, and the otters. She glanced up at John out of the corner of her eye. Yeah, there was a lot about this escape she found thrilling.

"Come on, crazy woman, let's get cleaned up."

"And catch fish," she said hopefully as she followed him to the water's edge.

"And catch fish." He sounded so defeated that she almost laughed.

CHAPTER 17

They took turns washing in the lake, while the other kept a lookout. Because Beast was worried that something would bite off his dick while he was in the water, he convinced Belinda they should keep their underwear on. It'd been partly true and partly out of desperation. He knew seeing her naked wasn't going to do anything for his self-control, and he was already on edge when it came to the woman. One false move and he would fall.

They dried off on the edge of the lake, using the two parts of the ripped sheet.

"I can't stand it," Belinda said from behind Beast. "I need to wash my underwear too."

He stilled. "You're getting naked?"

"Yes. If it bothers you, don't look, but I'm washing everything," she declared. "I don't know how well it will dry in this humidity, but I can't stand the dirt anymore. We can camp here for the night, can't we? I don't think the otters will be back, but if we camp away from the lake, we should be fine. I don't know what we're going to sleep on, though. Do you think this water is safe to drink? It should be, shouldn't it?"

He was becoming used to her incessant chatter when she was nervous. Sometimes, it even amused him, but right now, he was still focused on the naked part of their conversation.

"Are you sure about getting naked? Something might eat you." Yeah, he really shouldn't have put that thought in his head.

She laughed. "Don't be daft. Now, do you think we can drink the water?"

Beast tried valiantly to drag his thoughts away from her stripping off the last of her clothes. He could do this. He could keep his eyes off her. It wasn't hard.

"Not sure I want to drink water that had six huge, furry otters swimming in it," he said. Good, he sounded calm. In control. He broke out in a sweat, as he realised it wouldn't last.

"I don't see any bamboo," she said. "Our only option is lake water, and I can't remember how to make a filter. Oh, maybe there's a little stream going into the lake. We should look for one. Running water is cleaner than sitting water, isn't it?"

How the hell would he know? As far as he was concerned, water came in two forms—out of a faucet and in a bottle. He heard the rustle of clothes behind him, then splashing in the water. *Don't think about her naked. Don't imagine all that creamy, smooth skin. Don't think about what she'd taste like. Don't remember what she felt like coming apart in your hands...*

"Are you even listening to me?"

No. He wasn't. He was trying very hard to shore up his self-control, so that he didn't lift her naked body and impale her on his now painfully hard cock.

"Sure. Filter. Water. Something about a..." *Don't say bed. Don't even think about a bed.* "...place to sleep."

"Oh, John." A warmth seeped through him at the way she said the hated name, as though it was something precious.

He gave himself a mental slap on the back of the head, hoping it would knock some sense into him and stop him mooning over a Hollywood star. "I was too busy dealing with myself and excited to bathe. I didn't look at your back. You're all scratched and bruised."

He was wrapped up in his own thoughts and wasn't aware of her approach, until he felt her hand on his back. He froze, his whole world suddenly reduced to the delicate touch of her fingertips on his skin.

"That shirt was no protection for you on your slide down the slope."

He heard the sympathy in her voice. Empathy over cuts and bruises he barely felt. Sure, he was a bit banged up, but it was nothing compared to what he endured during a fight. "It's nothing."

"It's not nothing," she said. "Do you have any idea how easily things can become infected in this environment? I don't even have any antiseptic cream in my bag. Wait! I do have something that will help."

She ran off, and Beast turned to see what she was doing. It was a mistake. The woman was indeed stark naked. In one split second, the blood that enabled coherent thought drained to his already hard cock and made it throb with desperation.

Satin skin flowed over curves made for a man's hands to caress. Full breasts with dark pink nipples swung as she ran. And when she turned to dig something out of her tiny bag, Beast's mouth fell open at the sight of her nipped-in waist, gently flaring hips and perfect heart-shaped ass.

An image popped into his mind. He saw himself coming up behind her, running his hand down her spine, pressing between her shoulder blades until her breasts were flush against his bed. His black sheets would make her pale skin glow. In a soft, low voice, he would tell her to turn her face until her cheek rested on the mattress, her golden hair spread out behind her. That way, he could watch her face as he grasped her hips, pulled her up and angled her to just the right position for him to drive into her. She would gasp and flex around him, sending agonising ripples of delight throughout his body, a sweet agony of sensation he knew would be his addiction. And then he'd withdraw, slow, smooth, controlled, and listen for that breathless moan she made when he built her orgasm with his touch. And he'd—

"John?" Belinda was standing right in front of him. Within arm's reach. A frown puckering her brow.

He clenched his fists tight to stop from reaching for her. This was torture. Pure and simple.

"You're naked." The words were strangled, barely making it past his lips.

She shrugged. "You've seen me in underwear. This isn't a big deal."

"But. You're naked."

Now she seemed worried. "John, did you hit your head on the way down the ravine?"

Yes. But that wasn't the reason he couldn't think straight. No, that was the fault of the real-life siren standing in front of him. She was a temptation strong enough to lure any man to his doom. His eyes trailed down the graceful column of her throat, over her full breasts, across her flat stomach to the golden curls at the V of her thighs. Golden treasure that he'd touched but hadn't seen or tasted—yet.

"John? Answer me. Did you hit your head?" she said slowly, as though testing his ability to reason.

He could have told her it was a waste of time. His reason had fled the moment he'd seen her naked. "You're naked," he repeated because, honestly, that was pretty much the only thought in his head.

"Yes, John," she said softly.

She used the same tone doctors used when he'd woken up in hospital after a particularly brutal fight. She was worried, afraid of making his condition worse. Only she couldn't make his condition worse. His cock wasn't going to get any harder. It had reached its limit and was strangling in the confines of his pants. Damn, he wished he hadn't rushed to get dressed.

Slowly, as though trying not to spook him, she put a hand on his arm. His whole body shuddered with her touch.

"We're in the rainforest," she said. "The Amazon rainforest. Can you remember my sister's wedding? You were a guest because of your friend Joe, Julia's new husband. And then we were kidnapped. We think it was a real kidnapping, but there are some doubts. Now we're running for our lives and it's quite possible we're totally lost. Can you remember any of that?"

Yeah, it was time to step in before she started drawing diagrams of their predicament in the dirt with a stick. He took a step towards her and watched her eyes flare as the realisation that he was a man and she was naked in front of him hit her.

"I'll tell you what I remember, Hollywood." He moved his hands, one clasping her nape, the other the curve of her hip. It was almost as though they'd reached for her of their own volition. Beast couldn't have stopped them even if he'd wanted to. She sucked in a breath, and the noise was heady, making adrenalin surge through his body. "I remember having you on top of me." His voice dropped an octave and he saw her pupils dilate. "I remember the feel of your body against mine." The tip of her tongue peeked out to wet her lips and, at the sight, his legs almost went out from under him. "I remember how wet you were and how you gasped my name when you came." He stepped closer still, until his chest pressed against those hard nipples and her soft breasts flattened against him. "I remember thinking that we needed more." He lowered his head, until his lips were against her ear. "Do you need more, Hollywood?"

Her reply was a little moan that ripped through his body. She clasped his arms, and he felt her tremble and sway against him.

"Tell me you need more," he said against the shell of her ear, making her shiver.

"Please, John."

"I'll please you, baby. Promise," he whispered, and then he angled her head and took her mouth with his.

BELINDA WASN'T self-conscious about her body. Getting over being naked around people was something that happened pretty fast as an actress. The fact she had a bit of an exhibitionist streak helped too. When she'd decided to strip totally naked, she'd been thinking about washing her underwear. Mainly. In the back of her mind, a tiny voice wondered how John would react when he saw her naked. That same voice wondered if she could tempt him into carrying on from where they'd left off that morning.

She didn't have to wonder any longer.

Because his reaction was blowing her mind.

His kiss was demanding, without words, that she give all of herself over to him. There was no hesitation. Belinda wanted everything that John promised with his touch. Strong hands caressed her body as John held her tight, leading their kiss. Taking her away from everything. Taking her to a place where only this mattered.

His chest was hot under her fingertips. Muscles rippled and flexed as she investigated him. The urge to sink her teeth into those muscles and feel their strength was almost overwhelming. She wanted to bite, to taste, to tease. She wanted to know every inch of him.

Her hands found the waistband of his trousers, and she quickly unfastened them. He groaned into her mouth as she tugged his clothes over his hips, freeing him. And then he was in her hand. Thick. Long. Hard. She shuddered with need.

"I want to taste you," she said against his mouth. She did. She wanted him in her mouth. She wanted to trace the mushroom head of his cock with her tongue. She wanted to know his taste and exactly what kind of touch set him off.

He groaned. "Later. I promise. Later. But right now, I need to be inside you."

She understood. She felt the same. It was as though every touch since they'd met had been foreplay.

"Yes," she said, sighing, squeezing the hard, hot heat of his cock and feeling him pulse against her palm. "Yes."

He kicked off his shoes and clothes as she held him tight. "You're killing me, baby."

"Mmm, but what a way to go, huh?" She lowered her head and nipped at one of his nipples. The strange swirling tattoo that covered his left pec danced under her touch. He needed more tattoos. He had a body that should be covered in art. And then she could trace every single line with her tongue. Mmm, yeah, more tattoos were a good idea.

Strong arms turned her and pulled her back against his body. She felt his hard length against her lower back and rubbed against him. "I want to touch you," she said.

His hands came up to cup her breasts. Clever thumbs strummed her nipples. She let her head fall back to his shoulder and moaned.

"You touch me any more, baby, and this is gonna be over fast."

That was okay with her. The thought of him losing

control and being able to watch him explode was enough to make her shiver.

He chuckled and nipped her earlobe. "Put it on the list," he said, as though he'd read her mind. "We'll work our way through it once we're somewhere safe. Somewhere with a nice big bed."

"Promise?" She held his arms as he walked her forward, his hands teasing her breasts.

"Promise."

She turned her head and nuzzled at his throat. He smelled musky. It was tantalising.

"This is gonna be fast, but I promise you'll enjoy it and I'll make it up to you later."

"I like fast." She just liked touching him. It was electric.

He chuckled and turned her head to kiss her hard. She was breathless when he released her. Desire-darkened eyes bored into her, and she saw her own need mirrored in them.

"Bend over and hold on to the tree, baby. The ground is covered in ants and there's no way I'm laying you down on it." He gently put pressure between her shoulder blades, to bend her over a fallen tree. "Once we're out of here, I'm going to get you flat on a bed with black silk sheets and I'm going to take my time with every single inch of this glorious skin of yours."

She flattened her back and arched her backside out towards him. He ran his hand down her spine and over the curve of her behind.

"That's exactly how I want you." His hands smoothed over her skin. It felt like tiny bubbles shimmering over her. "You're so soft. How is that even possible?"

He massaged her hips and cheeks. All Belinda could do was close her eyes and sink into the sensation.

"Spread your legs, baby." His tone had turned guttural.

She did as he asked, and his fingers moved over her sensitive entrance, making her writhe and moan.

"So wet, just for me."

He seemed to be talking to himself, which was perfect, because Belinda was unable to concentrate on anything other than the wonderful sensation of his touch trailing through her sensitive folds. She arched her hips and pressed back into him, wanting more.

Her actions earned a deep, dark chuckle. "Don't worry, baby. I'll make you feel good." His fingers sank deep inside her.

A desperate wail of a moan escaped her, and her head hung down. "Please, John, I need—"

She felt a fingertip circle her clit, and the ability to talk was torn from her. She gasped and arched and writhed against him. She was so empty, clenching on nothing when she needed him to fill her.

"John." It was a wail.

"Okay, baby, okay." He withdrew his tormenting touch to soothe her by stroking her back.

Belinda didn't know whether she was grateful for the respite or desperate for him to continue.

"Damn," he spat out as he clenched her hips. "We used all the condoms to store water."

It took a minute for his words to register. Oh no, no, no, no. There was no way he was stopping. Not now. Not when she was desperate enough to lose her mind. "They're still good. Just a bit…baggy. You can make it work."

There was a second's silence. "Hollywood, I'm not putting one of those on my dick. Even if I got one on, they're stretched to hell and it could come off inside you. We have to wait."

He started cursing some more.

"No!" Her mind raced. "I'm clean. At least, I think I am. I never have sex without a condom. Go ahead, shove it in."

He barked out a hoarse, desperate laugh. "Be still, my heart. What about pregnancy? You want a baby Beast?" His tone was mocking.

For a second, everything within Belinda froze. Her mind filled with images. A little boy just like John, running around, driving her mad and going all alpha on the other kids in kindergarten. Yeah, that didn't sound so bad. In fact, it made her heart clench with a sharp stab of longing.

"You can't seriously be thinking about it?" John's frustration had a calming effect on her. "Are you on birth control?"

"No, it makes me gain weight. I'm sure it's the wrong time of the month to get pregnant." She looked over her shoulder at him, relieved to see that he looked as desperate as she felt. The veins in his muscles throbbed with his fight to stay in control. He wanted her just as much as she wanted him. "John, please, I need you so bad."

"Baby, you haven't even asked if I'm clean."

Her heart warmed—even in this, he was the protector. "Are you?"

"Yeah, I have regular check-ups." His eyes tore from hers and went straight to the temptation in front of him.

"Please, John, please don't make me wait. Don't put this off. I need you now. I'm going to lose my mind if I don't have you inside me." Every single word was true, and she hoped he heard it, because in that moment, there was nothing on the planet except this man and feeling him inside her.

He let out a long stream of inventive curses before he grasped her hips and plunged deep inside her. Belinda sucked in air. Her body bowed. So big. So deep. He filled up the empty space inside her. A delicious invasion. A taking. An owning. She was one with him. Complete for the first time in her life, rather than empty and longing. She was always longing for something to fill her, to take away the cold, dark place inside of her. And now she'd found it. It was a blessed relief. A wonderful, intoxicating relief.

"You ready for me, baby?"

It took a second for her to realise he wasn't moving. He was giving her time to become accustomed to him.

"Please." It was a gasp of need.

He didn't ask her again. Instead, he slid slowly out of her, letting her feel every inch of his long, hard length, and then he slammed back in. He kept up the same slow, brutal pace until her mind filled with a dizzying fog of desperation. Each plunging stroke drove her higher and higher, sending her spiralling off into the universe.

"Baby." He sounded strangled. "I'm not going to last. You gonna come for me?"

She couldn't answer; her mind was on the stars floating around her. It was on the great black void of peace she hovered in, as he tortured her with his touch, bringing her to the edge of ecstasy and keeping her there. She was on a precipice. Lost in sensation. Her body reacted on instinct, writhing against him. There was no coherent thought in her head, and she didn't want there to be. Each slow slide of his shaft against her sensitive sheath sent bubbles and sparks throughout her body. She was lost to them. Lost to him.

"You're going to kill me," he groaned, and she heard his voice as though it were coming from far away.

He leaned over her, pressing his front to her back as his arm snaked around her. Fingers found her swollen clit and teased. She clamped down on him. His fingers pinched. And she exploded. The stars inside her head turned into a show of fireworks and dazzling lights. She heard a grunt and felt John tense behind her, his hands tightened on her hips and then he exploded along with her.

It was perfection. In that moment, there was nothing but

Belinda and John, flying together. Joined in a way that made her believe she would never have to be alone again. It was sublime.

"Hey, Hollywood," John said in a soft, deep voice. "You with me yet?"

Belinda blinked several times as she looked up at his smiling face. Her body was limp. Sated. Wrung out. It took her a minute to realise she wasn't standing, bent over the fallen tree—instead, she was cradled in John's arms, her knees draped over his arm, her arms around his neck. He held her close to his chest.

"How?"

"You were out of it for a bit there." If he was making an effort to hide the smugness in his voice, it didn't show. "You're back with me now, right?"

She cleared her throat, wanting to put her cheek back on his chest and close her eyes. But she couldn't. The noise of the jungle intruded, along with the reality of their situation. This was no lazy weekend retreat with a lover—this was a dangerous hike to safety.

"I'm okay. You can put me down. I can stand." How he stood there, cradling her without showing any signs of strain, she didn't know.

His dark eyes sparkled. "I think I'll keep hold of you for a while longer."

"You don't think I can stand?" She was a little offended.

"Baby, you've been out of it for twenty minutes."

"Oh." She looked around as though searching for confirmation. "That's never happened before."

"Way to stroke a guy's ego," he said with a smile.

"Maybe it's hunger?"

"And there she goes, deflating it all over again." He started walking towards the water, holding her gently but firmly in his arms. "Let's get cleaned up and then we'll see about catching some fish."

Now that perked her right up. "We need the mosquito net. I think we could use it as a net to catch some. Failing that, I thought one of us could bleed a little and see if we can attract some piranha."

John stopped dead and glared at her. "That'd better have been a joke."

Belinda thought it was best not to reply at all. With a grunt, he strode into the lake, taking her along with him.

Ryan didn't have long before he needed to be back in the ballroom, coordinating the search party with Elle. But ten minutes was all he needed to see if, by some miracle, Esperanza had set up home in his room and was still waiting for him. Yeah, he didn't think it was a possibility, but he hoped she'd at least left her phone number behind.

"Hey, wait up," he called to Dimitri and Megan, who shared the cabana next to his. "I need a ride to my room."

Megan shifted onto Dimitri's lap to make space beside them in the back of the golf cart. It would probably have been faster to run the path to his cabana, but he didn't have the energy. Truth be told, he probably should have stayed an extra night in the hospital. But there was no way he could lie there while his team were looking for Belinda and Beast—and while Esperanza was possibly waiting for him.

Dimitri told the driver to go fast, and they shot off along the perfectly groomed path, complete with eco-friendly woodchip surface and solar lights along the edges.

"You should be in hospital," Megan said. "Your skin is grey and you look like a breeze could blow you over."

"Thanks," Ryan said, before saying to a grinning Dimitri, "You got everything you need for the search?"

"Yeah, you and Harvard did a good job of pulling equipment out of thin air. We're covered."

"Kevlar?" Ryan had called in a favour to get some vests for the team, but he wasn't sure if they'd arrived.

"Yeah. Not too thrilled to wear a bulletproof vest in this heat, though."

"Better than dying a painful death with a bullet in your back," Megan told him.

"My wife," Dimitri said drolly, "always bringing the sunshine."

The golf cart screeched to a halt outside their cabins, and Dimitri asked the driver to wait. "Ten minutes?" he said to Ryan.

"More than enough time." Ryan jogged up the two steps to the porch around his tiny cabin.

A surge of hope went through him when he spotted the *Do Not Disturb* sign hanging from the handle. Maybe she had waited. Maybe. He used his key card to unlock his door and swung it wide—only to be greeted by darkness and silence. He knew before he even stepped inside that the room was empty and she was gone. Of course, she was gone. What woman hung around for days, in the room of a guy she barely knew, waiting for him to come back?

Ryan flicked the light on and strode inside, scanning every surface, looking for a note. His heartbeat sped up when he spotted one on the nightstand. It was written on resort stationery, and he fell on it like a hungry lion with prey.

Dear Ryan,

I am so sorry. I want you to know that I would never have done this if I wasn't desperate. I will pay you back one day. I promise. Thank you for a wonderful time. It meant the world to me. Love, Essie.

Ryan read the note several times as his blood chilled. His head shot up to see the closet door ajar. He covered the distance in a few short steps and looked inside. The safe was open. And empty. His fist clenched on the note, crumpling it tight. She'd robbed him. Cleaned him out.

His passport, cash, backup phone, gun, ammunition, iPad —all gone.

His head started to swim as black dots appeared in front of his eyes, and he realised he'd stopped breathing. With great effort, he sank onto the edge of his bed and focused on breathing in and out, on calming the hell down, when all he wanted to do was put a fist through the wall.

She'd left him. Stolen from him.

He wasn't even sure which part made him angriest. This was seriously screwed up. The woman had cleaned him out and he was more upset over her running. He shook his head and went to check the rest of his room. His duffel bag was gone, along with a couple of pairs of jeans and some shirts. A quick look in his bathroom told him she'd helped herself to his toiletries and a couple of hotel towels.

There was a knock at the door, and Dimitri poked his head in. "You ready?"

"Nowhere near." Ryan had to fight the shame of revealing he'd been conned. "Remember the girl I brought back from the reception?"

Dimitri nodded. "Cute. Lots of hair. She was a waitress, right?"

"Yeah, well, she's also a thief." Ryan ran a hand over the top of his head. Damn, Lake and Callum were going to hand him his backside over this. "She cleaned me out."

Dimitri's eyes turned hard. "What do you mean?"

Ryan gestured around the room. "Look around. She even took my passport and backup gun."

Dimitri checked the room. When he'd finished scanning the bathroom, he turned to Ryan. "This doesn't add up."

"Which part? The part where she ripped me off, or the part where she screwed me first?"

"The part where she only took supplies for travel. Look." Dimitri pointed into the bathroom. "One of each of the towels is gone. The travel-sized shampoos and soaps are gone." He walked over to the closet. "Her clothes are here, in a pile with your laundry. But there are empty hangers, saying she took some of your clothes, but not all. If she was going to sell them, why not take all of them? You've got sneakers in here worth hundreds of bucks."

Ryan stilled as Dimitri's words pushed through his anger and humiliation. He looked around the room again. It was neat. She'd even made the bed and unpacked his bag onto hangers. This wasn't a hurried ransacking. She'd cared enough to tidy after herself.

"She left a note." Ryan handed it to Dimitri.

He read it and his lips thinned. "Your girl's in trouble." He passed the note back to Ryan. "Running, by the looks of things."

"She isn't my girl."

"Whatever. She's definitely the woman with your passport. That's going to be a shit-ton of stress to replace." Dimitri looked around the room, no doubt seeing what Ryan saw—evidence of a conscientious thief. "You reporting this, or hunting her down?"

"Oh, I'm hunting her ass down." And when Ryan got hold of it, he was going to spank it so freaking hard, she wouldn't be able to sit for a week.

What the hell? He meant he was going to lock her ass up in jail.

Yeah, that was what he meant.

"I'll help once we get back."

"Thanks." Ryan looked back at the note.

I will pay you back one day.

No kidding she would. If it was the last thing he did. Esperanza, *Essie*, would definitely pay him back.

MUCH TO BEAST'S SURPRISE, Belinda's idea of using the mosquito net to catch fish actually worked. While he dealt with their catch—which meant removing the heads, because Belinda insisted she couldn't cook or eat anything that was looking at her—Belinda built a fire. It was small, but big enough for their needs. She stabbed several Y-shaped sticks into the ground on two sides of the fire, then rested more sticks in the Y shape to make a grill. She then wrapped some small twigs in a wipe from her bag of many tricks and set fire to it with the matches he'd taken from their guard.

"The antibacterial wipe is mainly alcohol," she explained. "Makes a good fire starter."

He watched in amused bewilderment as she got the fire going. Her brain was a bottomless pit filled with random bits of information.

"You get that from the Bear guy?"

Her cheeks turned a rosy shade of pink that made him want to strip the sheet she was wrapped in from her body and make her scream all over again.

"No, I learned that by accident when I put some wipes too close to a candle and set my trailer on fire. It was on the set of a movie I did in Morocco. The fire put us behind schedule and made everyone mad at me." Big blue eyes blinked up at him. "I'm not allowed candles in my trailers now. It's written into my contracts."

Beast smothered a laugh. She looked so downhearted at the prospect of a life on set without candles.

"It's ready." She pointed at the fire. "Make me dinner."

With a shake of his head, he placed the five fish on the stick grill.

"I wonder what they are? I don't recognise any of them. My fish normally comes grilled and covered in sauce. Do you know what they are?"

"I'm not exactly a wildlife guy, Hollywood. They're fish. That's as far as I get with this."

"The most important part is that they're less likely to poison us than the unidentifiable fruit the monkeys keep throwing at you."

As though prodded by her comment, their monkey stalkers lobbed another piece of fruit at them. This one hit his shoulder. Beast looked up into the canopy. He couldn't see them, but he could swear the noise they were making was laughter.

"Bet monkey tastes nice too," he said.

"Don't feel bad. I'm pretty sure they aren't targeting you. You're just bigger and easier to hit."

"Thanks, I'm relieved." He watched the flames grow taller under the fish. He could smell it now, and his mouth watered. "You think the grill should be higher?" The flames were licking up and around the fish, and he worried they'd burn.

"I don't know." Belinda's brow puckered as she studied the fire. "It looks fine to me. The main thing is that they're cooking." She slicked back her still-damp hair, and Beast's cock began to stir within the tight confines of his underpants. Part of him wanted to say to hell with cooking and spend more time with her instead. The sensible part of him knew they had to eat.

He picked up a stick and poked at the fire because, well, that was what men did, right? It seemed important that he poke at the fire. As though he was doing something other than hanging out in his underwear in the middle of the jungle with a Hollywood actress he'd just made scream with passion.

As they watched, oil from the fish dripped down into the flames and fed the fire, making it spark and leap. The smell was wonderful. Belinda must have thought so too because her stomach rumbled loudly.

"Sorry," she said, her cheeks flushing again.

Another piece of fruit flew out of the trees and headed for Beast. This time he saw it coming and stepped to the side. Those monkeys' days were numbered.

"No!" Belinda screeched and lunged past him.

It was too late. The fruit hit the grill. The sticks, which were partly burned through, snapped. And the fish fell into the flames.

"Get it." She lunged for the fire, but Beast pulled her back.

"It's too late." He held her out of reach of the flames and they watched their only meal in two days go up in smoke.

"I'm beginning to really hate those monkeys," Belinda said.

"We can catch more fish." Although it was getting dark, and the chances of catching dinner before the light disappeared were slim.

Another piece of fruit landed on the ground beside them, and there was a loud rumble from above. As though a switch had been flicked, the rain started. It didn't come on gently, a few drops here and there hitting leaves around them. No, this rain fell in a torrent, as though someone had tipped a bucket over their heads. They were instantly drenched. The ground around them became a series of mud puddles, and the noise was deafening. It was no pitter-patter. This was the roar of a waterfall crashing down on the forest. Branches bowed under the weight. Plants flattened close to the earth and streams of water poured off leaves like faucets had been turned on everywhere.

"We need shelter," Belinda shouted over the noise. "We should have made shelter first. Instead of trying for dinner."

The water had doused the fire instantly, but the fish was unsalvageable. It lay in charcoal-black pieces amongst the hissing embers.

"The tree." Beast pointed to the V shape formed by the massive buttress roots of the kapok tree. "Get in there. We can use palms to make a roof. Keep some of this water off us."

She shook her head, water pouring down her face. The sheet wrapped around her was slick and transparent from the rain. "We can't be on the ground. It isn't safe. Most of the animals and insects are on the ground."

"Hollywood, we don't have a choice. This will have to do for now. Once the rain stops, we'll find something better." He rushed through the ankle-deep mud to a large palm and chopped off some of the leaves.

Belinda had obviously decided not to argue, as she was quickly gathering up their things and heading towards the tree. "The ground's turning to mud," she shouted. "We need to go higher or we'll get flooded out." She pointed up at the wide branches overhead. Two branches met close to the trunk, making what looked like a large platform.

Beast considered the option. They could climb up one of the massive roots and swing onto the branches. The space was wide enough to support them both for the night; although he didn't think sleep would be an option. The leaves spanning out above the branches would serve as shelter. It was better than being in the mud, but it was going to be a long, long night.

"Okay. You climb up first and I'll hand everything up to you."

She didn't hesitate. She hiked up her sheet, tied it in a knot at her hip and began to climb. Beast hovered underneath her, in case she slipped. She didn't, making it to the joined section of branches easily. Holding on tight, she leaned over and reached for their things. Beast tossed the bundle, wrapped in the other half of the sheet, to her, following it with their clothes, shoes and her tiny bag of wonders.

Against all reason, the rain actually got heavier. It was hard to breathe through the sheets of water pouring over him, and the ground was running with streams.

"Come on," Belinda called to him.

He didn't need to be told twice. He swung himself up onto the angled root, grabbed for a liana to help pull himself up and swatted at yet another insect trying to eat him. This one was a big black ant, about an inch long and unafraid. He squished it and hauled himself up the last few feet to the branches.

Then he stopped dead. The spot on his leg where the ant had bitten began to tingle and burn. He looked at Belinda, who was eyeing him with worry, clearly aware something was wrong.

"What? What is it?" she said.

The rain wasn't as heavy here, in the shelter of the tree, but it still ran over her face as though she was standing under a shower. Beast felt a surge of pain rush up his leg and looked down at the spot where the ant had bitten him. His calf muscle had large red splotches on it now, and when he touched the area, it was solid. Even a brush against the red skin was agony.

"I was bitten by an ant," he said as he broke out in a sweat.

She paled. "What did it look like?"

"Long, black, about this size." As he held up his fingers, he became lightheaded. A sudden rush of white-hot pain blasted through his body, making him double over in agony.

"Oh, this isn't good, this really isn't good."

He vaguely registered Belinda's voice as he struggled through the pain. It was like nothing he'd ever experienced. Blinding, all-consuming agony. His muscles spasmed and tingled. He felt nauseated and lightheaded. When the wave passed, he was left panting and clinging to the tree.

"John?" Belinda said gently. "Honey, I think you've been bitten by a bullet ant."

He worked to focus on her face as another wave of pain overwhelmed him. He rode it out as he gasped for air. When it passed, Belinda was holding him tight to keep him on the branch.

"I have to tie you to the tree. Otherwise you'll fall. Can you sit back against the trunk? You have to help me. We need to get you settled fast." Her face softened. "I'm so sorry, John. This is going to be bad."

Beast wasn't sure he could move at all, but he clenched his jaw and inched into position, just as the pain overwhelmed him again. He had to close his eyes as the world tilted. He thought maybe the trees were leaning towards him, and it was hot, so damn hot. His skin was on fire. When he'd ridden through the pain, he found Belinda had tied several nearby lianas around his waist to hold him against the tree.

"What?" he managed to get out. He wanted to know what the ant was. He wanted to know if the bite was deadly. He wanted to know who would watch over her if he was gone.

Another wave of pain hit him, and he couldn't say anything else. All he could do was moan through it and make it to the other side. When he opened his eyes, Belinda was right there.

She brushed his hair back from his forehead. "This won't kill you, honey. I know it feels like it, but I promise you it won't. I think you were bitten by a bullet ant. It has the most painful insect bite on the planet." She bit her lip as he felt another wave begin to build. "It can take up to twenty-four hours for the poison to work its way out of your system."

Beast let out a howl of curse words as his body spasmed again. He was shaking hard now, and the constant throbbing in his leg made him feel like it was going to explode.

"There's nothing we can do but get through it. Oh, John, I'm so sorry." She pressed his forehead to her breast and held him tight as spikes of pain pulled him under.

He didn't care what she told him. He knew he was going to die. The venom was going to rip him apart. He couldn't open his eyes anymore, as when he did, he hallucinated. The jungle was moving, closing in on him, pressing against him until it squeezed him flat and he couldn't breathe. He was grateful for the bindings, because staying upright on his own was not an option. With another grunt, he doubled over as far as the ropes would allow, as, one after another, the muscles throughout his body began to cramp.

When it passed, his head fell back against the tree and his eyes remained shut. All awareness of his surroundings was gone. All that remained was endurance, getting through each wave of pain as it built and crashed within him. There was nothing else. Nothing at all.

CHAPTER 19

Belinda was crying. Her tears merged with the rain and disappeared into the forest below. She'd managed to strap John to the tree, even though he weighed at least a hundred pounds more than she did and all of it was tense, pained muscle. It was agony watching him suffer, knowing there was nothing she could do about it.

The pain of the venom had stripped away his reason and his defences. She knew he would have hated her seeing him like this, helpless and weak. Each time a wave of venom worked its way through his body, he convulsed, grunting and moaning in agony. She knew he didn't see her any longer. He probably wasn't even aware he was still in the rainforest. Every now and then, he muttered something, but most of it was incoherent.

Belinda wiped at her face, but it was pointless. The water flowed over her in one continuous deluge. The light was fading fast, and the greens of the forest were losing their colour, turning to the shades of grey that made up twilight. Belinda fished into their makeshift pack and came out with the empty water bottles and condoms. She used the travel-sized dental floss from her handbag to tie a large leaf down at an angle, to funnel water pouring off the tree into the bottles. They filled up fast, and she was able to fill all of the condoms while there was still some light.

"Lying bitch," John muttered. "Lying, lying liar liar liar…"

Belinda scooted along the branch and pressed the water bottle against his lips, grateful that there was still enough light to guide her to his side. The last thing they needed was for her to fall out of the tree.

"Sip," she said. Even with the water soaking them, she could feel John's skin burn and knew he had to be sweating from the pain racking his body.

She'd expected to have to force him to drink, but he gulped at the water, emptying the bottle in no time.

"Beautiful," he whispered when he opened his eyes and stared straight at her.

Belinda gave a little hiccupping sob as she stroked his hair from his face. "You're a dangerous man, John Garcia. A woman could fall in love with you."

His face contorted and he surged forward, straining against the bonds that held him tight to the tree. Belinda wept as she checked the makeshift ropes to satisfy herself that they were not only secure, but that they weren't harming him in any way.

His head lolled back as the pain passed. "It's all an act. Two-faced hypocrite, liar, liar, liar…"

Belinda's heart ached at his rambling words. She hoped he didn't mean her; that it was just the pain talking.

"Never gonna know," he muttered. "Never gonna know. Nothing. I'm nothing."

"Shh." Belinda caressed his cheek, and his eyes opened. He was looking straight through her.

"They don't see," he said in a voice so earnest that it almost broke her.

"Don't see what?" she whispered.

"Me. They never see me. They only see the liar."

A low, agonised groan followed as his eyes snapped shut. Every muscle in his body was clenched tight, and his skin was so hot that Belinda could feel heat coming off it even without touching him. When the pain receded, he was panting and Belinda had refilled the water bottle. She pressed it to his lips again, and he drank the lot.

"Don't let her hurt me," he whispered when he was done. "See me. Somebody needs to see me."

"I see you, John," she whispered.

His face filled with fury. "Don't call me John!"

His body bowed in agony as another wave of pain hit him.

"Beast—it's okay, Beast. This will pass. I promise. This will pass. You're so strong. The strongest man I know. If anyone can handle this pain, it's you. Please be okay. Please, please be okay."

He was lost to her, groaning as he slumped against the tree between bouts of agony. All Belinda could do was keep the water bottle full and make sure they were both as safe as was possible. She kept the gun beside her, grateful that the way the tree limbs joined meant the area was wide enough for her to sit tailor-fashion, facing John. It was almost fully dark now, and Belinda could only make out John as a shadow in front of her. She tied another liana around her waist, securing her to the tree, hoping it would keep her from falling, in the unlikely event she actually fell asleep. Sometimes exhaustion could overwhelm a person.

"I'm getting out of here," John said.

Belinda couldn't see him now. Absolute blackness had swallowed them whole. "Yes, we are."

"Gonna live on the street, where nobody can hurt me."

She sucked in a breath but didn't say anything. She wasn't sure he would hear her anyway.

"They don't believe she hurts me." He sounded so faint, as though it was a whisper from his mind. "She's perfect. They only see perfect. But it's all an act. I know what she's like when the social worker leaves. Can't stay here. Can't take it anymore. Gonna live on the street and learn to fight. Nobody's gonna hurt me. I've done it before. I can find enough to eat."

He grunted and let out a low whine of pain. "Liar," he shouted into the night. "Liar, liar."

Belinda was grateful for the never-ending beat of the rain, because it swallowed John's words and kept them hidden from the people who hunted them.

"It's all an act," he mumbled before letting out an agonised howl.

All Belinda could do was cry for the boy he'd once been, as she prayed that the man he'd become would make it through the night.

CHAPTER 20

It was late in the evening by the time the helicopter had flown the entire search party back to the resort—empty-handed. Each of the teams went their separate ways, to clean up before meeting in the ballroom, to refuel and debrief. Ryan was well aware of the sombre yet determined mood of his team, and he wasn't looking forward to adding to their problems with his latest humiliation.

"Aren't you eating?" Elle said as she smacked a palm to his forehead. "Are you ill? I don't feel a fever."

Ryan brushed her hand away. "Not hungry."

Her jaw fell and she gaped at him. "When are you ever not hungry? You're always eating. Always." Her eyes narrowed. "What have you done?"

There was no point in denying it. "You'll find out same time as everyone else."

"Oh, Ryan," Elle said.

She patted his shoulder before pulling her seat closer to him at their makeshift meeting table. He knew, even as she tucked into her meal, that she was planning on jumping to his defence—no matter how dumb his screw-up had been.

That knowledge made his stomach clench even tighter. He had good friends. A good team at his back. And he'd screwed it up. Again.

Slowly, one by one, the seats around the table filled. Each member of the team stopped at the warm buffet set up in the corner and came to the table ready to eat. Every single one of them frowned in Ryan's direction, clearly perplexed by the empty spot in front of him.

"Okay," Lake said as he sat at the head of the table. "Dimitri, Harvard, tell everybody what you found."

Dimitri reached into his pocket and pulled out a torn piece of material which he lobbed onto the table. "We found that in a small clearing, stuck in the knot of a liana. The knot was tied tight around it. It looked like someone had used an old sheet to rig up a hammock."

"It could have been anyone, at any time," Megan said.

Dimitri shook his head. "We scoured the area. Two sets of footprints. One set made by men's dress shoes, and nobody wears dress shoes into the jungle. The other set were sneakers, but the person wearing them was at least half the weight of the dress shoe wearer. The prints from the sneakers were uneven, as though they didn't quite fit the person wearing them."

"Also," Harvard said as he pushed his plate away and clasped his hands on the table in front of him, "the tracks were fresh. Not long after we found them, the rain started and they were wiped out. It was definitely Belinda and Beast. They made camp there for the night but were long gone by the time we found it."

"We do know which direction they were heading," Dimitri said with a grimace. "It's just like Ryan said—they're heading straight for the mining operation."

Elle stilled with her fork halfway to her mouth. "Oh, that isn't good. I was going to show you this after we debriefed, but I think you should see it now." She opened the laptop that was sitting on the table beside her and tapped the keyboard, and an image appeared on the conference wall. "Those are the latest satellite images. There's been a lot of activity at the mining site. It looks like they're amassing people."

Lake ran a hand down his face—the first sign of agitation Ryan had ever seen the man make. "Rodrigo, what's your take on this?"

De la Cruz studied the images on the wall. "Helluva coincidence?" He looked back at the team. "I would say the cartel either know Beast and Belinda are heading straight for them, or they're gathering a hunting party."

Lake turned to Dimitri. "You only found two sets of prints at the camp, right?"

Dimitri nodded. "Yeah, but that doesn't mean the cartel didn't stumble on more evidence Beast and Belinda left behind somewhere else."

"I don't get it," Megan said. "Why chase their escapees? Why not cut their losses and get out of there?"

Violet answered, "Reputation. It's a powerful thing. The Martinez gang are building theirs, and they can't let anyone think they're weak. Losing their kidnap victims would undermine their reputation. They need to get Belinda and Beast back, and they need to make an example of them."

Megan's eyes went wide, and she turned to her husband. "That doesn't sound good. It means Beast and Belinda are going to suffer, right?"

"No, it doesn't." Dimitri didn't sound in the least doubtful. "Because we'll find them first."

"You are totally getting lucky after this meeting," Megan said with a beaming smile.

There were groans around the table. Dimitri only had to breathe to get lucky—this announcement was nothing new.

The doors to the ballroom slammed open and Belinda's parents rushed in, followed by Lake's wife Kirsty. The former lingerie model signalled frantically that she'd tried to stop them. Lake gave her one of his rare smiles before turning to the Hollywood power couple.

"Mr and Mrs Collins, how can I help you?"

"You can help us by stepping aside and bringing in the Peruvian police." Belinda's father's face was ruddy and his fists were clenched. "We need the authorities. We need the people who know what they're doing. The Peruvian police, the FBI. We need to contact the US and UK embassies." He took a step towards Lake, having to angle his head to look up at the ex-SAS specialist. "You've had long enough. This isn't working. We need the full weight of our governments behind this. We need the experts on the ground." He looked around at all of them, clearly furious and desperate, a disturbing combination that made everyone squirm in their seats. "This isn't a game. It isn't like the other jobs you do. This is serious. This is my daughter." His voice broke and his weeping wife rushed to put her arms around him.

Kirsty looked like she was going to start crying right along with Libby Collins, and she inched to Lake's side, looking for comfort. He stroked his hand down her back and gave her a look that held a wealth of private communication. Ryan's chest clenched as he watched them, and his thoughts went to Esperanza. As soon as they did, he felt sick all over again.

"Mr Collins, Mrs Collins," Lake said with compassion, "we're the people governments call in to deal with situations like this."

"You can't be the only people in the world who know what to do when someone's kidnapped," Stephen Collins barked. "I will not let my daughter's life rest in the hands of a company who is more concerned about its reputation than about getting the job done. This is about you thinking you're the best. You wanting to prove you're the best. I won't play those games. I want my daughter back. I don't care who's best to achieve that. I want everyone who's available here to help. And I want it now. Do you hear me? No more messing around. None."

Lake opened his mouth to answer, but Rachel put a hand on his arm and stepped in front of him, facing the Collinses.

"You know who I am. We've known each other for years," she said in that cool, clipped voice of hers.

"Yes. Tell me why I should trust a businesswoman and 'trust fund baby' with my daughter's rescue?" The words were vicious, but Rachel didn't even flinch.

She folded her arms over her suit jacket. "You shouldn't. You shouldn't even trust me to know who the best people are to rescue Belinda. I'm biased. I own a quarter of this company and I am not a security expert."

"Exactly!" Stephen Collins looked a little confused that she agreed with him.

"You do believe I'd tell you the truth, though, do we agree on that?" Rachel said.

He nodded slowly, as though he suspected she was leading him into a trap—proving that he did indeed know Rachel.

"Wonderful." Rachel nodded. "Then listen carefully, because I'm going to give you the brutal truth. I've been working as the team's liaison with local law enforcement, and you absolutely cannot trust them. We captured two of the kidnappers when we raided their camp yesterday. The local chief of police insisted on taking them into custody and taking over the rescue—before we could interrogate the men. Since then, there has been no information obtained from those men. In fact, by the time the men arrived at the police station, their lawyers were already waiting for them."

She took a step towards them. "Think about that for a second. The criminals didn't have time to call their representation. Which raises the question—who did? Not only that, but who knew which lawyers to call? Because these weren't any old lawyers, appointed by the court or picked out of the yellow pages—these were the lawyers kept on retainer by the Martinez cartel."

The blood drained from Stephen's face.

"On top of that, while Benson Security were out today scouring the jungle for Belinda and Beast, I sat in the local police chief's office and listened to him explain why the official rescue would take another couple of days to organise."

Noah and Callum moved a couple of chairs behind Belinda's parents who sat down, shaking as they did so.

"It's up to you how you go forward with Belinda's rescue," Rachel said. "You should know that Beast, as silly as his name is, is one of ours, and we will still search for him and bring him home, regardless of what you choose to do about Belinda's rescue. We will do this even though the police have told us not to, and we won't stop until we have the result we want. Now, what do you want to do?"

"I'm in love," Harvard muttered, drawing Ryan's attention. The American was looking at Rachel as though she was the second coming.

"Dude, you need help," Ryan whispered to him. "I'm sure we can get you some medication that will sort you right out."

Elle elbowed Ryan in the side as Harvard ignored him and continued to drool over Rachel.

"What about calling our embassies?" Stephen's bluster had gone, and he simply looked devastated. "Surely we should do that much, at least."

"If we call the embassies," Rachel said, "this will turn into a diplomatic nightmare. The British, American, and Peruvian governments will waste time trying to figure out how to work together. Time that we can't afford to waste."

The couple looked at each other, their eyes red. "Okay," Stephen said. "We do it your way."

"Sir." Dimitri stood and walked over to the couple. "I know what you're going through." He held up a hand when Stephen started to protest. "My sister was kidnapped and held for a year. I quit the Army to find her, and exhausted all of my resources doing it. When I crossed paths with Lake and his team, they should have sent me packing, but instead they offered to help." He folded his arms tight, and Megan stepped up behind him. She wrapped her arms around his waist and laid her forehead between his shoulder blades. Dimitri cleared his throat. "A few weeks later, we found her. We brought her home and now she's building a new life. If it wasn't for this team, she would have been lost to me forever." He looked around. "In this room, you have an Army ranger, a marine, two SAS specialists, a decorated army soldier, a CIA operative, police officers from two countries, one of the best computer hackers in the world, an expert on the Peruvian jungle and the cartels, and whatever the hell Rachel is."

Rachel arched an eyebrow. "You'd better hope you never find out, Dimitri."

Dimitri flashed her a smile before turning back to Belinda's parents. "Do you really think the local police would be better equipped to bring Belinda home?"

Stephen looked older by the minute. "What do you need us to do?"

"I need you to do the hardest job of all," Lake said. "I need you to wait."

Stephen nodded, wrapped an arm tightly around his wife and stood, pulling her up with him. "We'll be in our room."

Everyone silently watched as they left the ballroom.

"I hate seeing them like that," Elle said.

"The best thing we can do for them is our job," Lake said. "And do it well."

Ryan took a deep breath. "On that note, I need to tell you that I've screwed up."

All eyes swung to him.

"Explain," Lake said. He was back to being the predator everyone in the room knew him to be.

There was no hiding the mess Ryan had made. All he could do now was lay it all out for them and take the consequences. "The night Belinda and Beast were taken, I spent the evening in my room with one of the waitresses. I left her there when we went to search the rainforest. While I was gone, she cleaned me out. Took everything in my safe, including my backup weapon and passport."

Callum exploded. "Weren't you listening when I gave you the talk on the importance of never thinking with your dick?"

There was nothing Ryan could say to that, so he stayed silent.

"There's more," Rachel said. "Isn't there, Ryan? I think it's best if we hear it all."

Like he was planning to keep anything back. He wasn't that dumb. At least, he'd thought he wasn't. This situation might be the one that proved him wrong. "I asked around. No one knew who I was talking about. She wasn't hotel staff."

The air in the room became thick.

"You telling me someone got past our security?" Callum's face had gone heart-attack red, which wasn't a good sign.

"Yeah," Ryan said. "She waitressed all night. Collected tips, too. Chatted with the other staff. They all thought she was one of them, but management has no record of her." He ran a hand over his hair. "I think she was here to earn money. I don't think she was targeting us, or working for the Martinez cartel, but I can't know for sure. When I went over what was missing from my room, along with Dimitri, he noticed she took the sort of things someone would want if they were on the run. She left a note." He dug into his jeans pocket and tossed the note onto the table in front of Callum, who swiped it up. "She said she didn't have any choice but to rob me and that she would pay me back."

Callum glared at him. "We don't have time to deal with how much you've screwed up here, son. That will come when we get back to London. It's time you stopped thinking about your stomach and your dick and grew the hell up. You've risked your team and this whole operation. This affects your future with the company. You have to know that."

Ryan hung his head for a second before looking Callum in the eye. His boss wasn't telling him anything he didn't already know.

"Elle," Callum said, "you know what to do."

Elle nodded as she flashed Ryan a sympathetic smile. "I'll dig up everything I can on her. The hotel must have security footage with her in it. I'll get our facial-recognition software working on her. I doubt we'll find anything, but I can tap into local law enforcement to see if her details bring anything up on their databases."

"Don't get caught," Lake said.

"I never get caught," Elle said with an offended sniff.

Lake nodded. "In the meantime, if Dimitri is right and Belinda and Beast are heading straight for the gathering force at the gold mine, then we'll need to head them off before they walk into an ambush."

"Which means back into the jungle at the crack of dawn," Megan said.

Lake smiled at her. "Rodrigo, Callum, and I will go over

the map together and formulate a plan. We meet here at oh five hundred. Get some sleep."

He turned from the team to talk to Callum, and Ryan's shoulders slumped.

"It's going to be okay," Elle said as she squeezed his hand.

"Sure it is," Ryan said. "Let me know if you find anything on Esperanza." Then he turned and walked away, making sure he didn't catch anyone's eye as he did it.

CHAPTER 21

A couple of hours before dawn, the relentless rain stopped, just as abruptly as it started. John had passed out sometime during the night, which Belinda considered a blessed relief for both of them. Watching him suffer and being unable to do anything to ease his pain, meant she'd added a stream of tears to the deluge swamping the forest. Now, in the early morning light, he lay slumped against the tree trunk, breathing evenly.

Belinda wrung the excess water out of John's shirt and used it to wipe his face. He was pale, almost grey, with dark, vivid circles under his eyes. She stroked his forehead with her fingertips, tracing over his cheekbone to his jaw. He had a decent growth of hair now, which did nothing to soften the harsh angles of his face. Even the ravages of a night enduring agony couldn't detract from the strength he exuded.

Belinda pressed a kiss to his forehead. He would hate knowing she'd seen him this helpless. With a grunt, John writhed against his bonds, but he didn't wake. The waves of pain seemed to have lessened, and exhaustion meant he slept through the latest assault on his system. Above them, the troop of monkeys that seemed to have adopted him watched on as he slept. Belinda hoped the little devils wouldn't start throwing fruit at his head again.

The canopy had come alive as the first hints of sun touched the trees, and now it was a raucous maelstrom of noise and activity. Large red and blue macaws swooped overhead, going from tree to tree in search of breakfast. A gecko ran along the branch beside them and scurried up the tree, only to disappear in amongst the multitude of colourful orchids attached to the trunk. Behind her, in the lake, the giant otter family were back. They frolicked and played, calling out to each other as they did so.

If it hadn't been for their desperate circumstances, Belinda could have been in paradise. The plethora of colour and activity was enough to make her drunk on the experience for months to come. Unfortunately, she was fairly certain her most vivid memories of her time in the Amazon would be of fear, hunger and exhaustion. Her empty stomach gnawed at her ability to think. They needed food. They needed strength to carry on and make it to the river—if they were even heading in the right direction to find it.

She studied the lake and wondered if it was safe to try fishing again, with the otters in the water. A meal would go a long way towards helping John recover. She scanned the shoreline, looking for the best place to set up her makeshift net, and that was when she noticed that the forest floor was more colourful than usual. The weight of the torrential rain had brought plants, branches, and fruit crashing down to the ground, and the area was littered with the bounty. And it was a bounty, because in the middle of it all, Belinda could have sworn she spotted green bananas.

With a little whoop of excitement, she wrapped the damp sheet tight around her and grabbed the other half of the sheet to use as a bag.

"I'll be right back," she told John, even though he didn't even stir at her words. "I'm bringing breakfast."

With a grin, she carefully climbed down the tree and ran barefoot to the edge of the lake—keeping plenty of distance between her and the otters. She was working on the principle that if she ignored them, they'd do her the same courtesy in return. She picked up the bundle of fruit and burst into relieved laughter. They *were* bananas. She was fairly sure they weren't the kind you could eat raw, but she could cook them first. Surely it would be easier than their attempt at cooking fish? She surveyed the treeline. There were more than enough bananas there to keep them going for the rest of the day at least.

She danced around the area, picking up fruit and storing it in the sling she'd made across her body. If she lived to be one hundred, she would never look at a banana the same again. In fact, she might get one dipped in bronze and keep it on her mantel.

As she bent and reached for another bunch, the jungle went suddenly quiet and an icy chill swept through her. Slowly, Belinda stood, scanning the treeline.

But it was too late.

A hand clasped her throat as a knife pricked her side and she found herself pulled back against a hard body.

"I knew I would find you," a male voice said in heavily accented English. "You could not escape me, my English whore."

Miguel.

The guard who'd promised to rape her.

Panic assaulted Belinda, and she struggled, kicking back at him, scratching at his arm. The hold on her throat tightened until she was clawing for air.

"Keep fighting," he said against her ear. "I like it when they fight."

Belinda stilled, making him bark out a guttural laugh.

"I'm going to enjoy you," he told her. "You have spirit. Breaking it will be my pleasure. Where is your friend? Did he abandon you?"

Belinda's gaze shot to the tree where John was slumped over. If you didn't know he was there, you wouldn't have spotted him. He was in no state to help her. He wasn't even conscious. Miguel would kill him for sure.

"Yes," she said.

"Excellent." His hand tightened further, and dots danced in front of her eyes.

She was losing consciousness. He was killing her. She clawed at his arm, trying to pull it away from her throat, and he yanked her up onto her tiptoes.

"If you don't behave, I will make you bleed." He ran the flat of his tongue up her cheek as Belinda began to feel light-headed. She fought, struggling against him, desperate not to pass out.

"Maybe I will make you bleed anyway," he said. "I like blood. It can make things much more interesting."

The blackness of oblivion closed in on Belinda. Her hands and feet tingled, and she lost the energy to fight. She was dying. He was killing her. *John.* Who would look out for John?

Abruptly, he let go of her throat and her legs gave way. She gasped for breath as his arm circled her waist. He held her in place with a punishing grip on her breast. His fingers dug in tight, and she knew there would be marks. He pressed her back into his body, rubbing his hips against her, letting her feel the threat of his erection. Letting her know what her future held.

Belinda gasped for breath as her vision cleared. Her throat was aching and tender, and she knew there was no way she'd be able to scream—even if John was awake to hear her.

Miguel took a handful of the sheet between her breasts and ripped it from her. It fell to the ground, along with the sling full of fruit. She lurched forward, taking advantage of the second he wasn't holding her to try to escape. A hand twisted in her hair and pulled her back. The knife moved to her breast, the tip against her nipple. She felt a sting and whimpered. Blood ran down her breast and dripped to the forest floor.

"Beautiful. The red against your pale skin is beautiful." He ground his hips against her, yanking her back with her hair until her scalp felt like it was going to rip from her head. "Maybe I will make red lines all over your body and carve my own pattern into the famous skin of Belinda Collins."

"No, please. Please don't cut me." Her voice was a hoarse whisper, forced from a throat that ached with each laboured word.

"See, I knew you would beg. They all beg. Eventually." He pushed her forward with such force that she tripped and landed hard. Her knee hit one of the tree roots, which jutted out all over the ground. A sharp, hot streak of pain made her gag, and she knew she was badly injured.

Running was now impossible.

A sob escaped. She couldn't hold it back.

Miguel chuckled at the sound. He grabbed her hair, yanked her to her feet and threw her over the same fallen tree John had asked her to bend over the day before. Another pained sob escaped. Her knee barely held her weight. Her throat was on fire. Blood trickled from her breast. And still, she fought. She struggled against him, clawing at his arms, kicking back at him with her good leg. She managed to turn until she faced him and scratched at his face, drawing blood.

"Bitch!" With one almighty backhand, he struck her across the cheek and sent her back to the ground.

She hit her head on the log and her world tilted. For a second, she no longer knew where she was or what was happening. And then she felt a hand tangle in her hair and he yanked her back to her feet. Her knee gave out under her, and he held her up with her hair. It felt as though her scalp was being ripped from her skull. Belinda sobbed, barely able to see through the tears filling her eyes.

He pushed his face into hers. It was a contorted mask of evil intent. "Do that again and I will cut your pretty face."

He didn't wait to see if she understood. Instead, he shoved her over the log. The brittle bark bit into her stomach. Flesh scraped off her arms. A harsh hand smacked down in the middle of her shoulders, keeping her in place. He kicked her ankles wide. She pushed at the tree, fighting to get away. It was impossible. Between her injuries and the way she was balanced over the log, she was trapped. She sobbed, the noise tearing through her bruised throat. A hand twisted in her hair, keeping her in place, and the knife sliced deeper into her hip.

"Bitch! Stay still."

"John!" she screamed, but it came out as a whisper.

Miguel leaned over her, pressing his body along her back, his weight and strength making it hard to breathe. The smell of sweat and dirt and stale alcohol made her gag.

His tongue came out and he licked her face, tasting her tears.

"Salty." He laughed.

With blurred vision, she saw him stab the knife into the tree, just out of her reach.

"Please, don't," she begged. "I'll pay the ransom."

"I never wanted the ransom," he said.

He wedged his hand between their bodies. Belinda struggled as she sobbed, but she couldn't move, couldn't shout, couldn't do anything. He overwhelmed her and kept her captive far too easily.

She felt his fly zip lower, and his hand pull out his cock. It pressed against her behind, and she gagged. Her stomach convulsed and she vomited up water and bile, making him laugh. His hand slid over her backside.

"My famous whore," he said.

Belinda whimpered, clawing at the tree, trying to get away from him. Trying to get out from under him. She felt the weight of his body lift as his hold on her hair tightened. And then she felt him grasp his cock and rub it against her rear. Taking his time positioning himself. Enjoying her pleas for mercy. Knowing none would come. He was going to do it. He was going to rape her, and she couldn't stop him.

"No!" she wailed hoarsely. "No!"

It was pointless. No one could hear her bruised voice.

Nothing could save her now.

CHAPTER 22

Beast woke to the sound of monkeys screeching inside his head. Slowly, painfully, he opened his eyes to find they hadn't invaded his brain. They were jumping around on the branch above him.

"Go away," he grumbled.

The little bastards ignored him. John groaned as he tried to sit up, but something tugged at his waist, preventing him from moving. He looked down to find lianas securing him to the wide trunk behind him. Belinda. He cracked a smile but found even the slightest movement hurt his head.

He felt like he'd been hit by a Mack truck. Every single muscle in his body felt bruised and aching. Just untying the lianas was exhausting. He honestly doubted he'd be able to stand, let alone walk through the jungle. Which meant they were stuck where they were for the day. It also meant the chances of their kidnappers finding them would skyrocket.

Above him, the monkeys were going insane, making so much noise it was hard to think. It was early, barely past six, and he suspected Belinda was off taking care of business before she woke him. For some reason, the woman didn't want him to know that she had the same bodily functions as every other person on the planet. He smiled at the thought. Maybe it was an English thing. The English were a nation of prudes, weren't they? Anyway, no matter where she was, he had to track her down. They were still very much in danger, and he didn't like the thought of her wandering around on her own. First, he had to get some water into his body.

He reached for the water bottle she'd thoughtfully left beside him, and froze.

In the distance, in the clearing beside the lake, he saw Belinda.

And she wasn't alone.

Pure terror flooded Beast's system as he watched the guard from the camp strip Belinda and push her down. Beast cursed as adrenalin rushed to his abused muscles. He had to get to her. He had to stop this.

He pushed himself to his feet, one eye on the guy as he backhanded Belinda. She fell to the ground, going down hard on something and wailing with pain. Rage, like nothing he'd ever felt before, exploded within Beast, and then, just as suddenly, it cooled to a stark, deadly intent. The guard was dead. He just didn't know it yet.

Beast tried to take a step, but his shaky legs gave way. He cursed, holding on to the tree. He was stuck, trapped by his own weak body, while Belinda was being attacked. There was no way he could climb down the tree. No way he could run to save her.

The man grabbed her hair and shoved her onto her belly over the log. The same damn log where Beast had made love to her the day before. Somehow, knowing it was the same log made everything worse. He watched her fight. Watched her struggle. Why wasn't she screaming for him?

Fuck. Did she think he couldn't save her?

How the hell was he going to save her?

Something caught his eye at the water's edge, and he could have sworn he was seeing things. A huge black caiman lumbered out of the water. It must have been fourteen feet long. And its eyes were on Belinda and her rapist, drawn to them by the scent of Belinda's blood.

Beast tried to take another step and landed against the tree trunk, unable to do anything but watch, helpless as the guard struck Belinda across the face and she hit her head on the tree. He had to do something. Anything. The guard threw her back over the log and unzipped his pants. Belinda vomited. Beast felt like his heart had been ripped out of his chest and trampled into the dirt.

No. No. No. No. No.

He fought to make his legs work and almost fell out of the tree, watching as Belinda was brutalised, helpless to do anything to stop it.

It was a nightmare.

A fucking endless nightmare.

Beast had to do something. He had to do it now. He tested his legs. They held his weight better this time, but there was no knowing if he'd make it to her in time. The monkeys were going insane above him. Something howled in the distance. He thought he heard Belinda call his name, but it could have been his imagination.

He scanned his surroundings, looking for something, anything, that would help her, and then he saw it. The rifle. He cursed himself. He'd forgotten all about it. His brain wasn't working properly yet. He was too damn weak to think straight.

He threw himself onto his belly on the branch, snatched up the gun and aimed.

He didn't hesitate. Adrenalin gave his muscles enough strength to keep steady, and he took the shot.

It was true.

He watched the blood spurt from the guard's shoulder, saw him jerk back from Belinda. She didn't move, draped over the log like a rag doll. At least she was out of the line of fire. Beast aimed high and took another shot. This time, he hit the guard in the arm; spinning the man and making him stumble. The guard landed flat on his back, blood pouring from him.

Belinda struggled to stand, leaning her weight on the log. Even from this distance, Beast could see she was shaking. There was blood trailing down her side, her breast and from the corner of her mouth. She watched in horror as her would-be rapist tried to get up. To get at her. His feet slid in the mud and he went back down. He shouted something at Belinda, making her shrink into herself. He was going to go after her again. And Beast didn't have a clear shot this time.

"Run, Belinda!" he roared.

She stood frozen, watching her rapist. Beast didn't even think she'd heard him.

The guard got to his knees and reached for her. She was too far away, and he lost his balance. With a furious curse, he slid onto his back in the mud, his arm stretched out at his side.

And the caiman launched at him.

The guard had been so focused on his prey that he hadn't realised a much more powerful predator had him in its sights. The strong jaw of the caiman opened wide, and sharp teeth came down hard on the guard's arm. Even from this distance, Beast heard the sound of bone crunching. An unholy scream rent the air, driving the animals hiding in the canopy to silence. Belinda's hands flew to her mouth as her eyes went startlingly wide.

The guard kicked and screamed and struggled. The caiman was undeterred. He dragged the man straight into the lake. Beast and Belinda stared in horror as the water bubbled up in a cauldron of terror.

And then there was stillness.

Belinda stood immobile, staring at the water. Naked and bleeding. Alone. When she should never be alone.

"Baby," Beast called. "Come over here. Come on." He kept his voice soothing, afraid to scare her further.

She didn't move. He wasn't even sure she'd heard him. Beast pulled himself up to his knees. He had to get to her.

"Belinda," he shouted.

No response. She was frozen in place.

With sheer determination and a clenched jaw, Beast half slid, half climbed down the tree, landing on his knees on the ground. He held on to one of the buttress roots and pulled himself to his feet, grateful that he didn't fall straight back down. On shaky limbs, one agonisingly slow step at a time, he made his way towards her, keeping one eye on the lake in case another prehistoric reptile crawled out to get them.

Beast fell over twice more as his shaky limbs gave way. It took an eternity to get to Belinda. All the while he kept talking to her, letting her know he was coming. Making sure she was, at least on some level, aware of him.

"Look at me, baby," he said. "Don't look at the water. There's nothing you can do about that now. Look at me."

She didn't take her eyes from the calm surface of the lake. Now that he was closer, he could see she was shaking violently. Shock was setting in, making her feel cold even in the humid heat of the jungle.

"It's okay, Belinda. I'm not going to let anyone else hurt you. You're safe now."

He carefully wended his way past root joints and over shrubs as he catalogued her injuries. Her left knee was swollen, and her right hip had a bloody red line where the bastard had sliced into her flesh. Her left eye was swollen and red. There was a bloody nick on the skin near her nipple. The corner of her bottom lip was split and bleeding. There were scrapes on her hands, stomach and forearms. And around her throat there was a ring of fingerprint bruises. Beast wanted to drag the guard back out of the water and kill the son of a bitch all over again. Death by caiman was too good for him. Beast wished he could have sliced him into tiny pieces and drawn his suffering out for as long as Belinda's skin stayed bruised.

"It's gonna be okay. I'm gonna clean you up and we'll get out of here. You did good, baby. You fought him and distracted him. You bought us time. You did real good."

He closed the scant few feet between them and gently placed his hand on her shoulder. She jerked away and spun to look at him, terror on her face.

"It's okay, baby. It's me, Beast."

Her bottom lip trembled. "John?" Her voice was a strained whisper, testifying to the damage done to her throat.

"Yeah." His heart clenched. "It's John. Come here, baby, so I can hold you and convince myself you're still alive."

He expected to have to keep on coaxing her, but with an agonised sob, she threw herself into his arms. He staggered, and they went down to the ground together. Belinda curled into him with her arms up and her hands tucked under her chin. He wrapped her tight and cooed to her as he listened to her weep. Each pained gasp and sob broke something inside of him. Never before in his life had he wanted to take away someone's pain the way he wanted to take Belinda's. If he could turn back time and face the guard himself, he would do it in a heartbeat.

"It's okay, I'm here," he whispered as he stroked her hair.

"It's not like the movies, John," she said, each word a desperate croak. "It's not like the movies. Nothing like the movies. Nothing."

"No, baby, it isn't." He swayed slightly, rocking her; aware that his muscles were weakening now that the initial burst of adrenalin was wearing off. He had to get them back up into the tree, where he could keep her safe until he was stronger.

"Nothing like the movies," she muttered again.

"Belinda, baby, we need to get back up the tree. Can you do that for me?"

She shook so hard that he wasn't even sure she could hear him.

"Belinda, we're safe in the tree. We need to go back there until I'm stronger, then we'll get out of here. I need to clean your wounds, too. Remember, you told me it's important to clean wounds in the rainforest."

Still nothing but painful little sobs and lots of shaking. There was only one card left to play.

"Baby," he said softly, "I really don't feel so good, and I'm worried I'll pass out here beside the lake."

She stilled, then her head lifted and red-rimmed eyes looked up at him. "Are you still in pain?"

"Some," he said. Although the waves were faint now and he barely registered them.

"Okay." She swallowed, then winced, making him fight another burst of rage. "Okay." She looked back at the tree. "We can do this." It sounded like she was trying to convince herself.

John laid it on thick: "I'm gonna need some help. That ant bite knocked me out."

She wiped the tears from her eyes and said, "Lean on me, John. I'll help you."

Just like that, he knew he was falling in love with this woman.

He cupped her cheek and pressed a kiss to her forehead. "I know you will, baby. I know you will."

Getting back up the tree was harder than getting down, but they made it. If it seemed strange that Belinda was still naked and Beast was only wearing underpants, then neither of them noticed. All Beast could see was the evidence of Belinda's ordeal.

He made her sit with her back to the tree while he cleaned her wounds using water from a bottle she'd filled and his damp shirt.

"This cut on your hip is deeper than I thought it was," he told her as he gently cleaned the wound.

He hated that the guard had left a mark on her. Hated that she was in pain. Hated that he hadn't been able to save her before the asshole had laid a hand on her. All those years training to wipe out bastards like the guard and he hadn't even been there when it mattered.

A small hand wrapped around his wrist. "Stop it," she whispered. "You saved me. That's all that matters. You. Saved. Me."

"Baby," he said, "I didn't save you fast enough. He should never have gotten his hands on you."

"You were out of it. You did everything you could."

He couldn't stop himself—he slowly closed the gap between them and gently pressed a kiss to her sore lips. "Never again, Belinda. I can't let anything bad happen to you ever again."

Her smile was shaky as her eyes filled with tears. "Ever is a long time, John. I don't think it will take that long to get out of the jungle."

"I'm thinking you need someone to watch over you when you're out of the jungle, too. You seem to attract trouble." It was a poor attempt to lighten the mood.

She sucked in a breath. "Are you saying I'm the reason that man tried to rape me?"

What? "Hell no." He gently touched her chin, angling her face up. He wanted her to look him in the eye. "No. Do you hear me? No. You didn't ask to be kidnapped. You didn't ask to have some asshole try to rape you. This is on them. Not you. They're evil bastards who think they have a right to do whatever the hell they want. If it wasn't you, it would have been someone else. This is not on you. Don't even think that. Got me?"

"I get you." Tears filled her eyes and spilled out to roll down her cheeks.

Beast gently brushed them away with his thumbs. "I hate that I wasn't there to stop this from happening."

"I do too," she said as more tears fell. "But it isn't your fault any more than it's mine."

He barked out a mirthless laugh. "That's damn hard to swallow, isn't it?"

She gave him a woeful nod.

"Come here," he said gruffly as he sat beside her and pulled her into his lap.

She clung to him as she sobbed, each sound shattering a

little more of his heart. He cooed nonsense to her and stroked her arms, back and hair. He wanted to take away every single mark on her body. He wanted to wipe it clean and make it easier for her to get past what had happened.

He knew the cuts and bruises would eventually fade, but the scars inside would be there forever. They never healed. He knew this from experience. He also knew that you could live around them. You could use the internal scar tissue to make you stronger. You could become better knowing you were a survivor. Not a victim. A survivor. He could teach her that.

"It gets better, baby. Trust me, you'll get past this."

"I can still feel his hands on me," she said through tears. "I feel h-his, h-his *part* pressing against my backside. He was so close when you shot him. A second more and he would have been inside me and I would never have been clean. How do you clean deep inside, John? How is it possible? Why am I the one who feels dirty when he's the one who was vile? It doesn't make sense."

Her words were lost in yet more tears. Beast held her close, as tight as possible. It wasn't enough. All he could do was listen to her cry and clean her wounds. Care for her. But it wasn't enough to wipe the slate clean for her. He wished there was something else he could give her. But there was nothing. Or… Maybe…

He swallowed hard, breaking out into a sweat at the thought. Could he give her that piece of himself to help her feel better? Damn, he was shaking at the thought of sharing his secret. Even though he'd learned the hard way that the past had no power over him, he still broke out in a sweat. He'd chosen to be a survivor. The shame of what had been done to him wasn't his shame. That was on the abuser. Not him.

"You'll get past this," he said. "You'll use it to make you stronger."

"How?" She sounded hopeless, and it stripped the last of his hesitancy.

"Because I got past it," he said hoarsely. "That's how I know."

She stilled in his arms as his words penetrated. Slowly, she looked up at him, and Beast steeled himself. Would he see disgust in her eyes? Pity? He pushed the thoughts out of his mind. They had no place in his head. What she felt was on her. Her pity, or disgust, or judgment didn't affect him. He chose who he was and how he dealt with his past.

"The woman," she said softly, startling him. "She hurt you. The liar. The one who acted in front of other people but hurt you in private. She was your foster mother, right?"

His mouth opened and shut a few times as his mind raced. Had she investigated him? No, she hadn't had time. Plus, he was sure there was nothing on record anywhere about what had happened.

"How do you know?" He hated that he sounded vulnerable. He wasn't vulnerable. He was strong. He'd chosen to be strong when he was a teenager, and it hadn't changed since.

She reached up and stroked his cheek. "You were delirious last night. You said stuff."

Beast swallowed hard. It didn't mean anything. This secret wasn't his shame. It was his mantra. He lived by it.

"Yeah, it was a foster mother. She sexually and physically abused me. The authorities loved her because she acted like the perfect, caring parent to their faces. But when they weren't looking, living with her was hell." He recited his story in a monotone, watching her face for reaction.

"That's why you ran away and lived on the street." The sadness in her eyes made him ache.

"I did talk a lot last night, didn't I? Yeah, that's why I lived on the street."

"You were only a child."

The way she said it melted his heart. She felt for him. She was aching for the child he'd once been. It was an astonishing revelation. No one had ever hurt for him. Never felt *for him*.

"I'm not a kid now, baby. That's why I'm telling you this. You'll get past what that evil asshole did to you. You'll get past being kidnapped. You'll become stronger. You'll thrive. This won't stop you, because you're a survivor."

Her smile was everything. It warmed him like the sun. "Like you. You're a survivor. You're the strongest man I've ever met."

Damn, she was stealing his heart right out of his body. His throat tightened as emotion built to a crescendo inside of him. He had to lighten things before he burst. "Not with insects. With insects, I'm a wimp."

"We never talk about that, remember?" Her eyes sparkled with more than tears.

He kept his eyes on her face as she leaned into him and pressed her lips to his. "Thank you for telling me. It helped."

"Good," he said as he held her close. "That's good."

And then they sat there, letting the sounds of the jungle wrap around them like a soothing blanket.

"We need to move soon," Beast said. "The gunshots would have been heard for miles."

"Five minutes," she said. "Then we'll go. I need five minutes."

His arms tightened. She needed this. Time in his arms. Time wrapped in his protection. And he would give her as much of it as he was able. He suspected he'd always give her his protection. No matter where life outside of the rainforest took them, when Belinda called, he would drop everything and run to her. The knowledge settled something inside of him, and he relaxed against the tree.

He felt Belinda's muscles ease and knew that she'd crashed from the adrenalin that had helped her fight. Exhaustion overwhelmed her bruised body and she slipped into sleep. Beast kissed the top of her hair and held her tight. In his arms. Where he suspected she was born to be.

CHAPTER 24

Ryan and Elle studied the latest satellite photos of the mining area, and what they saw wasn't good.

"There are way more boats at the mine than there was yesterday," Elle said as she looked up at Ryan. "Is he assembling an army?"

"Looks like it," Ryan said.

Something was going on for sure. But what? He was missing something important. He knew it. He had that tingly feeling in his gut that told him something more was going on. For a long time, Ryan had thought that feeling meant he was hungry. Now that he'd lost his appetite, he knew it meant something else.

"Can you zoom in on the mine?" He stood close to the image on the wall. "As close as you can get without losing sharpness."

Elle did as he asked. Ryan studied the close-up, hoping the answer would jump out at him.

"What's worrying you?" Elle came up to stand beside him, laptop in hand.

"Apart from the fact he's amassing an army?"

"Apart from that."

Something caught Ryan's eye. He pointed at the wall. "Zoom in on that, will you?"

As the image became clearer, Ryan froze.

"That's a satellite uplink dish," Elle said, sounding just as worried as Ryan felt. "It's attached to a mobile broadcasting unit."

"Yeah," Ryan said. "The son of a bitch is going to broadcast whatever he does to Belinda and Beast."

"He's using them to build his reputation," Elle said.

"No, he's going to use them to make people fear him." Ryan turned his back on the image. "He's taking a leaf out of the ISIS playbook and he's going to televise their torture."

"He wouldn't…" Elle trailed off, because from what they'd learned of the guy, that was exactly what he would do.

"We need a new plan," Ryan said. "I don't think we'll get to Belinda and Beast before they hit the river. That's a lot of ground to cover, and the rainforest is dense. It's like looking for a needle in a haystack." The last time he'd heard from the team, there hadn't been any sign of the couple. He checked the time: two hours until sunset. The chances of finding them now were slim. Soon, Ryan would have to make the call as to whether the search teams camped in the jungle for the night or he brought them home to regroup for the morning.

A regroup was beginning to look like the most feasible option.

"This is going to turn into a massacre on the river, isn't it?" Elle said as Isobel, Callum's wife, stomped into the room, clearly furious.

"Not if we can stop it," Ryan said, with his eyes on Isobel.

She strode up to them and held out her hand. There was a phone in it. "I took this from the entitled idiot."

As if she'd summoned him, Belinda's brother crashed into the ballroom. "Give me my phone back," he demanded.

Ryan ignored him and took the phone. "Why did you take it?" he asked Isobel.

"Because I overheard him arranging a press conference."

Ryan's stomach fell as he turned to the actor. "You want to explain this to me?"

The kid at least had the sense to realise he was treading on thin ice. His face paled and he took a step back, away from a tightly coiled Ryan.

Daniel held out his hands as though to fend Ryan off. "I was helping."

"Tell me you haven't already called in the press." This whole operation was going to hell in a handbasket.

"Having the world's eyes on Belinda will keep her safe. If the kidnappers get her again, they won't dare hurt her with everyone watching."

Ryan could barely contain his rage. He strode to the image on the screen and pointed at the mobile broadcast unit. "They want the world to watch what they do to your sister. You've played right into their hands. Now nothing will stop them from putting on a show where Belinda is the star."

Daniel lost all colour, bent over and started to gag.

"Get him some water," Ryan snapped at Isobel, who had the good sense to realise he wasn't mad with her. She went to the bar, grabbed one of the water bottles the hotel kept there for them, unscrewed it and thrust it under Daniel's nose.

"Drink," Ryan ordered him. "Then tell me exactly who you called so we can figure out how much damage control we have to do."

"I thought I was helping," Daniel whined.

Ryan didn't say anything at all. It wasn't worth the energy he would expend doing it. Things had just become a whole lot worse for Belinda and Beast. And Ryan feared that there wasn't a whole lot Benson Security could do to stop it.

CHAPTER 25

It had taken a lot longer than they'd planned to break up camp on their tree platform and head out into the jungle. Mainly because Belinda had crashed after her ordeal. She'd woken in John's arms, traumatised, sore and very, very hungry. She didn't mention the bananas to John, because the thought of gathering them again made her want to vomit. Guess John was right and she wasn't at starvation point after all, because nothing would have made her eat them now.

They moved even slower through the rainforest than they'd done before their time at the lake. Not only because John was still recovering from the damage the insect bite had done to his system, but because Belinda's knee could barely hold her weight. John had fashioned a crutch out of a stick he'd painstakingly examined for lurking insects. The stick was long enough to fit under her arm, where it forked out on an angle, making it painless to lean on.

They'd wrapped strips of water-soaked sheet around her knee, in an attempt to keep the swelling down and give it some support. Now the bindings were warm and Belinda was wishing for ice. A nice, long soak in a Jacuzzi wouldn't have gone amiss, either. And the biggest pizza she could get delivered. She dreamed of pizza in her normal life, one of those foods that was mainly carbs and disallowed on her strict diet; but now, in the jungle where she was so hungry she could cry, she would have given anything to have a Chicago pie, loaded with pepperoni. Her mouth watered at the thought.

John had offered to catch fish for her again before they left, but she couldn't bring herself to eat anything from the lake where someone had died—even someone as evil as the man who'd attacked her. All she wanted to do was get as far away from that spot as possible.

"How're you doing?" John said from behind her.

He'd told her he was bringing up the rear to guard them. She suspected it was so he could catch her if she began to topple. Unlike Belinda, who got weaker with every step she took, John's strength returned as the last of the venom worked its way completely out of his system.

"Fine," she said, because what else was she supposed to say?

The shoes she'd stolen rubbed her feet raw. Her side throbbed where the asshole had stabbed her. Her face throbbed and she could hardly see out of her swollen eye. Her throat ached, which made talking painful. And her knee just plain hated her. It was in full rebellion. It didn't want to be part of her body anymore. It was fed up with playing nice. It just wanted to rest.

Like that was going to happen anytime soon.

"Fine my ass," John muttered, which made her smile.

"Yes, your ass is very fine."

"Stop talking." He sounded amused. "Let your throat heal."

"It's hard," she said. "I talk when I'm nervous."

They'd skirted the lake of death, as Belinda now thought

of it, and were heading in the direction dictated to them by John's expensive watch. Belinda was very much aware that they weren't covering ground fast enough, and evening was going to hit them sooner than they would like.

They walked on for about an hour, stopping only to replenish their water supply from an outcrop of bamboo. It was hard going. The heat and humidity were getting to Belinda. She felt like she was walking in a sauna and breathing in thick, sticky jelly. It reminded her of James Cameron's *The Abyss*, where Ed Harris breathed in this oxygenated liquid so he could dive deeper than ever before. She'd hated that movie; she'd actually had problems breathing just watching it.

Mosquitoes hovered around her continuously now, and she didn't have the energy to bat them away. She didn't have the energy to do anything at all, other than force one foot in front of the other and pray they made it out of the rainforest alive.

John suddenly grabbed her arm, jerking her out of her maudlin thoughts. He pressed a finger to her lips to keep her quiet. Belinda's heartbeat shot into overdrive as she heard the noises he'd noticed before her—there were people in the forest. John tugged on her arm and signalled for her to crawl into a narrow space between two fallen tree trunks. The tree trunks came up to Belinda's shoulder and were covered in moss. The space around the trees was overgrown with large palms, giving them plenty of cover.

Belinda bent over to examine the space between the logs. It was teeming with ants, but none of them dangerous. She used part of the sheet they still had left to gently, quietly brush as many of the insects out of the way as possible.

John stilled when he realised what she was doing. Belinda pulled on his shoulder until his ear was close enough to whisper. "Not poisonous."

He seemed relieved. He took the sheet from her, finished clearing the area as much as was possible and then laid the sheet out like a mini picnic blanket for her to sit on. Holding on to his arm, Belinda lowered herself into the gap, checking every nook and cranny for lurking threats. As far as she could see, the small area was free of snakes, poisonous frogs, or insects that could kill them.

The people were closer now. It was hard to miss their approach—they weren't even trying to be quiet. They crashed through the bushes, snapping branches, hacking at trees, crunching everything underfoot.

A male called out in Spanish, and Belinda looked to John for a translation. He pressed his lips to her ear and said, *"You see anything?"*

Belinda's fingers curled into John's arm as a chill went through her. Were they looking for them?

John stayed beside her but angled his body to best protect them. He crouched, ready to spring at the first sign of trouble. The rifle was in his hands and the machete lay on the ground beside him.

"Nothing," another man shouted back, and John translated. *"This is a waste of time. It's getting dark. I say we go home before it's too late."*

"We can't go back empty-handed or the boss will skin us," yet another man said.

"Well, it's pointless carrying on. We'll never find them in this."

"The boss won't believe you," the first man said. *"He thinks he would have found them easily."*

"He thinks he's king of the jungle," the third man said, making them all laugh.

"He's a bastard, that's what he is," a new man said. *"I wouldn't want to be in that actress's shoes when he gets his hands on her."*

"He won't get you," John whispered to her once he'd finished translating. "I promise you, he won't get you."

Belinda closed the distance between them and pressed her forehead to his shoulder. She believed John, she did. She knew he would do everything within his power to keep her safe. He couldn't save her from her memory, though. Memories of the attack at the lake flooded her mind. She could feel the guard's hands crawling over her body. She could hear the lust and violence ooze from him as he whispered to her. She couldn't do that again. She couldn't let any of those men touch her. She couldn't.

John pressed a kiss to her hair. He was tense, vigilant, ready. It was easy to lean on him, to trust him to care for her, and she needed that. She'd reached the end of her own resources.

There was more shouting. John didn't translate, and the only word Belinda recognised was "tequila."

"They're setting up camp for the night," John whispered against her ear. "Stay quiet and they won't even know we're here."

Belinda couldn't help the shiver that passed through her. It looked like they were going to spend the night, in the dark, on the ground, with their enemies right beside them. She wasn't sure she could do it.

"You can do this, baby," John whispered, as though he'd read her mind.

She shook her head. She was weary, bruised and emotional. The beauty of the jungle was gone for her now. All she wanted to do was go home.

"Yes, you can." He was so adamant in his belief that she was almost convinced.

They sat, unmoving and silent, as they listened to the men set about clearing the ground behind the palms that flanked the two fallen trees. They couldn't be more than ten feet away from John and Belinda's hiding place, making it impossible for them to sneak past the men's camp without being caught. Even if they did manage to slip away, it would be dark and they would only get lost, or worse, eaten when they stumbled over something they shouldn't have. No, it looked like they were stuck for the night. Stuck in their tiny shelter, hoping that nothing deadly crawled over them. At least, with the two tree trunks flanking them, there was no chance of a tapir walking over them.

The men built a fire, and smoke wafted out into the jungle as they settled down around it for the night. John slowly, and silently, inched into a sitting position beside her. He put his mouth to her ear.

"We're close enough that the fire will keep the predators away from us too."

He was right. It was a welcome plus in a situation that was perilous. The smell of cooking meat and fish wafted towards them, making Belinda's stomach rumble loudly. She pressed her hands to it and hoped they wouldn't hear.

John wrapped an arm around Belinda's shoulder, and she leaned into him. She closed her eyes and tried not to breathe in the smell of cooking food. So close and yet so far away. It was agony. They sat there, listening to the men, as night fell. The light of the fire close to them meant that they weren't swallowed by darkness. It also scared away the predators. Apart from the odd insect, they were left alone. Every now and then, John would give her a summary of what the men were saying. They'd moved on from boasting and posturing, to talk of women. She didn't care. She pressed her cheek to John's chest and let the sound of his heartbeat drown out everything else. Its steady rhythm soothed her and, against all odds, she fell asleep.

CHAPTER 26

Beast sat still, leaning against the log and holding Belinda while she slept. He knew that exhaustion, trauma and hunger had made her weak, and sleep was a good healer. Food would be better. And that was exactly what he intended to get for her as soon as the men fell asleep.

He listened as they stoked the fire. Their conversations became increasingly offensive the more they drank. By the time they bedded down for the night, not one of them was sober. Beast gave them plenty of time to fall into a deep sleep. Which they did without problem. The men weren't worried about danger. The fire was roaring and they were well armed. Beast knew this because they'd spent quite some time boasting about all the things they'd do to a jaguar if it attacked them that night.

Once he was certain everyone was sound asleep, he slowly, carefully lowered Belinda to the sheet beneath them and then crept out of their hiding spot. After nights spent moving around in complete darkness, it was easy to see clearly by the light of the fire. He took his time sneaking up on his prey, although even if he'd crashed through the brush, he doubted they would have heard him. They were out cold. Drunk, well fed and reassured by the flames.

There were four camp beds around the fire, the kind with canvas stretched over a lightweight metal frame. Each held a sleeping man. For a minute, Beast was tempted to take his knife to each of them. They'd were definitely part of the kidnapping gang and showed no compunction about taking Belinda back to their boss. He would have liked to say his conscience stopped him from killing the men in cold blood, but really it was more of a practical decision—he wasn't sure he'd be able to kill them one at a time without waking the others.

He tiptoed around their camp, noting everything he saw. Two men slept cuddled up to empty bottles of booze. One man was snoring loud enough to wake the dead. And the last had fallen asleep with his hand down the front of his pants. Beast scanned the area, especially around their beds, looking for supplies. There was nothing.

Frustration made his gut clench. There had to be something somewhere. And then he spotted them. Four canvas daypacks hanging in a clump from a nearby tree, wrapped in mosquito netting to keep out the bugs. A tight smile spread over his face as he made his way to the bags.

They weren't large, so Beast cut the netting and took all four. As he turned to go back to Belinda, one of the men groaned and tossed around on his bed. Beast froze, waiting for him to settle. He didn't. Instead, he struggled out of bed and staggered towards the nearest tree to empty his bladder. Beast ducked low, using one of the other men for cover. The guy staggered back to his bed and landed on it, face first. He was sound asleep within seconds. Beast didn't hesitate. He was on his feet and rushing back to Belinda before anyone else could wake up.

She was exactly where he'd left her, curled on her side on

the dirty sheet, her blonde hair fanned out around her and that silly silver dress catching the golden light from the fire, even though she'd had the sense to turn it inside out. He'd had to cut one of the legs off her stolen jeans to bandage her knee, and she'd insisted in smothering the exposed skin in mud before they set off into the forest. She told him it would help keep insects off her.

It was hard to believe he was looking at the same woman who walked red carpets in millions of dollars' worth of diamonds. A woman who wore dresses that cost more than the average person spent on a car. A few days ago, he would have sworn there was nothing more to Belinda Collins than premieres and photo opportunities. Now, he knew better. As he crouched beside her, it occurred to him that she hadn't complained once during their escape. Not once. She'd kept on going, weathering everything that came at her and staying strong no matter what she had to endure. No one would ever guess that the sunny princess of Hollywood had a spine of steel. But she did. And she was smart, too. They wouldn't have made it this far if it hadn't been for her.

Beast's chest felt strangely tight at the thought. Belinda Collins was pure, solid gold. A treasure. And he couldn't help but wonder if she'd even look at him twice once they got out of the jungle. It gave him a shock to think that he would want her to look at him. They were poles apart. Yet he couldn't imagine meeting a more interesting, strong and capable woman than the one asleep at his feet.

He took a breath and banished his wandering thoughts. If they wanted to put some distance between them and the men, they had to get moving—and he knew she wasn't going to like travelling at night.

"Belinda," he whispered, stroking her hair from her face.

Her eyes snapped open and she froze. She blinked twice before she realised who was with her.

"John?"

"Hey, baby, I'll help you sit up." He put his hands under her arms and tugged her into a sitting position.

"What's going on?" She kept her voice barely above a whisper. Beast held up the bags by way of an answer. Her eyes went wide. "Did you kill them?"

He would have reprimanded her for thinking so little of him if he hadn't had exactly that thought. "Not this time. I robbed them."

"Are they still there?" She looked over in the direction of the fire.

"Yeah, they're out cold."

She nodded and looked back at the bags. "Is there anything to eat in there?" The hope in her voice almost broke his heart.

As quietly as he could, he opened the first bag and rummaged inside. It was difficult to see anything but shadows inside, so he pulled out each item to look at it. There was a Bible, which made him arch an eyebrow at Belinda. Guess having faith meant something different down in the jungle. Where he came from, it meant you *didn't* align yourself with someone who was pure evil. Next out was a roll of toilet paper, which Belinda hugged to her as though it were precious. Then came some spare ammo for the rifle. Matches. A flashlight, which made Beast grin. And two nut bars.

He held up the bars as if he'd struck gold. Belinda grinned, snatched one, ripped the paper off and devoured it. Beast wasn't far behind. They were finishing up when one of the men started coughing. Beast and Belinda stilled, staring at each other, their ears straining to hear what was happening. Beast peeked over the tree trunk and saw one of the men roll out of his narrow bed, only to groan and go back to sleep on the ground.

He turned to Belinda. "We need to get out of here."

She immediately started shaking her head. "We'll die. Something will eat us. Or we'll get lost."

Beast held up the flashlight. "I can still see my compass. We don't need to go far. We do have to put some distance between us and those guys. When they wake and find their packs gone, they'll go hunting. We need to be somewhere more secure."

She bit her bottom lip as she thought about it. It was plain to see that logic was warring with fear.

He leaned forward and pressed a gentle kiss to her lips. "It will be okay," he told her. "I won't let anything happen to you. We have to do this, baby. You know that."

She stared into his eyes as though searching for reassurance. She must have found it, because she gave him a terse nod. "Okay. Tell me what to do."

"That's my girl." He couldn't resist kissing her again. "Let's get out from between these trees."

He backed out of their tiny clearing, dumped the bags at his side, then leaned back in to help Belinda get out. She handed him her walking stick first, which he put beside the bags. Then he supported her as she got to her feet.

"We don't need the flashlight yet," Beast said. "The fire gives off enough light to make out where we're going. Just take it slow. Make as little noise as possible and watch where you're stepping."

She nodded.

Beast kept one eye out for the men on the other side of the bushes as Belinda wedged her walking stick under her arm.

"How's the knee?" he said.

"It's stiff. I can do this, though."

It was also painful, if the tight lines around her mouth were any indication. She gave him a determined look that made pride swell within him. This woman was stealing his heart, and up until he met her, Beast wasn't even sure he had a heart to steal.

"You go first," he said. "I'll bring up the rear. Once we're clear of the fire, use the flashlight to lead us out of here." He flashed the light on his watch, long enough to get a direction from his compass. "That way." He pointed.

Now that she'd committed to going, Belinda didn't hesitate. She made her way straight in the direction he'd indicated, taking her time to get over obstacles with her walking stick.

It was slow going. Once they were far enough away from the fire that they couldn't even see shadows anymore, she switched on the flashlight and they carried on. Eyes of every size reflected back at them from the shadows of the forest. Overhead, an owl screeched. The noise was followed by scurrying all around them as small animals ran from the predator. The flashlight made a large spider's web glitter and sparkle. It was nestled in the V of a tree, and sitting in the middle of it was a hairy tarantula. Beast couldn't help but shudder, and was glad Belinda had her back to him. He was fairly sure he'd lose some man points for his developing arachnophobia.

There was a flurry of activity above them, and Beast ducked just in time as a cloud of bats spiralled towards them at dizzying speed. Belinda looked back at him once the bats were gone. She waggled her eyebrows and grinned widely. Even with her bruised and swollen eye, there was no hiding the delight she took in the sight.

Beast shook his head at her, but his lips twitched with the need to smile back. Instead, he urged her forward.

Almost an hour later, he decided they were far enough away from the cartel's men to set up camp for the rest of the night.

"Do you think you can climb a tree?" Beast asked Belinda as she finished off the last of her water.

"I can try."

He was beginning to realise that sentence summed Belinda up. She would try damn hard at anything that came her way.

"Okay, let me scout around and see what I can find."

Without a word, she handed him the flashlight. "Don't go too far." She looked at the stolen bags. "Maybe there's another flashlight in there." Her voice was still hoarse, but she didn't wince every time she spoke anymore. Beast took that as a sign she was healing.

He crouched down and opened the first bag. "Medical kit," he told her. "Two bags of Brazil nuts."

"Gimme!" Belinda waggled her fingers at him, and he put a bag in her hand.

She fell on the nuts like they were the finest cuisine, even though it was clear that swallowing caused her pain.

Beast clenched his teeth at the sight. His anger at her suffering wouldn't help her any.

"You were right," he said as he rummaged in the bag. "Another flashlight." He handed it to her. "A shitload of condoms." He looked up at her. "What the hell did he think he was going to do out here?"

"Jaguars beware," Belinda said through a mouthful of nuts.

Beast smiled as he shook his head. Crazy woman.

He pulled the next bag over. "Bingo." He grinned up at her. "A hammock." He pulled out the string hammock and handed it to her.

"You think it will hold both of us? It looks like one of those shopping bags from the seventies. The kind that stretched out of shape as soon as you put something in it. I've seen the photos. My mum loved those things." She stilled and looked at him. "Do you think she's okay? She's probably out of her mind with worry. Mum doesn't deal well with stress. And Dad, Dad thinks he can order the situation to fix itself. Lake Benson won't like dealing with my bossy father." She bit her bottom lip. "They are looking for us, aren't they?"

Beast stood and put his hands on her shoulders, making her look up at him, wanting her to see exactly how serious he was. "Damn straight they're looking for us. Your family wouldn't allow anything less, and my boys will rip this jungle apart until they get to us."

She relaxed beneath his touch. "You're right. Of course you're right. We just have to make it to the river, and then we'll be easier to find."

What she didn't say was that neither of them knew if they were heading in the right direction to find the river.

Beast crouched back down and raked through the half-empty bag. "You're going to love this. Catch." He tossed his find to her.

"Chocolate," she whispered with genuine awe before looking at him. "I'll save it for when we're in the hammock. It can be our reward."

It was on the tip of his tongue to tell her she could be his reward, but thankfully, he realised how corny that would sound and stopped himself.

The last bag held another bottle of booze, some snack food, a mosquito net that was in much better condition than the first one they'd stolen, and insect repellent. Better late than never, Beast thought as he looked at the can. It was obvious from the things these guys had packed that they hadn't expected to be in the rainforest long. Which made Beast think they were closer to the river, and civilisation, than either of them had thought.

"I'll string up the hammock." Beast took it from her.

"I'll stand here and eat," Belinda said solemnly. He arched

an eyebrow, and she flashed her killer smile. "Don't worry. I'll save you some."

He chuckled as he looked for two decent trees, close together, that would suit his purpose. It wasn't hard to find what he wanted—they were surrounded by trees. He was so busy working on putting the hammock up that he didn't pay enough attention to what was going on around him. It was a dumb mistake.

"Uh, John," Belinda called softly. "Don't move."

A chill ran straight through him, and his first thought was another damn killer insect. Instead, he felt something large brush against his leg. Slowly, he looked down and saw a long, hairy creature lumbering beside him. The animal scraped at the ground, sniffing around with its long, tapering nose, before its tongue darted out to chase the insects scurrying on the rainforest floor. Anteater. Beast slowly studied its body, noting the thick neck, long hair and massive bushy tail. It had to be six feet long, and it was eating the very thing Beast detested—insects. They could have used this guy the night before.

When he looked over at Belinda, she was grinning again. Beast couldn't help but grin back. Nothing kept the woman down, and nothing stopped her from finding joy even in the worst of situations.

The anteater shuffled around Beast, completely uninterested in his presence. Once the creature had cleared the area of as many ants as possible, it disappeared through the bushes.

"It was so cuddly," Belinda said when she came over to him.

"Hollywood," he said, letting out a sigh, "you need a keeper."

He finished tying up the hammock and stung a liana between the trees above it, the way Belinda had taught him, then threw the new mosquito net over the line, making sure it covered the hammock completely. Belinda silently handed him each of the packs, as well as their last water-filled condom.

"Get into bed," Beast said gruffly, when they'd finished securing everything under the mosquito net.

She looked worried for a second before her face flushed. "I think I'll sleep in my clothes tonight."

Beast understood immediately. He cupped her cheek and looked her in the eye. "You do whatever makes you feel safe, Hollywood."

"It isn't you." Her cheeks had to be burning now.

"No, you want to be prepared in case someone else stumbles on us." He got it. He'd spent years sleeping on the street and always felt safer with as many clothes on as possible.

Her eyes welled up. "Yes. That's exactly it."

Beast stroked her cheek and tipped her chin gently up to him, so that she would look him in the eye. "It's okay, baby. I'll sleep in my clothes too."

Her eyes became glassy with tears, and she blinked them back. "Maybe there's some antiseptic cream in the medical kit. We can dress my cuts."

"Good thinking." He pulled the small bag out of the pack.

They took a few minutes to slather the cream over every wound on her body. There was a compression bandage in the kit, and Beast used it to bind her knee. Antihistamine cream was next, and they took turns dabbing the insect bites on each other's bodies.

"We're a matching pair. Both of us a mess," Belinda said with a mixture of amusement and tears.

"Couple of days and this will all be gone."

"Yeah," she whispered.

She was losing hope; he heard it in her voice. The jungle

was taking its toll on her, and the trauma of that morning's attack was far too fresh.

"Done," she said, handing the cream to him. "You get into bed first and I'll climb on top of you." He moved to do exactly that, and she put a hand on his arm to stop him. "Maybe we could get undressed. It would be more comfortable. But keep our underwear on?"

"We can do that if you want, baby. There's no pressure either way."

"Yeah, I want to. Everything rubs at me. It might help me feel better. But…" She looked around. Their surroundings were swallowed in shadow. The flashlight only illuminated the tiny pocket of space they occupied.

"I'll keep the gun close. We'll hear anything that comes at us, long before it gets here. You'll be safe."

She nodded. "Can you help me to get my clothes off? My knee won't hold my weight."

"Anything for you, Hollywood." He was beginning to think he meant every word of that literally.

He slid the dress over her head and hung it over the line above their bed, under the mosquito net. She'd long ago discarded her bra, and the marks on her breast from where she'd been held and cut were stark on her pale skin.

Beast clenched his jaw and pressed his lips together tightly to stop from saying something about the marks. She didn't need to hear it. Not now. He crouched in front of her and gently removed her shoes, taking care not to jar her swollen knee or the hip with the knife wound. He hated seeing the damage that had been done to her and couldn't wait until it had healed and the physical reminders of her attack were gone. Gently, he pressed a kiss to the dressing covering the knife wound.

"I don't feel it," Belinda said softly.

"I still hate him for it."

"Me too," she whispered.

"Ready?" he said as he stood.

She nodded, and Beast quickly kicked off his shoes and took off his shirt and pants. She eyed his underpants.

"You don't have to keep them on because I'm keeping mine on," she said.

"Yeah, baby, I do. I don't trust those monkeys with low-hanging fruit."

She seemed surprised when she laughed, and Beast couldn't help but grin at her.

"Get your ass in bed," he said gruffly. "We've got four hours until daylight, and we need some sleep."

"You first. I don't want to be crushed."

Beast climbed into the hammock, then steadied Belinda as she climbed in beside him. She didn't hesitate in sprawling on top of him and snuggling close. Her legs straddled him, her arms tucked in at his sides, her breasts flattened against his chest, and she nuzzled against the crook of his neck until she found a spot she liked. Once settled, she let out a contented little sigh that melted his heart.

"Can I sleep on top of you?" she said.

He smiled, noting that she'd asked once she was settled. "You can sleep wherever you like, baby."

With his arms wrapped tight around her, he closed his eyes and hoped for a miracle. Because he suspected they'd need one to get out of the rainforest alive.

CHAPTER 27

"This is why civilians shouldn't be allowed anywhere near an operation." Callum's face had gone red, and he looked like his head might explode. "What the hell were you thinking calling the press in?" He took a step towards the actor and Daniel flinched.

Isobel stood right in front of him and patted his chest. "We talked about this. You aren't in the SAS anymore. You have to deal with civilians and you can't kill everybody who annoys you. Now, calm the hell down."

If Ryan hadn't been mad enough to spit, he might have found watching tiny Isobel take on her raging husband amusing. As it was, he didn't see anything funny in their situation. It had been a long day. The team were tired and hungry. They'd barely had time to clean up before they met to debrief, and now they were dealing with yet another setback. Callum was only saying what everyone else was thinking.

"I'm sorry," Daniel said. "I was helping."

That didn't calm Callum down any. His fists clenched and his eyes narrowed. Isobel took one look at his face and launched herself at him. She wrapped her arms around his neck and her legs around his waist and held on like a limpet. Callum had no choice but to hold his wife.

He looked down at her, clearly exasperated, and opened his mouth to tell her so.

"Don't you dare," Isobel said. "You won't punch him with me here, and you know it."

There was a chuckle, and everyone turned to see Elle snapping photos of the pair. "For the company brochure," she said, and laughed while Callum growled.

"Okay," Lake said, and there was instant silence. "You contacted the press. What exactly did you tell them?"

All attention focused on Daniel. He cleared his throat. "I, uh, told them Belinda had been taken and that the baddies had asked for a ransom."

Ryan groaned and pinched the bridge of his nose with his good hand. Now *he* wanted to punch the guy. *Baddies?* Daniel was calling the cartel baddies. Like this was one of his movies and he'd ridden in to save the day. Yeah, the baby actor needed punching.

"Did you tell them who took her?" Lake asked.

Daniel nodded. "The Martinez cartel."

"Where did you arrange for this press conference to happen?" Callum said. "Is this one of those phone-in things?"

As soon as Callum said the words, Ryan knew it was the exact opposite. He shook his head. The guy was dumb as dirt.

"I, uh, told them to meet me here," Daniel said. "They're coming in the morning."

Callum looked down at his wife, who was still wrapped around him. "Can I hit him now?"

She slid down his body and stepped aside. "Have at it. He's a bloody idiot."

"Let's not hit the wealthy and famous actor," Rachel drawled from where she was perched on a stool beside the bar, flicking at her phone screen. She was dressed in a cream trouser suit. The jacket buttoned up and it looked like there was nothing beneath it. Her nails were bright red to match her four-inch pumps, and her face was perfectly made-up. This was Rachel. In the jungle.

"What time did you say you'd talk to them?" Lake said.

"Breakfast?" Daniel didn't sound sure, which was a worry.

"Then we have to get out of here before they turn up, or we'll end up searching the jungle with the press on our tail."

"We have another problem," Dimitri said, and Belinda's brother looked relieved when the attention moved from him. "The Martinez men are out in force, herding the pair towards the mining operation. We stumbled on a couple today. After some persuading, we discovered they had orders to either force the pair to head for the river or take them straight to Martinez. I wouldn't be surprised if they'd already found Beast and Belinda. According to our source, the Martinez brother had every man in their operation out scouring the jungle."

"Did your source survive your *talk*?" Lake asked.

"Absolutely, boss," Dimitri said. "We take internal memos seriously in the London office. Julia printed the one about no unnecessary killing and posted it on the noticeboard."

Lake's lips twitched, but he didn't break out a smile.

"What did you do with the bastards, then?" Callum said, cutting to the chase, as usual.

"We left them where we found them," Dimitri said solemnly. His eyes glittered as they looked over at his search partner, Harvard. "Didn't we?"

Harvard nodded, equally solemn. "When we left, they were secured to a tree and unharmed."

Ryan shook his head. The morons had staked the cartel members out like offerings to the jungle predators.

"I think you might need to write a new memo," Rachel said to Lake. "Maybe add more detail this time."

Dimitri and Harvard grinned at each other.

"If the cartel doesn't already have Beast and Belinda," Ryan said, "there's a good chance the pair will stumble into them anyway. Elle and I figure they have to be just hours away from walking straight into the mine. One way or another, things are coming to a head at that mine tomorrow."

"We need to go back in tonight," Lake said.

"Damn it to hell," Callum said. "We only just got back."

"We don't have a choice. The cartel is closing in on them and the press are going to start arriving at dawn." Lake shook his head at Belinda's brother. "If they wait that long. I wouldn't be surprised if a helicopter or two turn up tonight. We can't be here when they arrive. It will make everything harder."

"I thought I was helping," Daniel whined, and Megan turned to him and hit him hard. Right on the jaw. Daniel hit the floor.

"Don't talk," Megan ordered him before turning back to her team.

"I wanted to hit him," Callum said.

"What was it Violet said? You snooze, you lose?" Megan grinned at their boss.

"We can't go in by air tonight," De la Cruz said. "Can't see to land."

"We'll take the boat," Lake said. He looked over at Ryan. "Think you can drum up another at short notice?"

"No problem." Ryan pulled out his phone and sent a text. He had a boat on standby, just in case. "It'll be ready to go in half an hour."

Lake nodded at him. "We'll go in from both directions and drop teams north and south of the camp. We'll work our way in on foot and get there before the sun rises." He turned to the youngest Collins, who was still on the floor. "You will not speak to the press. Under any circumstances. Are we clear?"

Daniel rushed to assure Lake he was very clear, all the while keeping an eye on Megan.

Ryan felt a tug at his arm and turned to find Elle looking up at him.

"I need you to look at something for me." Her unusually serious attitude set off alarm bells in his head.

"Sure." He followed her over to the end of the large table where she'd set up her workstation.

She hit some keys then turned the laptop towards him. "Is that Esperanza?"

Ryan sucked in a breath as he saw the woman who'd used him and run. The photo showed her in a yellow T-shirt, her smile wide, as she looked straight into the camera. "Yeah."

Elle nodded and brought up a new screen. "Her real name is Esther Redgrave. She's an Australian national who went missing almost a year ago while trekking through the Andes." Elle gave him a look that was equal parts compassion and trepidation.

"Spit it out," Ryan said.

Elle licked her lips before continuing. "She was on the holiday of a lifetime." She glanced at Ryan before turning to the screen. "With her husband."

It was like being punched in the gut. Ryan actually took a step back before he righted himself. She was married? She'd played him. Slept with him. Stole from him. And she was married? He ran a hand over his face, wondering if this could get any worse.

"I'm sorry, Ryan," Elle said softly.

"It's fine. Give me the rest." He knew from the way she was hesitating that there was more bad news to come.

"On the same day she went missing, her husband's body was found at the bottom of a ravine, outside of Cusco."

Ryan locked his knees to stop himself from collapsing. "She killed him?"

"That's what the local authorities think."

His throat was dry, and it took a couple of attempts to swallow. He knew he should say something, but he couldn't formulate any words. She was a murderer? He'd let a murderer get close enough to bed him and clean him out. Hell, he didn't deserve to be part of Benson Security. He was as big a screw-up as Belinda's brother.

He felt a hand on his arm and tore his eyes from the laptop screen to see Elle's sympathetic smile. "If it's any consolation, she didn't have a previous record."

He shook his head. "Yeah, it's a great consolation that her first foray into crime was to kill her husband."

"I think there's more to the story than meets the eye," Elle said.

Ryan didn't care. She'd made a fool of him. Damaged his standing with his team. Put their operation to find Belinda and Beast in danger. So, no, he didn't give a crap about any mystery surrounding her husband. He only cared about one thing.

"Is she involved with the Martinez cartel? Did she have anything to do with this kidnapping?"

"No," Elle said. "I'm certain the timing was pure coincidence."

"Good." Ryan nodded and straightened his shoulders. In that case, he was done with Essie, whoever she the hell she really was. "I need to make sure that second boat is here on time."

Elle held out a hand to stop him. "I think there's more to the story, Ryan. I think she's in trouble."

"Damn right she is." Ryan pushed past Elle. "She killed her husband and stole from me."

"No. I think *she's* in trouble," Elle called after him as he walked away.

Elle could tell Esperanza's—no, *Esther's*—story to someone else. As far as he was concerned, she'd taken enough from him already. He didn't give a damn if she was in trouble. All he cared about was helping his team and getting the kidnapped pair back home safe. He'd learned his lesson. He wouldn't be that careless again. From now on, he was going to be all about being professional. That way, no more women could take advantage of him and make him look like a fool to his teammates.

He stalked over to where Callum and Lake were discussing the operation with the rest of the team. He nodded at them, pulled up a chair and put *Esperanza* out of his mind for good.

They woke at first light. After they were dressed and had condensed what they needed into one pack for John to carry, they shared the chocolate bar for breakfast. Neither of them seemed inclined to talk. It was as though the day loomed over them. Belinda felt the jungle pressing in on her. With each agonising step she took, it became harder to see things to delight in. Instead, it was a world of danger and treachery, ready to pounce and eat her alive. Even the colourful macaws couldn't lift her mood. All she wanted was to go home.

The compression bandage on her knee helped somewhat, although it still hurt to walk, especially over ground that was uneven and littered with obstacles. The wound in her side throbbed with fiery pain, and she suspected it was infected. Not from the jungle, but from the dirty knife that had been used to cut her. She didn't mention it to John—there was nothing he could do about it—and she'd lathered the site in antiseptic cream and hoped for the best. If there had been antibiotics in their stolen medical kit, she would have taken them, but the only medication she'd found was aspirin. She'd taken two, hoping they'd help her walk on her swollen knee.

"We can stop here for a few minutes," John said as he looked back at her. "Get our bearings. Make sure you drink enough."

Thanks to her bamboo trick, they had plenty of water. They needed it. The heat sucked the moisture out of their bodies with an unrelenting greed. Belinda didn't argue; she sat on the nearest tree stump beside her, took the water bottle John handed to her and drank. It didn't matter how much she drank—she still felt as though she were dying of thirst.

John gave her a look that said he was worried about her, and she answered with a smile that made the cut on her lip sting. He crouched in front of her, tucking her tangled hair behind her ear. His face was soft, his eyes tender. She blinked back the tears that sprang to her eyes.

"Don't be nice to me right now," she said. "I think I would crumple."

"Me? Nice? You're thinking of a different man, Hollywood. Tell me who he is so I can introduce him to the Beast." He flashed his tattooed knuckles at her.

She traced a fingertip over the letters. "When did you get this done?"

"When I was fourteen. I won my first underground fight and I wanted to celebrate."

"Fourteen," she said softly. "So young. At fourteen, I was in a high school for the performing arts and worried I wouldn't get the lead in our Christmas production."

"Did you? Get the lead?" His voice was tender.

It was hard to imagine him fighting to survive on the street while she chased boys, discussed lipstick with her friends and dreamed of becoming the next Ingrid Bergman.

"Yes," she said. "It led to a role in a West End play. My first professional job."

"At fourteen?" He sounded impressed.

She nodded. She still remembered the excitement of winning the role. Her mother had spent weeks going over the part with her, helping her master the nuances of the character. Her father had attended rehearsals with her and subtly, for him, given directorial advice to everyone who'd listen. Belinda had wallowed in their support. She'd soaked up their attention and thrived on it. All the while, at the same age, John had been alone on the streets.

"Don't feel bad for me, Hollywood," John said, proving yet again that he could read her mind. "I had good things in my life too. At fourteen, I met Joe, Grunt, Harvard, and Noah. They never once looked at me differently because I was a street kid. Harvard's mother took me under her wing, shouted at me until I went back to school, then hounded me until my grades were acceptable to her. Joe's mom fed me every time I turned up at her house, which was a lot. That woman can cook. Noah's parents let me sleep in his room more times than I can remember. And Grunt, well, even as a kid he was the size of a house. He mainly scared the crap out of anyone who gave me a hard time."

She smiled, lifted his hand to her mouth and took her time kissing each of the letters. They were precious. They were marks testifying to his survival. She gathered her courage and looked him square in the eyes. What she saw there, the emotion in his gaze, made her heart swell. "I don't want this to end when we get out of here," she whispered.

She was laying her heart on a platter at his feet, hoping he didn't trample all over it when he ran from her.

He turned his hand over in her grasp to thread his fingers with hers. "Baby, we live in different worlds."

"Then we make a new one. One that fits us both."

"I don't think it's that easy. People will talk about you. They'll wonder what you're doing with someone like me. They'll think there's an angle I'm playing, and they'll dig into my past. What will happen once all those tabloid reporters find out I'm the son of a hooker? How will you cope with that? Hell, I don't even know how I'd cope. Being with me will damage your reputation, Hollywood. Maybe even your career."

"That's rubbish." Like she would care if it did. People could think what they liked. She projected an image for them anyway. None of them really knew her. Their opinions counted for nothing. "Don't make excuses, John. If you don't want to be with me, say so."

"Now, isn't this sweet?" someone said from beside John.

They jerked apart. John was on his feet. He spun towards the threat and found a gun pressed against his chest. Belinda gasped as the blood drained from her face. They'd been caught. It was over. They were going to die.

The man shouted something over his shoulder in Spanish then smirked at John. And John moved like lightning. His fist struck out, hitting the man in his throat, while John grabbed the gun with his other hand. He twisted it away from the man as he grasped his throat, gasping for breath. He collapsed to the forest floor.

John turned to her, put a hand under her arm and hoisted her to her feet.

"Run," he ordered her. "Lean on me. But run."

They set off, racing into the jungle, letting it swallow them whole. They heard shouts behind them, sharp orders snapped in a language Belinda wished she'd taken the time to learn. John dragged her along, but Belinda knew she was slowing them down. Every few steps she took, her knee gave way. She wouldn't last much longer.

"There." He pointed at a tree with the gun. "Up the tree. We can hide. Or defend ourselves if necessary. Hopefully they won't even see us." He didn't wait for her answer before he was lifting her into the tree. "Go as high as you can."

He was close behind her. Together they climbed until John put his hand on her arm and stilled her. She was out of breath, gasping for oxygen in the thick soup that made up the Amazon's air. Her knee was agony. It throbbed continuously, sending sharp streaks of pain up and down her leg.

"Down." He pushed her flat to her belly on the thick branch beneath her.

A second later, he was on his stomach on the branch next to hers. The leaves surrounded them, hiding them from above and below. Voices drew closer, and Beast motioned for her to stay silent. Belinda held her breath, afraid even that would alert someone to their presence. There was the unmistakable sound of something crashing through the foliage, and then Belinda heard people beneath them.

She waited, praying for a miracle as the men shouted to each other in Spanish. There was some sort of commotion, and then they ran past the tree where Belinda and John hid. Her heart beat so loud in her chest that she was sure everyone could hear it. It was a drum, summoning her attackers to her position. Calm—she had to be calm. She inched her hand towards John and wrapped her fingers in his shirt at this side.

And then they waited.

THERE HAD BEEN FIVE MEN. Now there were four. Beast had taken one out, and they weren't happy about it. They shouted to each other as they frantically searched the forest, looking for any sign of Beast and Belinda.

Beast was painfully aware of Belinda's ragged breathing. She was in pain. Her leg was worse than she let on, and she was running a fever, which told him her body was fighting an infection. Probably from one of the knife wounds the bastard had given her. She needed a doctor. If things got worse, she'd need a hospital. Time was fast running out for them.

The sounds of the men crashing around faded into normal jungle noise. They'd run ahead of Beast and Belinda's hiding place, thinking the pair were still running. Beast kept an eye on the time and waited. They couldn't stay up the tree indefinitely. This wasn't the first team of men the kidnappers had sent into the forest to find them. These men weren't the ones Beast had stolen from the night before, and from what he'd overheard, there were other teams out looking for them too. The leader of the kidnappers had offered a reward for whoever managed to return them to him. Their chances of making it out of the forest without getting caught were getting smaller by the minute.

Beside him, Belinda shivered, in heat warm enough to cook chicken. She was definitely running a fever. He looked over at her and noted that her cheeks were flushed and her eyes were a little glassy. She smiled at him, and his heart melted. For a woman who understood dramatic timing, she'd sure picked exactly the wrong moment to tell him she wanted a future outside of the jungle. He'd given her the sensible answer. It was not the one he'd wanted to give her. His newly discovered heart had told him to hold on to her and never let her go.

"Is it safe now?" she mouthed.

Beast checked his watch; forty minutes had passed. If the men were going to head back towards them, they would have done so by now.

"I'll go down first, make sure it's clear." It also meant he could hold her up. She didn't look like she had the strength to climb down a tree.

She nodded and fell silent again. Beast was worried. His Belinda wasn't quiet. His Belinda chattered when she was scared. He trailed his fingertips across her forehead on the pretence of brushing her hair out of her eyes. She was burning up. Beast swallowed hard. His medical knowledge was about as good as his jungle craft. All he knew for sure was that he had to get her to help, and fast.

Slowly, he shifted to his feet and made his way down the tree, stopping every couple of feet to listen. He signalled Belinda to follow, watching carefully when she did. Her usual agile movements were awkward and stiff, a sure sign that things were getting worse. Together, they made their way to the ground, where they stood still and listened.

Belinda swayed against him, and Beast put and arm around her to steady her. "Can you walk?" There was no way she could run.

She nodded, but her eyes told him she wasn't sure.

"There's no need, Señorita," someone behind Beast said in Spanish. *"We can carry you."*

Beast froze. Belinda's eyes went wide and she started shaking. Two more men stepped out from behind the wide tree and came up behind Belinda. Beast felt the muzzle of a gun pressed to the base of his skull.

"I saw what you did to my friend," the owner of the gun said. *"I will not be so stupid. Do not turn. Do not move. Or my friends over there will kill the woman."*

Belinda didn't understand what he was saying, and she looked at him for translation. "John?" she whispered as she held tight to his arms.

"Do what they say, baby. Everything is going to be okay." He kept his voice even, imbuing it with as much confidence as he could muster, hoping she'd take his lead and remain calm.

She nodded, her eyes filling with tears. She knew this was bad. How could she not?

"What are you going to do with us?" he asked the man in Spanish.

"Take you to Martinez. He's been looking for you. You ran out on him before he was finished with you."

"He won't like it if you hurt the girl," Beast said.

"No. But he doesn't care about you." Beast felt a harsh blow to his kidney and doubled over in pain. *"Disarm him,"* the guy barked to his friends.

Someone ripped Beast's pack from his shoulders. Another took the knife from his belt. His arms were dragged behind his back and tightly secured before the man behind him shoved him forward.

"Don't do anything stupid or we will take it out on the girl. We were told not to hurt her," the man said as he stepped forward and leered at Beast. *"We weren't told not to use her."*

"John?" Belinda sobbed, tears streaming down her face as one of the men held her back. "John?"

"I'm okay," Beast said when he could breathe again.

Belinda was swaying, her cheeks red and her eyes glazed. Beast took a step towards her. It was too late. Her eyes rolled back and she crumpled to the ground.

"What's wrong with her?" one of their captors demanded.

"She has a fever," Beast said. *"She needs medicine. Water."*

The man studied Belinda, who lay crumped on the ground. No one moved to help her. One of them toed her with his boot, making Beast growl.

"Don't." The gun was pressed harder to his head. *"Don't harm her,"* Beast said. Nothing would stop him if they did. No amount of binding would keep him from them.

"I don't think it's an act," the man who'd toed Belinda said. *"We have to carry her."*

The men leered at each other before one of them lifted Belinda and hefted her over his shoulder. She hung like a rag doll, and Beast let out another low growl.

"Be careful with her."

The men laughed at him.

"*Move.*" He was shoved in the back with the barrel of a gun. "*Martinez is eager to see you again. Don't worry. We aren't far from him now.*"

Beast didn't care who was waiting for them. All he cared about was the sight of Belinda dangling sick and vulnerable over the shoulder of the man in front of him. Even if he had to die to do it, he was going to find some way to get her out of this in one piece.

CHAPTER 29

Belinda wavered in and out of consciousness. She felt as though her skin was on fire, yet it was suddenly very cold in the jungle. Thirsty—she was so thirsty. She caught snippets of activity around her. For a while, she'd been upside down, then she'd been tossed to the ground. She remembered landing, the jolt to her knee making her scream. After that, there was laughter and someone roared her name.

John.

She struggled to open her eyes. The world had toppled. The sky was to the side of her and the trees had gone. *Sky? Blue sky?* After days of endless green, she couldn't believe what she saw was truth.

"She needs water," John said in a harsh, desperate voice. "Somebody give her some fucking water!"

She felt a hand under her arm, and the world righted itself. She blinked several times as someone pressed a bottle of water against her lips. She grasped it with both hands, gulping until it was finished.

"More," she whispered, and another bottle was placed in her hands.

She felt as though her body had turned into a giant sponge, soaking up each precious drop of water. Her head slowly cleared and her surroundings came into focus.

She was in hell.

The green of the Amazon Jungle's trees and plants was gone, replaced with an endless sea of red earth and mud. Hundreds of trees had been uprooted and left to rot where they fell. Their leaves were gone and their skeletons lay caked in mud. Mounds of dirt loomed up all around them, like giant anthills. In front of her there were vast, gaping craters filled with brown water. In the middle of one, a large makeshift raft sat abandoned. It had bamboo poles poking out in all directions, holding up pipes and supporting a ripped tarpaulin roof. Alongside it was what looked like a large metal conveyor belt. And around it, in the mud, were several empty pots and basins. At the side of the crater were a few crooked huts, made of strung-together bamboo with straw-covered roofs. The only piece of colour in the whole area was the blue of the tarpaulin.

It was a scene of utter, thoughtless devastation. But the thing that shocked Belinda the most was the lack of noise. There were no insects buzzing around, no birds singing, no monkeys calling to one another. This land was dead. Lifeless. Empty.

"John?" she said in a hoarse whisper. She cleared her throat and shouted, "John!"

"I'm here." The sound of his voice made her want to cry with relief. "Let me get to her. She's sick."

There was a scuffle, and a man with a gun shoved John to his knees beside her. She threw her arms around his neck and held on tight.

"It's okay, baby. We'll get out of this."

"Oh, I don't think so." A man crouched in front of them, and she recognised him immediately as the kidnappers' leader. "I have something much more interesting planned for you."

He grasped Belinda's chin and turned her face towards him. John shot forward, but a guard clamped a hand on his shoulder and kept him in place. He growled and struggled for freedom, and Belinda noticed that his hands were secured behind his back.

"Who did this to you?" The leader sounded angry that she'd been hurt. In her dazed and confused mind, she wondered if it was because he didn't want his property damaged, or because he'd wanted a clean slate to mark for himself. "Tell me." His fingers tightened on her jaw, making her gasp.

"Miguel!" she said.

He released her, and she fell back against John. "*Estúpido!* Miguel never understood patience." He trailed a finger down Belinda's cheek as the guard tightened his hold on John. "Tell me, Señorita Collins, did Miguel get inside that famous body of yours, or did your lap dog stop him first?"

John fought to get at the man. The leader nodded at the guard holding him, and the guard struck John with the butt of his gun. He slammed into the mud in front of them. Belinda gasped and reached for him as the world tilted yet again. Her hands were shaking, and it was hard to focus on anything being said.

"Tell me." The leader grabbed a handful of her hair and yanked her attention to his face. "Did Miguel fuck you?"

Fury coursed through her, giving her clarity. "Do you mean did he rape me? He tried. He was eaten by a caiman for his efforts."

There was a moment's silence before the leader threw back his head and laughed. He shouted to his men, and they all laughed too. The leader let go of her hair, and she hurriedly reached out to help John get back onto his knees.

That small effort sapped every last reserve of strength she had left, and she slumped against him.

He was breathing hard, fury emanating from him. She placed a hand on his arm, a small comfort in a situation that was woefully out of their control.

As she watched, a man came up to stand beside the leader. He acted as though he was also in charge, rather than one of the men the leader ordered around. Now that she studied him, her slow, aching brain noted the family resemblance. The two men had the same bone structure and the same dark, greasy hair.

"Who are you?" Belinda said before she could censor her words.

With identical flat, malicious gazes, they turned their attention to her.

"Forgive me for not introducing myself," the leader said with clear amusement. "I am Angel Martinez, and this is my brother Diego. This"—he held up his hands and motioned to the devastation—"is one of our gold mines. And you"—he pointed at them—"are about to become the stars in our first ever live broadcast. I am sure you feel honoured."

Belinda shivered and slipped down into the mud. The Martinez brothers laughed before shouting orders at their men. They were no longer interested in their captives.

"John," Belinda said softly, "I don't feel so good."

And then the world went dark again.

Belinda's head landed on Beast's thighs as he knelt in the mud. With his hands secured behind him, he couldn't even touch her. She was clearly burning up. Her face was flushed and her eyes had been glassy before she passed out. Her body was fighting a virulent infection and her injuries had weakened her. Each time she lost consciousness, John worried it would be the last and she wouldn't wake up again. She needed medical help. And she needed it fast.

He glanced around the mine. They were in an older part, one that had obviously been exhausted of its resources. The only men in the area now were members of the Martinez cartel. In the distance, closer to the river, he saw the busyness of mineworkers, dredging the sandy banks in search of more gold. Beast knew they wouldn't help them. They were captors, the same as him and Belinda, men at the mercy of the gangs.

He spat mud out of his mouth as he watched a small tractor drag something through the mine, something the Martinez brothers were salivating over. Behind Beast, the guard had lost interest in watching him, although he still kept his gun trained on Beast's head. In his lap, Belinda stirred.

Beast looked down at her. She was beautiful to him, inside and out. He wished he could tell her how important she'd become to him during their intense trek through the jungle. He wished he could take back his reaction when she'd asked to spend time with him after this was over. He wished he could comfort her and let her know how much she comforted him. But he couldn't. Not here. Not in this place.

She opened her eyes and stared up at him. "John," she whispered.

Her blue eyes softened when she looked at him, and he knew it couldn't be an act. They were past acting. The jungle had stripped them raw, and nothing was hidden any longer.

"You okay, baby?" It was a stupid question, but it was all he had.

"I want to go home." Her eyes filled with tears, and John knew she didn't hold out any hope of it happening.

"*Put them against the hut and come help,*" Diego shouted to the guard behind them, the one who was more interested in the tractor than in guarding them.

The man didn't hesitate. He grabbed Belinda's arm, pulled her to her feet and thrust her against the ragged little hut that sat a few feet behind them. She landed with a thump and a cry of pain. John clenched his teeth, flexed his bound fists and silently promised retribution to the grinning guard. The guard turned to grab John, but he was already on his feet. He strode to Belinda and sat at her side. The guard smirked before he called to a man near them, telling him to cover the captives, and then he went to help his bosses.

Belinda was crying as she curled into Beast's side.

"I'm sorry, baby. I'm so sorry." He was sorry he hadn't been able to protect her better. Sorry she'd been hurt. Sorry he couldn't think of a way out of this mess.

"It's okay," she said.

And then she slumped against him again. Beast looked up into the laughing face of the guard who now held a gun on him.

"*No stamina,*" the man said. "*White girls never have enough stamina.*"

Beast wished he could wipe every single one of these men from the face of the earth. He scanned the area looking for some way out. Someone who could help. Anything to get them out of this mess alive.

And then he felt it.

He froze. Belinda's fingers were working the knot on the rope that secured his hands behind his back.

He looked down at her. She seemed completely unconscious, exactly as she had been earlier. She lay against him, her head hanging, her limbs limp. All except for the hand behind his back. The one picking at the ropes.

CHAPTER 30

"We've got four hostiles standing watch at the treeline," Lake said over the comm system Ryan had in his ear.

Ryan had fought to take part in the mission this time around. His arm was still in a sling, but he couldn't stay at the hotel while everything was going down in the jungle. In the end, Lake had agreed to let him man the second boat, to free up someone else for the on-the-ground search party.

He'd been sitting in that boat, idling on the river around the bend from the gold mine, for hours. After the team had regrouped and refuelled, they'd split into teams and Callum and Ryan had dropped them off on the riverbank, as close to the mine as they could get without tipping off the Martinez crew. The teams had then made their way on foot, through the jungle, to the mine.

It was late in the morning now. The teams had been on the ground for hours. They had to be exhausted. Yet they carried on, fuelled by adrenalin and determination. Ryan felt the tension build with each update he received. One way or another, things were coming to a climax soon.

"Six on the south side," Dimitri reported.

"Eyes on target?" Callum said from his spot on the opposite side of the horseshoe where he manned the other boat.

"Nothing yet," Dimitri said.

"Nothing," Lake said.

"No," Grunt said.

Ryan picked up his satphone. Elle was keeping the line open for them. "Anything showing at your end?" he asked.

"No signal coming from their broadcast unit," she said.

Which meant that whatever the Martinez cartel had planned for Beast and Belinda, it hadn't started yet.

"We've got trouble at base," Violet said over the satphone. "The press has arrived. We've got four helicopters on the hotel lawn."

Ryan pinched the bridge of his nose with his good hand. It had been expected, but he didn't have to like it. Mainly he was just grateful that they'd turned up later than expected.

"Get the hotel security staff to deal with them," he said. "Secure everyone in the ballroom. Make sure you have all the Collins family where you can see them, in case one of them decides to hold a press conference."

"It's being done," Violet said tersely. "I know what I'm doing. This was a courtesy call."

Ryan let out a sigh. Just what Benson Security needed— another team member with a chip on their shoulder and a permanent bad attitude.

"Eyes on target," Grunt said, and Ryan's heart almost exploded from his chest.

"Report," Lake barked.

"They're in the centre of the camp. Bound. Wounded. Belinda is unconscious."

Ryan knew every member of his team was wondering the same thing—had they arrived too late?

"Status on the ground?" Callum said.

"Twelve hostiles surrounding the targets," Grunt said. "All armed. Miners in the pits nearest the river."

"Can you get to the targets?" Lake asked.

"Negative," Grunt said.

"I need more detail," Lake said.

Noah said, "They're out in the open, about a hundred feet from the treeline and surrounded by mud pools. There's a digger dragging some equipment up from the river to the site of the targets. The brothers are focused on that and not on our people."

"Has to be the broadcast unit," Ryan said.

"We don't have a clear view," Noah replied.

"Five more hostiles joined the party over here," Dimitri said.

"We got boats coming in fast," Callum reported.

"No time to waste. Move in," Lake said. "Keep it quiet."

"Roger," each signed off before going silent.

Ryan felt an itch under his skin that demanded action, but this was as close as he'd get to seeing any. He had to trust his team to get the job done and get their people out of there—before the Martinez brothers managed to broadcast the situation around the world.

CHAPTER 31

Beast felt the rope around his wrists loosen, and he could have kissed Belinda. Not one person looking at them would have guessed she was awake and working to free them. He made a silent vow that if they got out of there alive, he would never again say anything derogatory about her acting skills. The woman was extraordinary.

"To the left of us, behind the shack, there's another hole," he whispered, trying to hide that he was talking from their guards. "You hear me, babe?"

She patted his back to let him know she'd heard.

"When I make my move, run for the hole and jump in. Take cover. I'll get you when it's over."

She tensed for a second before hanging limp again. Then she started writing letters with her fingertip on the back of his shirt.

N. O.

"You have to," he said, hoping she would hear his urgency. "I can't fight and watch you at the same time. You have to trust me. I'll get us out of here."

Her finger moved again. *G.U.N.S.*

"I'll take care of them," he promised. *Somehow.*

His plan was to pummel a guard, remove his weapon and fire on anything that moved. Simple. But hopefully enough to get them out of there. The river was too far away; their only option was making it back into the trees and hiding until help came. Because he *knew* help would come, and they had to be alive when it did.

He scanned the surrounding area, trying not to make it obvious what he was doing. He counted at least fifteen men, all armed and all taking orders from the Martinez brothers. There was no way he could fight his way out of the situation with Belinda being ill. Their best hope was to hit hard and fast, then run and hide.

"Baby," he whispered, "if something happens to me, if it doesn't look like I'll make it, head for the forest. Hide until the team from Benson Security find you. They're looking for you. I promise you that. All you have to do is stay alive until they find you. Promise me. Promise me you'll do what I tell you. Promise me you'll run if it looks bad."

The answer was fast in coming. Her fingers stabbed at his back.

N.O.

"Damn it, Belinda. Do as I fucking tell you."

N.O.

He let out a frustrated hiss. Her hand was shaking as she wrote another word on his back.

L.I.V.E.

"That's what I'm telling you, you stubborn woman."

They sat in silence as Beast kept an eye on the men charged with watching them. Their attention kept straying to the vehicle making its way through the mud towards them.

He let out heavy breath. "We both live. We do what it takes."

She gave him a little nod that he barely felt, but definitely registered. All he could do was hope that she ran when she saw he was gone. Because, given the odds, Beast didn't think the fight he had planned would achieve much more than create a diversion for Belinda to get away.

The guard turned back to them, and Beast couldn't risk saying anything more, even though there were things to say. He wanted to tell her how much she meant to him. How much their time together had changed him. He wanted to tell her that she made him want to let go of his prejudices and be a better man. He wanted her to know that he'd made a mistake. She was right. Whatever they'd forged between them in the jungle was too important to end when they left it. He wanted a chance with her to see where it went. He'd never wanted anything more in his life. But the time for telling her these things had passed.

Now, all they had was one last desperate bid for survival.

The tractor vehicle that everyone focused on made its way through the mud and around the water-filled craters. Beast might not have a great love for the rainforest, but the Martinez crew had stomped all over it and ground it into dirt under their boots. Beast suspected they enjoyed treating the people around them exactly the same way. He'd seen the looks on their faces once too often in his life—the brothers enjoyed watching other people suffer.

Behind the tractor, there was a large, sealed trailer, with several doors and hatches on it, for people to open and access whatever was stored inside. As it came closer, the trailer turned, and Beast saw the back of it. He stilled. He knew exactly what was attached to it. It was a satellite uplink dish. The kind he'd seen time and again on the boardwalk of Atlantic City. The kind used by TV stations when they were reporting live.

Beast's eyes shot to the Martinez brothers, who oozed

glee as they stared at the truck. And Beast knew. He knew they planned to make an example of their recaptured kidnap victims.

And they were going to do it on air.

"This is going to go fast," he told Belinda. Because there was no way he could wait for a better time. There was no way he could take the chance that they'd brutalise Belinda while they broadcast it around the world. "Be ready. I don't care how you do it but get to cover."

"*Stop talking,*" the guard ordered him.

"*She's out cold,*" Beast said in Spanish. "*It isn't like she can hear me.*"

The conversation attracted the attention of the brothers, who prowled towards them. They had identical looks on their faces—evil anticipation.

"*Wake her up,*" Diego ordered the guard.

The asshole took great pleasure in unscrewing the cap off a water bottle and dousing Belinda. She jerked up, sputtering as though she'd been forced awake.

"It's time," Angel said. "Señorita Collins is going to put on one last performance for us, and then this will all be over."

"You're going to return us to our families?" Belinda asked. She sounded both scared and hopeful.

Beast knew it was an act. She knew the Martinez brothers had no intention of handing them over to anyone.

"But of course," Martinez said with a smile that was dead. "You are worth ten million dollars to me." He paused and arched an eyebrow at Beast. "Each."

It was clear he knew Beast wasn't some big-shot direc-tor, and it amused him. The Martinez brothers' amusement was the least of Beast's concerns. His eyes kept returning to the men unloading the trailer. They pulled out camera equipment and started to set it up in front of him and Belinda.

"What are you doing?" Belinda said. "Why is there a camera?"

She sounded confused now, and Beast knew it wasn't an act. Her fever was raging. He could feel the heat coming off her skin as their arms pressed together.

"I'm going to film you," Angel said. "You like being filmed, don't you, Señorita Collins?"

Belinda started to shake. She looked up at Beast. "What?" Her eyes were glassy and unfocused.

"Come here!" Angel snapped at Belinda.

Her head lolled towards her captor and she frowned as she tried to focus. Beast wasn't going to let that happen. No matter what. Belinda wasn't getting anywhere near the brothers.

"Now," Beast roared as he shot to his feet.

He launched himself at Angel without a backwards glance at Belinda. All he could do was trust that she followed his instructions.

And that, no matter what, she stayed alive.

"Move in now!" Grunt bellowed over the comm.

Ryan jumped as the sound blasted through him.

"Report," Lake snapped.

"Beast launched an attack on the Martinez brothers," Noah said in a rush.

A gunshot rang out, making birds take flight over the forest.

"Use full force," Lake said. "Get in there. Get the job done. Ryan? Callum?"

"Taking position now," Ryan said as he started the boat.

The team were past the stealth stage. Now the boats would get as close as they could to the mine to pull their people out as fast as possible.

"Ryan?" Elle sounded hysterical, which wasn't like her. "Ryan, are you there?"

He reached for the satphone and pressed the speech button. "I'm here."

"The Martinez unit is broadcasting. They've hacked a local news network."

"Belinda? Beast?" Ryan manoeuvred the boat around a tree growing on the edge of the river.

"Beast," she said. "Beast is fighting one of the brothers. I can't see Belinda. Someone is saying something. Damn it, I can't speak Spanish. Does anyone here speak Spanish?"

"I can!" There was the sound of movement as Ryan skimmed over the water.

On the bank opposite the mine sat half a dozen caiman, relaxing in the sun. They lifted their heads and stared at him as he passed.

Kirsty's voice came on the line. Ryan knew she'd spent a lot of time in Spain during her modelling years. It made sense she could speak the language. "Someone at the mine is narrating the fight," she said. "They're telling us that the Martinez cartel are to be feared and they deal ruthlessly with those who oppose them." She paused. "That would be fine and dandy if it didn't look like the Martinez guy was getting the crap kicked out of him by Beast."

"Two down," Lake said in Ryan's ear.

"One down," Dimitri said. "Harvard, watch your six."

"Got it," Harvard said calmly.

"Oh no," Kirsty said. "The guy just told everyone that two hostages had dared to escape the Martinez cartel. They've hunted them down and are going to show the world what happens to anyone who goes up against the cartel. He says that after their boss is done teaching Beast a lesson, he's going to make Belinda Collins scream on TV."

Ryan let out a stream of curses as gunshots rent the air.

"They know we're here," Dimitri said.

"Who has eyes on Belinda?" Lake said.

There was silence.

"Grunt. Get to Belinda," Lake said. "You're the closest. Noah, take out any threat to Beast."

"Roger that," Noah said.

"The rest of you," Lake said, "mow them down."

There was a pause, as though the world took a breath, and then an explosion rocked the forest.

"That would be one of their boats," Callum said with satisfaction. "I'm taking out the rest."

"I'm coming in to help," Ryan said.

"Don't get in my way, son. I'm in a killing mood."

Ryan smiled as Elle's voice came over the phone. "The press camped out outside the resort have heard the news about Belinda. A couple of teams are rushing to their choppers. They're heading your way."

"Got it," he told Elle before speaking to his team. "Be aware. Beast's fight is being televised. Reporters are on their way."

"Roger that," Lake said. "You heard him. First man to take out the broadcast unit wins a bottle of Scotland's finest."

"Or woman," said Megan.

"Or woman," Lake said. "Now let's get this done."

BELINDA WAS MOVING IN A FOG. But she *was* moving. As soon as John jumped up and launched himself at their kidnappers, Belinda got to her feet and half limped, half ran to the edge of the gaping hole behind them. Everyone's attention was firmly focused on John. No one had been watching her.

She threw herself over the edge of the muddy crater, sliding down the steeply sloped side and straight into the water. It was deeper than she'd thought it would be, and she kicked hard, fighting with what little strength she had left, to keep her head above water.

Above her, it sounded like the world was ending. Gunshots blasted. Something exploded. Men shouted. Someone screamed. She was suddenly in the middle of a war zone. Her heart thumped hard and fast as she panted for breath. The water was cooler than the humid air and helped clear her head some. It helped her get past the stabbing pain in her side and the continuous throb of her knee. In a moment of clarity, she remembered John telling her to run for the trees. An impossibility if she couldn't climb out of the bowl full of muddy water. The sides were steep and muddy, and she was certain her knee wouldn't hold up in an attempt to climb them.

She trod water, in a circle, looking for a way out, and spotted one. There was a ladder lying against one of the slopes. It was made of bamboo tied together with rope. But it would do. Fighting through the pain thudding in her head, she forced herself to swim towards the ladder. Each stroke was agony. The cut in her side ripped open, letting dirty water in, and her leg felt like it was a lead weight attached to her body. She panted, struggling to stay afloat and make it to her destination. Above her, the gunfire continued. Was John alive? Had he been shot? She shook her head, instantly regretting it when her vision blurred. He had to be alive. There was no other option.

An eternity passed, but she reached the ladder. Exhaustion almost dragged her under the water as she clung to the side of the hole. Out of the corner of her eye, she saw something slip into the water. She stilled, fear making her heart beat loudly in her ears. The water rippled. Something was coming for her. And it was getting closer. With a sob, Belinda summoned all the strength left in her. She struggled to pull herself out of the water, clawing at the dirt, huffing out moans of desperation when it came away in her hands.

The ripple on the water was getting closer, heading straight for her. With one last desperate push, she managed to haul herself up onto the muddy slope. She held on to the ladder as she snatched her feet from the water—just as something long and dark slid past them. Belinda didn't know what it was, but it circled around for a second attack.

Muffling her moans of pain, she pulled herself up the rickety ladder. Even the smallest pressure on her knee sent shards of pain throughout her body. Running for the treeline was going to take a miracle, because Belinda was sure she wouldn't even be able to stand. She made it up two rungs before she heard a splash. She looked down in time to see a large snake disappear back into the water. Shaking, she pulled herself up another rung. And then another. In her mind, the ladder seemed to get longer with each rung she conquered. Her body was leaden, her head disoriented. Spots danced before her, and she feared she would lose consciousness again.

No, not now!

Visions of sliding back into the hole to become food for the snake assaulted her. She shook them out of her head and lost her grip on the ladder. She frantically grasped for a rung and pressed herself against the ladder when she caught hold of it. Another explosion rocked the ground beneath her, making the ladder slide down the slope towards the water. Belinda bit her lip hard to stop herself from screaming. She clung to the top rung as the ladder stopped its slide. Belinda forced her eyes open to see how far she'd slipped. Not too far, but the rim was further away than it had been before the explosion. She attempted to wipe tears from her eyes and only succeeded in clogging them with mud. She could still make it over—if her leg held.

Angry men shouted above her. But none of them were John.

Please, please, please, please, please...

She prayed, silently begging God to save John.

To save the man she'd fallen in love with.

The man who was sacrificing himself to save her.

Please.

She put her hand on the rim of the crater. There was nothing close to hold on to. All she could do was press her palm flat and use it for balance as she climbed up to stand on the top rung. Her body lay flat against the steep slope as she took each step up to the top. Slowly, her head breached the edge of the pit, and she gasped. The mine was on fire.

The hut she'd sat against with John was ablaze. The two vehicles in the clearing were destroyed, and bits of metal lay scattered on the red, muddy earth. Men ran frantically, firing shots at an enemy Belinda couldn't see. Not two feet from her, lay the dead body of the guard who'd been watching over them. His head was turned towards her, and his blank eyes stared straight at her, while his spilled blood soaked into the red clay.

Belinda felt bile rise at the sight and squeezed her eyes tightly closed. The action made her sway with dizziness, and she forced them open again. She deliberately kept her gaze from the body as she searched the clearing for John. There was no sign of him.

A shout snagged her attention. The sound of flesh hitting flesh grew loud. Two men barrelled into the clearing. They were covered in mud and blood.

And one of them was John.

CHAPTER 32

"Now," Beast roared at Belinda before he launched himself at Martinez.

He had only two thoughts in his head: kill the brothers, save Belinda. He hit the man in front of him, one punch to his jaw, another to his stomach. Angel kicked out, hitting Beast in the knee, and making him slip in the mud. Instead of getting back to his feet, he used his position to tackle Martinez. He grabbed him around the waist and pummelled his kidneys until he was certain the guy would piss nothing but blood *if* he survived this fight.

Something hard struck Beast's back and sent him to his knees, forcing him to release Martinez. Beast glanced behind him to find the other brother wielding a length of wood. Movement brought his head back around, just in time to see Angel kick at his head. Beast ducked, rolled and punched at the guy's crotch. Angel howled and toppled.

Diego roared and rushed him. Beast rolled out of his way, in time to avoid the plank aimed at his head, but not fast enough to miss the kick to his ribs. He felt a crack and knew they were broken.

Angel struggled to his feet, and Diego rushed Beast again. There was a blast, sending all three men flying. Beast landed hard on the edge of the crater he'd told Belinda to hide in. He shook his head, fighting against the ringing in his ears and the disorientation that overwhelmed him. He had to get up, had to be ready. Glancing into the pit, he saw Belinda reach for the ladder leaning against the steep muddy side.

Good.

He had to fight the urge to rush to her aid. Fear for her was a taste in his mouth, one that made him nauseated. She was running on fumes, fighting pain and fever, terrified she was going to die. Beast had to trust that she would do as they'd agreed, because the Martinez brothers were bearing down on him.

He pushed away from the side of the crater and jumped to his feet, ignoring the sharp pain in his ribs, knowing that showing weakness was tantamount to conceding the fight. He was born for this. He'd been fighting on the streets of Atlantic City since he was barely a teen. And every single one of those fights, every professional match, was practice for this one.

He clenched his fists and charged for the nearest brother. Diego was unsteady on his feet, still shaking his head to get over the blast. Beast took him to the ground, straddling him while he punched his face, over and over again, until he went limp beneath him. The bastard was still breathing. Beast lifted his fist, knowing a punch to the throat would finish Diego off, when something slammed into his shoulder, sending him back into the mud.

It took him a second to realise he'd been shot. Blood poured from his arm, but he didn't feel the pain. There was too much adrenalin in his system to allow it. He flexed his fist. It still worked. He'd worry about the bullet wound later.

With a grunt, he clambered to his feet as Angel came at him. His arm was out in front of him. In his hand was a gun.

Diego groaned and rolled to his side. It was enough to distract his brother, who turned to look at him. Beast dove behind the burning news van, got to his feet and ran. Shots rang out, pinging against the burning metal, as Angel fired wildly. Beast saw Angel pull the trigger and nothing came out. He tossed the gun at the flames. Beast ran at him, pushing him into the middle of the clearing.

It was a whirl of fists and feet. Beast reeled at the blows, but didn't feel them. That would come later. If he survived. He punched at Angel's head and watched the blow hit true. Blood spurted and his head swung wildly. Beast didn't wait. He followed the punch with a death blow to the throat, crushing Angel's windpipe and sending him to the ground.

There was no time to gloat over the body. Beast whirled to face the other brother, only to stop dead. Diego was on his feet and pointing a gun straight at Beast.

"This is for my brother, you bastard!" He pulled the trigger.

There was a moment when time stood still. Beast watched shock spread over Diego's face. The gun fell from his hand as his other hand pressed to his stomach. Bright red blood mingled with the mud covering him. He looked down at the blood and then crumpled, knees, shoulders, face hitting the ground.

Beast swung around to see who'd fired, and his heart stopped. Belinda was lying face down, half out of the crater. Her arm was stretched out and there was a gun in her hand. Beside her lay the body of the guard who'd watched over them. His weapon was missing. Belinda had used it to save Beast's life.

Beast ran for her, sliding in the mud as bullets whizzed around him. He didn't care. He didn't know who was firing or why it was happening. All he cared about was Belinda. She didn't move. Not even a twitch. He couldn't see her breathing. She couldn't be dead. She couldn't.

"Belinda!" he roared as he slid to his knees in front of her.

He pulled the gun out of her hand, put his hands under her shoulders and dragged her up and out of the pit. She lay limply in his arms. Beast tried to wipe the mud away from her face, but there was too much on his hands. He was only making it worse. Frantically, he felt for a pulse and almost broke into tears when he found one. She was alive.

He clutched her against his chest, holding her there for a second, just one second before he had to pick her up and run for the trees.

"Beast," someone shouted.

Beast snatched up the gun he'd taken from Belinda and aimed in the direction of the voice.

"It's the cavalry, asshole. Try not to shoot us."

Through the smoke billowing from the burning vehicles, two overly large forms appeared. They strode towards him, materialising like angels sent from heaven. Grunt and Harvard.

"I hope to hell you're real," Beast said. If this was a hallucination, he was going to shoot someone for sure.

"Good to see you alive, buddy. I knew the jungle was no match for the Beast." Harvard crouched beside him. "How's she doing?"

Beast looked down at Belinda. "Not good. She needs a doctor."

Harvard pressed his comm link. "We have the targets. They're breathing. We need immediate medical attention. Somebody want to commandeer one of those pretty press choppers?"

Beast looked up at Grunt, who towered over them, a gun in each hand, scanning their surroundings for a threat.

"What took you so long?" Beast said.

Grunt looked down at them and grunted. Harvard and Beast grinned at each other as the sound of rotor blades filled the air. Beast held Belinda tight. His mind was made up. He was never letting her out of his sight again. There was no way he'd be able to live through it. Belinda Collins was stuck with him, whether she liked it or not.

CHAPTER 33

Belinda woke to a wonderful realisation—she wasn't in the jungle anymore. She knew this because the oppressive heat and heady aromas of the forest had been replaced by cool, lavender-scented air. Instead of the sound of chattering monkeys, chirping birds and buzzing insects, there was only the hum of an air conditioning unit and a gentle, distant beeping. Beneath her, the harsh textures of tree bark and dirt had been replaced by clean, soft cotton.

But more than cool air and clean sheets, the presence of a large body lying beside her made her heart race. The body was warm, solid and familiar. Belinda didn't dare move or open her eyes for fear she was imagining things. Which, considering the fog in her head and the throbbing pain in her temples, could be a very real possibility. Her memory was hazy, coming to her in fits and starts.

She remembered clawing her way up the ladder on the side of the crater. She remembered the dead guard lying at the top of the hole, staring at her sightlessly. She remembered the ferocious fight between John and one of the Martinez brothers. Both men had been covered in mud and blood, and they'd launched themselves at each other with terrifying violence. She remembered John standing over the body of the brother as he fell. And then…the sight of the second brother, rising from the mud and pointing a gun straight at his back. She hadn't thought. She'd only reacted. She'd snatched the gun from the man beside her and fired. After that, she remembered nothing at all.

"You might as well open your eyes. I know you're awake."

Belinda's eyes popped open at the sound of the deep American accent she adored. She blinked against light that felt like ice picks stabbing into her brain and waited as his face came into focus. He was lying on his side with his head supported on his hand, and he looked at her with a dark intensity that made her smile.

"Is this real?" she said. "Did we make it out of there?"

A delicious smile softened his face and made her want to trace his lips with her fingertips. But she didn't move, afraid it was all just a dream.

"Let's go over it one more time," he said. "The kidnapping was real, not fake. The rescue was real, not fake. You're here with me now. It's real. Not fake." His eyes crinkled and sparkled, making her heart race.

"Where is here?"

"Cusco hospital." He reached out and brushed the hair from her face. "You gave us a fright there for a while."

"How long is a while?"

"Two days." He made it sound like an eternity.

There was a cut on his cheek, taped with butterfly strips. His right eye was black and blue.

"We're a pair," she said. "Do you have other injuries?" She looked down his body, but couldn't see any evidence.

"Couple of cracked ribs and a flesh wound on my arm. Nothing I can't cope with."

Her stomach sank. "Flesh wound?"

"It's nothing. A scratch. How do you feel? You were pretty out of it for a while. They've been pumping you full of antibiotics and fluids."

Belinda did a mental inventory of her body. "I don't feel too bad. Tired. Weak. My knee is still sore. But that's about it."

"You're on painkillers. You dislocated your knee. They had to operate to fix it. You'll be fine, although it might take a while." The words he didn't say hung heavily between them —things could have been a whole lot worse for both of them.

She swallowed, her mouth dry. "What happened? I remember up until climbing out of that hole. I had a gun. Did I...?" She couldn't say the words. Part of her, a bigger part than she'd like to admit, didn't want to know if she'd killed a man.

"Did you save my life?" He leaned in and kissed the tip of her nose. "Hell yeah. You know what that means? I owe you a life debt. You're stuck with me until I repay it."

A surge of hope shot through her, but... "That isn't a real thing, John. It's a plot device used in old westerns."

"Nope, you're wrong, baby. It's a real thing. I can't leave you until I've paid the debt." He was solemn, but his eyes burned with sensual intent.

"How long do you think it will take to pay this debt?" Her voice trembled, betraying just how important his answer was to her. She wanted him to stay. She wanted to try for something special together outside of the jungle. She wanted a chance at making this thing between them work, at getting to know him when something or someone wasn't trying to kill them. She wanted it so badly that her heart actually ached from it.

"I'm thinking that it's gonna take a lifetime, Hollywood."

Her hand moved then. It curled in his blue T-shirt, tangling in the material above his heart. "Don't say that if you don't mean it." She couldn't bear it if he was teasing. It was far too important to her.

"I mean every single word. You asked me for a chance when we got out of the jungle, and I thought you were mad. The world would laugh at us, an MMA fighter with a Hollywood princess. They'd hound us every step of the way, making life hard for us. But I learned something important while we were out there."

"What?" she whispered, barely holding on to her courage to ask.

"I learned that you aren't a Hollywood princess—you're Belinda. And you can cope with whatever the world throws at us."

She sucked in a breath. "And you're the strongest man I've ever known. You aren't your past, or your profession, or where you were born. You're just John."

"Only to you, baby, only to you."

"Oh, for goodness' sake, what have I told you?" someone snapped from the doorway, and Belinda looked up to see her mother barrel in. There were tears in her eyes. "Get out of that bed right now, or I'll take a shoe to your backside."

"Crap, it's your mom again," John whispered. "You gotta save me, baby. I don't know what to do with her."

His face became a blank mask as he ignored her mother's order. Instead, he scooted up until he was sitting against the headboard. Then he reached down and slid Belinda up to lean against his side. It was unclear to Belinda whether he wanted to keep her close because he'd missed her, or whether he was using her as a shield against her mum.

"That boy doesn't listen to a word I say," her mother complained as she hurried around to the opposite side of the bed to John. Only Libby Collins would call John a boy. Her mum pulled Belinda, ever so gently, out of John's hold. "I was so worried," she said, her voice cracking. "I thought we'd lost you." And then she enfolded Belinda in that special hug only a mother knew how to give.

"I'm okay now." Belinda fought the urge to weep like a child. "John saved me."

"From what I hear, you saved him."

Belinda smiled. "We saved each other, Mum."

She breathed in her mother's special fragrance, a strange blend of roses and Earl Grey tea. She would bet that her mum was staring John down. She didn't interfere. If he was serious about sticking around, then he'd have to get used to her family. And, unfortunately, her family took a lot of getting used to.

"You're awake!" Belinda looked over to see her grand-mother, Patricia, standing in the doorway. She was dressed in a chic red jumpsuit, with oversized wooden bangles and Audrey Hepburn sunglasses. Behind her was Patricia's best friend, Alice, who was dressed like a bag lady.

The two of them rushed into the room and crowded around Belinda and her mother, wrapping them both in a massive hug.

"Family hug," her grandmother shouted. "Don't break the invalid."

Another set of arms joined the rugby scrum, and Belinda looked up into her sister's tear-filled eyes.

"I thought you were on honeymoon," Belinda said.

"I was." Julia sniffed. "Until I found out about your kidnapping—on the news." She cast a glare over her shoulder at her husband, Joe, who was talking with John. "He knew and he didn't tell me."

"I was protecting you," Joe said with a shake of his head.

"I'm not talking to him. I might never again," Julia said, which was a worry, as she was the most stubborn person Belinda knew. If anyone could pull off a threat like that, it was Julia. "When you back the car into a bollard, it's okay not to tell your wife. When her sister's kidnapped and then lost in the jungle—you tell your wife. It isn't rocket science."

"Belle," her father boomed, and like the Red Sea, her family parted to allow him access to her. "Never again, you hear me? My heart can't take it. Never again." He blinked back tears as he wrapped her in a bone-crushing hug.

"Can't breathe," she joked.

There was a growl. "Step back, Mr Collins. She only woke up and she's still fragile."

John. Watching over her. Protecting her from her family. He was woefully misguided, although very sweet.

"Listen here, Mr Beast," her father said. "I'll damn well hug my daughter any time I like."

John didn't like that one bit. He opened his mouth to protest, but Joe put a hand on his arm and shook his head. "Family," Joe said. "Just go with it."

John stepped back, but he clearly didn't like it. He looked a little lost, and a lot alone, out there on the edge of the room while Belinda was surrounded by people she loved. She held out a hand for him. "Come here," she said.

He was by her side in a second, holding her as though she were a lifeline. Her father watched the interaction with a frown before looking at John.

"You and I are going to have a little talk about your intentions towards my daughter," he said.

"Dad," Belinda said.

She briefly wondered if she should fake a fainting episode to clear the room and head her father off, but her family knew her too well and wouldn't be fooled.

John stared her father down. "I have nothing to hide. I intend to stick to her like glue for the rest of my life."

Belinda's mother gasped, her grandmother feigned a swoon and Alice got stuck into a box of chocolates someone had left beside her bed.

"In what capacity?" her father demanded. "Her body-guard? Her lover? Her husband? What?"

"Now I'm wishing I was still in the jungle," Belinda whined as she looked up at John. "Don't answer him. It's none of his business."

"It's an easy answer, baby," he said, his eyes still on her dad. "The answer is all of the above. I'm going to be her bodyguard, lover and one day, her husband."

Belinda's mouth fell open. "You can't know that."

"Baby, we had an intense start. We saw the worst of each other. We know more about each other than some couples know after years together. So, yeah, I can know what I want."

"You haven't even said you love me. How can you talk about marriage when nobody's mentioned love?"

"I was kinda hoping for some privacy for that part."

"Too late now," her grandmother said as she dug into the chocolates with Alice.

Belinda glanced around the room to see everyone watching them. She swallowed hard. "I see what you mean." As much as she loved her family, she wished they were far, far away right now.

The door opened and her brother strode in. He saw she was awake and came straight to her. He took her free hand in his. "Belle, I am so sorry about the press."

She blinked at him. "What about the press?"

He looked at her for a heartbeat, then flashed his killer smile. "Nothing. No worries. I'm glad you're okay." He pulled her in for a quick hug before heading over to lean on the wall. He looked pleased, as though he'd managed to get away with something. Belinda made a mental note to find out what, after she regained some energy.

She must have looked like she was fading, because John shooed everyone back and fluffed her pillows. He handed her a glass of iced water, then placed a pillow under her damaged knee. She couldn't take her eyes from him; she was mesmerised by the way his muscles flexed as he cared for her. When she did eventually drag her eyes away, she found all of the women in her family grinning at her, and the men scowling.

"What?" she said.

"Nothing," her mother said. "We'll talk about it later."

"Hey ho," someone called as the door opened again, and Elle walked in, her laptop under her arm. She was followed by Lake, Callum and Rachel.

Everyone shuffled around to make space for them, and even though Belinda suspected she had one of the largest private rooms in the hospital, it was starting to feel a little crowded.

"How are you feeling?" Lake asked. Out of the three owners, he was the only one who was house-trained.

"Claustrophobic?" Belinda said, looking around the room.

Lake's lip twitched. "We'll get out of your hair as fast as we can. First, we have news."

There was a heavily pregnant pause.

"Oh, for goodness' sake," her grandmother said. "We're supposed to be the dramatic ones. Spit it out."

Lake smiled. It was small, but Belinda definitely saw it. "Okay, we know who was behind your kidnapping."

Belinda sucked in a breath and reached for John. He sat on the bed beside her and put his arm around her, tucking her in to his side.

Callum watched the move carefully. "Does this mean you're saying no to our job offer?"

"This means you talk about Belinda's security with me," John said.

"You taking a wage?" Callum asked.

John stiffened. "No. I have investments and you're going

to let me moonlight for Benson Security—when I'm not with Belinda."

"Got it all figured out, then," Callum said. "Nice of you to let us know how we can fit in with your life."

"Give it a rest," Joe said. "You know you're going to take him up on the offer." He grinned at John. "Welcome to the team."

Belinda angled her head to look up at him. "What just happened?"

"Nothing important, baby." John turned to Lake. "Who was it?"

"Elle?" Lake said.

Elle fiddled with her laptop before switching the TV on. "I managed to trace the money in your driver's bank account to the people who paid him to arrange the kidnapping." Belinda felt the blood drain from her face at the thought of Brian betraying her like that. She'd believed they'd had a friendship, and she'd been totally wrong. John stroked her arm, aware that she was trembling, and his comfort helped.

"We handed the evidence we dug up to the police, and they made an arrest." She pointed at the TV with the remote. "I recorded this earlier. Thought you might like to see."

A CNN news report filled the screen. In the corner of a live feed from an L.A. police station was a head shot of a director she'd worked with the previous year. The banner at the bottom of the screen read: *Ethan Stratford—arrested in connection with Belinda Collins kidnapping.*

Belinda sucked in a breath and her heart raced. John pulled her closer, as though he could protect her from what she was about to see.

The reporter stood in front of the police station doors and looked into the camera. *"This morning, Hollywood director Ethan Stratford was charged in connection with the kidnapping of Belinda Collins and her friend John Garcia. Sources tell us that the director not only arranged for the kidnapping to take place but is also suspected of feeding money into a Peruvian cartel."*

"That little worm," Belinda's mother said. "I never liked him. Rubbish director, too."

"It is believed," the reporter continued, *"that Stratford arranged to have Collins kidnapped as an attempt to drum up interest in his new movie. The movie, Ransom, was shot with Collins early last year and is due for release in the fall."*

"I'll call our lawyers," Belinda's father said. "When I'm through with him, no distribution company on the planet will touch that movie. I promise you, sweetheart. It will never see the light of day."

"Thanks, Dad." Belinda flashed him a grateful smile.

"The movie plot follows a kidnap victim played by Collins," the reporter said, *"and it is believed that Stratford thought having the actress kidnapped in real life would add authenticity to a movie that has had a slew of unforgiving early reviews."*

"Unforgiving?" Belinda's mother snorted. "They slaughtered him. And he deserved every word. You were the only thing in that whole mess worth watching, darling."

Belinda wasn't sure that was any consolation, but she flashed her mother a smile anyway. There was a commotion on the screen behind the reporter, and the doors to the L.A. police station opened. Ethan was escorted out, handcuffed between two cops. Reporters pressed in on them and were held back by more police. As the reporters shouted questions at the director, Belinda stared at his face.

There he was, the man behind it all. The person responsible for their suffering. The person who'd sold her to men who would rape her, and kill her and John. And for what? For a movie?

"Turn it off," she said to Elle. "I've seen enough."

The screen went black as Belinda pressed her face to John's chest. The overwhelming feeling of betrayal, of being used to save someone else some money, was too much to bear.

"Don't worry, my love," her gran said. "That little skunk is going to jail. I've been in jail. It's no picnic. And he isn't as sturdy as I am. He's a skinny little thing with no backbone. I give him two days before someone makes him their pet. And I totally mean that in an unwillingly sexual way."

"Gran!" Julia said.

"What?" Gran said with genuine confusion. "We want him to suffer, don't we?"

"That's not the point," Belinda's mother said. "You aren't helping. And you were only in a holding cell for two days. You're hardly an expert."

"I still have nightmares," Gran said dramatically.

Belinda tuned her family out as she turned her face towards John; she was barely holding it together. "John," she whispered, "can you make them leave now?"

"Sure, baby." He kissed her hair. "Okay, everybody out. Belinda's had enough, we're done here."

She could only imagine what his face must have looked like, because not a single person argued. Instead, there was the noise of people shuffling out of the room and then there was silence.

Belinda clung to John. "I'm so sorry," she said as tears fell, wetting his shirt. "This was all my fault. You were kidnapped because of me. Because that man used us for a publicity stunt."

John gently but firmly held her chin and lifted her face to him. "Don't ever apologise to me for something somebody else did. You hear me?" There was fire in his eyes.

She nodded and then her bottom lip trembled. "I trusted him. I trusted my driver and my bodyguards. I trusted them and I was wrong. How do I know who to trust now?"

"You can trust me," he said. "I'll weed out the rest."

She lifted her hand to his cheek as she stared into those intense, pale eyes of his. "I do trust you," she whispered.

"Then trust this too, baby. Sometime in that jungle, I fell in love with you. Not the actress you give the world, but you. Belinda Collins." He placed her palm flat over his heart. "You own this now. I will always stand between you and harm. Always. So, trust me. Trust me to look out for you. Trust me to love you. Trust me to stand with you no matter what life brings. Trust me."

"John," she whispered as tears fell. She lifted her face to his, wanting his lips, and he gave them to her. The kiss was soft, slow, gentle. Each touch of lips to lips was a word. A promise. A declaration of hope.

"I do trust you, John. Don't you know I love you? How could I not? I don't know what the future will bring for us, but I do know I don't want to let you go. I love you, John Garcia. I love *you.*"

She gave him the words against his mouth and went willingly when he deepened the kiss. A lot had been taken from her during her time in the jungle, but what she'd gained far outweighed the loss. She'd come away with the greatest prize of all.

She'd come away with John.

ABOUT THE AUTHOR

I'm a Scot, living in New Zealand and married to a Dutch man. I write contemporary romance with a humorous bent – this is mainly due to the fact I have an odd sense of humour and can't keep it out of anything I do! If I wasn't a writer, I'd like to be Buffy the Vampire Slayer, or Indiana Jones. Unfortunately, both these roles have already been filled. Which may be a good thing as I have no fighting skills, wouldn't know a precious relic if it hit me in the face and have an aversion to blood. When I'm not living in my head, I'm a mother to two kids, several pet sheep, one dog, four cats, three alpacas, two miniature horses, eight guinea pigs and an escape artist chicken.

It was wise to call John Garcia by his street name—Beast. Unless you were Belinda Collins—she could call him anything she liked.

"Honey?" She padded into the kitchen of their house on the south coast of England. She wore cut-off jean shorts and a pink *I Heart NYC* vest. Her hair was in a messy bun on top of her head. She was beautiful.

"What is it, baby?" He looked up from the notes Callum had sent over for their latest job. It seemed simple enough, but after a few jobs with Benson Security, he'd learned that could be deceptive. It was always best to check the information twice and be as prepared as possible. After years working on his own as a cage fighter, he thrived on being part of a team. Having his childhood friends around him didn't hurt either.

"What was it you took from the guard's pocket in the compound, can you remember?" Belinda said as she walked over to him and sat in his lap. She put her arms around his neck and nuzzled at his jaw.

She'd decided to take a year off from acting, movie

promotion and TV appearances. She told her agent it was a year to come to terms with what she'd experienced and to reassess her direction. She'd told him that she needed time to get used to the fact that no matter what she did, for the rest of her life, every single story about her would include a sidebar detailing the kidnapping. The way to cope with that kind of infamy was to claim ownership of it—her words, not his. And she was doing that by writing a screenplay about their experience. She already had a studio interested in it, even though it was a fictionalised version of events and she had no intention of playing the lead in the movie.

"It was matches and a dead cell phone, baby," he said, then took the opportunity to kiss her senseless while she was there. He loved that dazed and needy look she had when she opened her eyes straight after his lips left hers.

She blinked up at him, and there it was. Gold. Pure gold. He'd found treasure no amount of digging in the Amazon would unearth.

"Thanks," she said breathily. "Now, can you describe your feelings when that spider jumped on your chest?" She gave him an innocent, wide-eyed look.

He wasn't fooled. She was yanking his chain. "What did I tell you? We never mention that. Which means it will *not* be included in your movie."

"But John, I can't miss out a scene like that. In fact"—she stood and sauntered away from him, swaying her hips—"I was thinking I'd make it more dramatic. Maybe have him cry like a baby, or better yet, wet himself with fear."

"Over my dead body!" He shot to his feet and launched himself after her.

She ran through the house squealing with delight, as Beast herded her towards their bedroom.

His woman. His life. His home.